THE EDEN PROJECT

Elizabeth Noxon

ISBN-13: 9781709471803

Cover design by: Lauren Giordano

Library of Congress Control Number: 2018675309
Printed in the United States of America

To my sons, Bradley and Eric, with love always

1

I was 17 when I stepped into our greenhouse where I loved to think in silence. I took a few moments of my Saturday morning to escape from the final pressures of senior year, as I chose the fresh produce carefully, with much of it not ready to be plucked from its source of nourishment. These little growing fruits were like me, just about to be separated from familiarity. Only I was about to be thrust into the unimaginable.

I remember it was a cool, gusty spring day when the silence was broken too soon. The distinct sound of the door creaked open behind me, causing me to jerk and drop the bag in my hand. "Sienna! Oh, good, you are here," Mom said latching the door behind her so it wouldn't blow open in the cold wind.

"Mom, you scared me!"

"So sorry, but I just couldn't wait to show you this. I grabbed yesterday's mail just now. Look—you got something from The Powell Scholar's foundation." She waved an envelope into the air.

"Oh, really?" She reached out her hand to me, and I took the envelope and opened it. It was a card with the PS logo on the front. I flipped it open and read, "Congratulations, Sienna Yardley! You've been selected as a recipient of the Powell Scholar Award for your senior science project. The Board would be honored by your presence at the annual ceremony on April 15 at the Hotel D'Ruse,

Chicago, 6 p.m. Formal attire. We look forward to your celebration." Mom read it while standing next to me. Her smile was beaming.

"Congrats, honey! This is wonderful. I'm so excited for you!" She gave me a quick hug.

"Thanks, Mom." I stared at the elaborate invitation in my hand.

"You earned this and should be thrilled, honey. This will open so many doors for you and just in time, too. Later today, let's figure out what you'll wear."

Mom's phone pinged with a message. "Shoot. I'm going to head back to the house and take care of this. Let's talk later." She turned, flipped up her hood, and was out the door.

Her patients contacted her at all hours of the day and night. I held the invitation, settling into the quiet once again. Of course, I'd heard of the prestigious Powell Award from our science teacher. He told us about it from the beginning of our projects, and it wasn't out of reach for me and many of us. Excitement rushed through me. My two years of hard work would be recognized. I wondered who would be there, and if I would have a chance to present my research.

My science project that had won was on the development of an herbal medicine for Alzheimer's prevention. I started it in the greenhouse we had built on a tight schedule. Mom had insisted on methodically ordering and planting dense, nutritious foods, and we hastily grew our food as more food supply production problems loomed from water issues. Along with hearing the latest medical scares—novel viruses and other new diseases—from Mom, a doctor, the news headlines screamed at us about toxins in the air, cyberattacks, and foreign countries testing missiles. The onslaught of doomsday messages made my head spin. So, naturally, when I was faced with choosing a senior science project, I considered what I could grow in the greenhouse that would help cure disease. My nana, Dad's mom, had the early signs of Alzheimer's, and I had found a small study on the internet on how herbs were showing promising results on slowing memory loss. I knew I had to dig for possible answers. I was afraid that Dad, my sister, Willow, or I would get it, too.

Moving away from family meant independence, something I dreamed of. I was about to graduate high school and was accepted to all of the top universities across the country. But if I moved away, my sister, Willow, would be alone, and Mom and Dad might ignore the very things that allowed us to thrive. The award would put me in front of the world of medical scientists, possibly offering more opportunities for research. I thought of what I could be and what I could discover. Little did I know things would change sooner rather than later.

I left the greenhouse that day realizing that I could tap into new potential, being faced with opportunities and the chance to meet new people and make new friends.

Looking back, it was all supposed to happen this way. Me in the safety of my space, with the world changing so rapidly around me that I was finally caught up in the swirling of time and purpose. The Powell Award announcement was literally a piece of paper that newly defined my life.

2

Two weeks later, I found myself standing in the same room with world renowned scientists for the Powell Scholars Award ceremony, which celebrated high school scientific geniuses.

I stood up straight while my heart raced, adrenaline surging. It was Saturday night, and I was about to face a crowd of other kids on my level. For years I'd tried avoiding it, but in a way, I was ready to be free—to be my true self with others like me.

I stood next to my parents in the security line at the upscale Chicago hotel. Mom and Dad were in their element, rubbing shoulders with other researchers and academics, always challenging each other with who was onto the next biggest discovery.

I wasn't a celebrity—I wasn't an influencer and my project didn't have millions of views. I was, though, like everyone else in line, a genius. It was the choice of words we used that gave us away. The few friends that I had would never use the words *insidious* or *contrite* or *ostensibly* in a sentence.

An alarm blared, making me jump—at least, as much I could in two-inch heels that were suffocating my wide feet. I was used to my roomy cleats or running shoes.

I covered my ears with my hands to muffle the repeating loud screaming pitch of the security alarm. Its familiar sound echoed in my head as I stood in the checkpoint line, something I'd done a million times before. I leaned to look around the person in front of me for a better view. When I practically breathed down his neck, he turned around to look at me with wide eyes. He was a teenager, too.

A tall, thin, bald man with some scrawny facial hair was pulled off to the side. A security guard spoke to him, looking him up and down. Others in line shuffled and held their bags tightly. Only an idiot would challenge security.

Behind the scenes, probably in a special VIP security line, scientists and medical researchers had arrived, zipping through without much question. Everyone needed to be scanned and bags checked to keep the crowd as safe as possible. In the past, bad things had happened at events like this. Things that were seared in my memory forever. People got mad and pulled out guns and ammunition of all kinds for unthinkable reasons. A renowned scientist might say something controversial, and when it got out into the media and pissed off a zealot, anything could happen. Everyone was on edge. Diseases were wiping out thousands of people, natural disasters were clearing out whole towns, crazy long winters were killing crops, and the list went on.

About three-and-a-half minutes went by of standing completely still. I knew timing down to the second—instincts, I guessed. Seriously, what was this guy ahead of me thinking? He'd never get away with sneaking in a pistol or some other weapon. I clutched my purse closer to my side, then quickly patted it down for my phone. It was there. My shoulders relaxed.

Another officer was called and approached the man. There was a discussion over items in his bag and he was led away from the screening area. I looked back at Mom and Dad who were also clutching their bags. Dad pulled out his tablet and began to furiously type, snapping a picture of the guy. Like he could do anything about it anyway. Dad was always taking pictures of people and stuff. He didn't trust anyone and never had since his identity was stolen five years ago. It had changed our lives. Now we lived on constant high alert, with security in our home and cars but I wasn't sure I felt any safer.

When I was patted down—chest, middle, butt, ankles, inseam—I shivered, then grabbed my bag after it was screened. Taking a deep breath, we followed the signs to the ballroom. I glanced around at the faces in the crowd: young, smiling, white, all with perfectly straight teeth. I didn't recognize anyone, and as the crowd thickened, Mom and Dad drifted away in the sea of people. They must have seen someone they knew and were sucked into the flow. No surprise.

I followed the stream of people. When we ended up in a large banquet room, a waiter offered me some champagne. I told him I wasn't old enough, but he just smiled and handed me a full glass. My fingernails were painted nicely to cover up their rawness, thanks to Willow, who had painted them that afternoon. We'd sat on the porch, and I let her pick the bright pink glitter. She always chose something bolder than I did, which I liked. Her body was fragile but her personality bold. I looked at my nails again and felt like they weren't my hands as I wrapped my fingers around the fragile crystal. I stood, alone, wondering if I should sip the champagne.

"Go for it, Sienna," someone said when I brought the glass to my lips.

"Ah…" I sipped slowly. "Hey, Kellen. You get some?"

Kellen, my science lab partner, was endlessly trying to impress me. "Me? You bet. Looking for my second." He winked, his mouth curling at the corner, as he took a piece of shrimp off his plate. Kellen looked older, at least in his twenties, wearing his tuxedo with his hair combed back.

"So, we're in the right place?" I asked, before taking another sip of the bubbly. It tickled going down my throat. I thought I saw Graham Glenbrook, a famous researcher in the field of biomechanics. I pointed to him, but Kellen didn't see me and kept eating like a sixteen-year-old.

"We are. I can't believe it, either. Shrimp and champagne flowing, steaks for dinner, five desserts to choose from, this is insane. And all for a high school awards ceremony," he said, leaning closer to me. I tilted away from him before sneezing—he was doused in cologne. His intuition and quick wit engaged me in the lab, but he was awkward making small talk. He'd crack stupid jokes or say things that weren't true, like the time he told me he played ice hockey and his team won the state championship. I knew for a fact he had never played hockey.

"Whoever planned this evening has some serious cash and isn't afraid to advertise it." I looked around the room.

"Whoever has this much money is freakin' awesome. I wanna be their friend." He leaned in again and whispered, "You look amazing, Sienna."

"Thanks. Where are we sitting?" I looked down at my drink, and the waitress approached with appetizers. Kellen was handsome, his strawberry blonde hair slicked neatly back, but I wasn't in the mood to deal with his insecurities.

Staring at the entrance to the ballroom, I waited for my parents, whom I had now located. They were lost in conversation as usual.

The band finished tuning and started playing. Kellen followed me as I navigated my way around the room to find my table and seat. We were at the same table, sitting next to each other. Figured. I guessed since we went to the same school and were science partners, they'd sat us together. Everyone else was a stranger. Adults sat together, too, on the other side of the room. Finally, I noticed Mom smiling and in her glory on the stage, mingling with the other professors.

The room buzzed when a man on stage took the mic. "Welcome, students! We are pleased you've come to be recognized for your scientific efforts this year. We've had some phenomenal achievements and are thrilled to share these with your peers and professors around the region. You've all worked so hard. You're the crème de la crème! Please sit down and enjoy your salad, and then we will begin the program between courses. What a special evening for us all."

Applause erupted and the band began playing again as the waiters and waitresses served us salads and rolls.

"Can't wait for these geeks to tell us all about their research crap. They'll go on and on and on. At least the food looks good. Do we get more champagne? Wine or beer?" Kellen spoke through his mouth full of chewed-up salad. I thought he truly did want to hear what they said but was trying to sound cool around the other kids.

"Yeah, probably boring as Latin class," I said sarcastically, giggling. I was thirsty for more drinks, and the champagne was making me feel a little giddy. I cleared my throat. I really did want to meet some of the famous researchers. In fact, I'd been dreaming of a moment like this, where I'd mingle with super smart scientists who actually wanted to talk to me, to hear what I had to say and what I thought.

Kellen and I were at the top of our class. We called ourselves third years and went to school year-round, taking fast track classes. We could go on to university after we did a two-month internship. Even with advanced honors and placement classes, school had few challenges for me. I considered myself lucky, since most of my friends struggled through regular classes. I just understood stuff, and quickly, too. I asked the teachers questions they couldn't answer, and I didn't do it to piss them off. Well, most of the time. Sometimes I did when they were being jerks. They didn't know everything.

Kellen and I ended up in the same college-level physics class and entered our project in a state contest. We, and the whole school, expected us to win, and we did. It was my idea, and it was brilliant. We piloted a new mix of herbal medicine that we grew in my garden, to help diminish the effects of Alzheimer's.

We finished eating our salads and the man who I assumed was a professor took the mic again as the music stopped. The stage lights made his bald head shine and made his bright red nose more prominent. I noticed the guy spit as he talked. Spit balls formed at the corner of his mouth, forming like tiny spider eggs in a window corner. Disgusting.

"Welcome, ladies and gentlemen! Congratulations to you all for earning your seat at the table tonight." He smiled, more spit balls forming. We applauded for each other. Mom was on the stage, all smiles, looking at me. I guessed she was presenting one of the awards.

"We will announce the award winners shortly after dinner. You've worked hard so deserve a nourishing meal before we begin." The man said chuckling, though no one else laughed. "But before we dig into our surf and turf, I'd like to turn the mic over to Dr. Simon who would like to share another reason for our gathering tonight. A very, very exciting point of business!" More spit flew as his voice raised and cracked with excitement.

"Good evening! I'm so pleased to be here and to be a part of this amazing evening," Dr. Simon said into the microphone, his tone quiet and controlled. His wiry, blonde hair was thinning on top, and his small lips made a little circle as he sucked in air before going on. "Take a look around if you haven't already. Each of you is special, especially made, I should say. Your parents dedicated themselves to you." He paused and took a deep breath, which we could hear through the microphone.

As I listened to Dr. Simon speak, I gazed at the girl sitting across from me and the kids next to her. Their skin was sun-kissed and light brown, and they had large, colorful eyes, outlined with long lashes. No acne or scars or even a hair out of place. All displayed adorable smiles, perfectly white, straight teeth, and all were wickedly smart.

He continued slowly, "Designing you, that is. You are part of an elite group of zygotic genomes—engineered technology babies, or designer babies, born out of the carefully orchestrated Eden Project."

The room was dead silent, as if a dark cloak had been thrown over all of us. A fork clanged against a plate. What...was...he saying? I looked at Kellen and the others at the table. There was an awkward silence before kids began exchanging words of disbelief.

The doctor's smile quirked as he soaked in our reaction and then looked back at the scientists on stage.

My mom was there, with her hands together about to clap, giddy with excitement. What the hell had my parents done? I wanted to shake them, but then Mom looked back at me and her smile faded. I shot her dagger eyes, right through her core.

A boy slammed his hand onto the table and stood up. "This has got to be a joke, right?" His voice was deep and melodic.

Kellen leaned over and whispered in my ear. "You think this Simon geek is full of shit?"

I stared at the young group in the room, my throat tight and suddenly dry. "What does a designer baby mean?"

"Really, you, Sienna, of all people have to ask?" Kellen said sarcastically.

"I know, I know." I thought for a moment. Kellen knew, too. Our parents chose our traits before birth, so all imperfections, mutations, and undesirable traits were removed. I glared at Mom and Dad who were now standing next to Dr. Stevenson. Sounded great, right? Then why was my stomach in knots?

"You got it. So, we are virtually perfect—and with all of the teens in the room at the cusp of procreation, we'll force negative human traits into extinction." Kellen paused to soak in the extent of his statement, then took a big gulp of water.

"This does explain some things," I whispered.

In a matter of seconds, the room erupted. Everyone started shouting and asking Dr. Simon questions.

"Is this true?"

"What does this mean?"

"Who am I really?"

"Could my parents really do this?"

"Why am I finding this out now?"

"This can't be possible!"

"How could anyone let this happen?"

"This is freakin' unreal!"

"Who are you?"

Dr. Simon held up his hand, signaling everyone to stay calm and listen. When they didn't, he shouted into the microphone. "Please, please quiet down! I have more to say."

My legs started to shake, first slowly, then for some reason, my right leg more violently than my left. I placed my right hand forcefully on my thigh to hold it steady.

After two more attempts to gain our attention and another woman on stage yelling at us to calm down, gradually everyone quieted. Dr. Simon began talking as if this was all so organic, but his words began to slur together as if he was mumbling.

"Your success this past year in science research affirmed to us that you're all ready to take on the task of our new project. Well, actually, it's a contest." He paused and took a sip of water, his beady eyes flowing over the crowd of confused young faces. "This is the project you were all born to live out, and you will all live well past 115 years. Today is your day. Today is a celebration of what's to come. Here's to our future designers who will save the world from disease and disaster and create generations of genetically perfect humans. Cheers! Cheers to you all—a toast for our future. To YOU, the Designers!" He shouted into the mic so loudly that I covered my ears and buried my head on my lap, squeezing my eyes closed.

When I opened them again, everything was blurred, but I could faintly make out Mom and Dad raising their glasses in the toast. Their bodies were a blob, just their arms sticking up. I didn't realize that I was holding my breath until I opened my mouth and gasped for air. My lungs hurt, then filled up as I gasped for more.

Dr. Simon quickly turned and raised his hand to the band to resume playing. He and the other adults on the stage, Mom and Dad included, stood together at the front and motioned for us to stand. One group at a table rose, then another, while others refused, and a few left the room. One girl cried out loud and ran. We looked like a bunch of freaking robots.

This was ludicrous.

Kellen stood and then grabbed my elbow to help me up. He raised his glass and forced mine up into the air. The trumpets blared.

My parents smiled and clapped, like good little scientists. Everyone applauded until finally the music stopped and Dr. Simon took the mic again.

"Ladies and gentlemen, thank you. Please, please stay and have a seat. I'd like to now introduce J.M. Stevenson, MD, Ph.D., researcher and physicist with Onyx Pharmaceutical Labs."

A woman stepped forward her dark hair tightly pulled back. She nudged up her round wire rimmed glasses She cleared her throat and lifted her mic to her lips. "We are all so grateful and excited to finally celebrate this evening with you. Your accomplishments this past year have exceeded our expectations. We are delighted to now share with you a new contest I think you'll embrace whole-heartedly. Your fierce competitiveness will only foster more scientific and medical success."

Her smooth voice and calm assurance quieted the dazed crowd. We sat, and I gulped some water. Though I was looking toward the stage, I was unable to focus on the very tall and lean woman in command. She paced the stage, shifting the mic to her other hand.

"You see, our underlying mission is to find a cure for major health and environmental problems before we self-destruct," she said, wetting her full lips before continuing. "Each of you will be receiving a notice in a few days outlining your new project for this contest. You will have six months to present your findings before we will meet back in this room. We are confident the competition will be tough. We anticipate there could very well be several of you who find treatments or even cures."

She cleared her throat. "The most successful student will win a large sum of money along with access to their own research lab, assistants, and all the equipment and technology needed for further work. Whatever the winner wants, she or he will get. We have the resources to back you." Dr. Stevenson paused for a minute. "It's all in your hands now."

She stepped to the center of the stage and extended her thin arm, fanning it across the room to encompass us.

"I think she's so excited she peed her pants!" Kellen said.

I was still in shock. My legs twitched again, but I managed to whisper back, "Is she serious or just plain crazy?"

"She's a scientist wanting to save the world."

Sounded impossible. It was a big world, but there were some incredibly smart and powerful people in the room.

"She may be on to something." He wiped his sweaty hand on his napkin, and I did too. I expected to have a fun evening, accept an award, and go back to my normal life. Now I was a "designer baby" and had a high stakes contest to complete in record time. I reached for another gulp of water as my stomach churned.

"What do you mean, Kellen?" My hands were still sweaty.

"Are you kidding? You're smarter than me."

He was right on more than one point. Yes, Stevenson was onto something and I wasn't buying into it, and yes, I *was* smarter than him.

"We have a chance to really do something immensely powerful *and* make a ton of money. Perfect combo. She knows how we think." Kellen smiled. My mind spun.

Stevenson continued to pace the stage, going on to tell us we would each be assigned a mentor who would help us get started and who had completed some preliminary work, so we'd have a base point to begin. This would help with our time constraints. Yeah, whatever. Her expectations were sky high and so crazy unrealistic that drinking a tall cup of coffee 24/7 to get the job done was a fantasy.

I sucked in a deep breath. My outfit was sticking to my back and legs. I abhorred this. I had kicked off my shoes long ago and now couldn't find them under the table. Leaning over to feel for them, my stomach lurched. My salad and roll felt like they were in my throat. I sat up quickly and swallowed hard. I was uncannily aware of my body, the body in which my parents had chosen every detail. It tingled, on the way to being numb. My life was a sham. I slumped back into my chair, my head aching.

My parents, Skylar and Landon Yardley, fricking designed me—chose my sex, my eye and hair color, my height, my athleticism, my IQ. The day I was conceived was all leading up to today—for me to have a part in saving the world from humans destroying the world. A reboot of Eden, a second chance for utopia. But really? Could we save this massive world that was spiraling out of control?

Now I couldn't hold back. I ran barefoot from the table to the bathroom, trying to hold down my partially digested food. The shrimp cocktail, the arugula with blue cheese...ugh, initially so tasty and now so, so bad. I leaned on the bathroom door, ran into a stall and leaned over. It shot out quickly and my stomach churned, the knots seeming to tighten. The secret hurt, my stomach clenched, and I hurled until there was nothing left.

"Are you okay?" another girl in the bathroom asked politely.

I flushed the toilet. "Not really..." I blew my nose.

"This whole thing is crazy. I had to get outta there, too," she said. I flushed again. "Agree. Too much for me," I managed to squeak out. I wiped my face again and opened the stall door.

"Who's she kidding? Just because we're designer kids, she thinks we can cure diseases in six months?" she sneered.

Another girl washing her hands piped in, "But they said we're elite. That's cool!" She laughed, throwing her head back.

"Seriously?" the first girl asked.

"Yeah, I mean, like we're crazy smart, right? And our parents designed us this way, so why shouldn't we be able to solve some of the world's crises? I'm in. This is our ticket to a better life." The second girl fussed with her silky black hair in the mirror until it lay perfectly on her shoulders. Her bluish gray eyes were mesmerizing, and her full lips balanced perfectly below her button nose with each nostril's edge rounded at a slight angle that gave her a most interesting, China-doll look.

I felt like crap and washed my hands for at least five

minutes.

"Just think, we'll have access to only the best. The best mentors, the best technology, the best databases...do I have to go on? You guys get it."

"Yeah, you're right, and the money," the first girl said, sounding more convinced. "Like, there's billions invested in this contest. Pharma companies, hospitals, other billionaires. Think about how much these scientists will get out of it, too."

"You're so right!"

These were crazy designer girls talking now. It was like I was on some other planet with my ears ringing.

I took the escalator down to the first floor and stepped out to the front of the hotel to get some fresh air—though, what air was truly fresh these days? Things were getting worse quickly. Our air quality was terrible, with inversions all the time in the city and the smog lingering sometimes for days. Cancer was spinning out of control with all of the environmental problems, while new forms were discovered every month. It was like we were digging our own graves. Actually, we were more than halfway down into our graves, holding on for dear life.

I wanted to run far away, but I was kind of tired from being sick. I had to face my parents, grill them on how they could design me and then not tell me themselves. I hated them. They'd made me hear it from a freaking professor. What more were they keeping from me?

I held my stomach and bent over, but nothing was left. Instead, I dry-heaved, my sides contracting hard. I coughed and closed my eyes, willing the pain to subside, gathering myself.

I'd left my purse at the table and realized my shoes were there, too. I had to go back in.

I stumbled back to the table, letting my hair fall over my face to cover my red eyes. If I had to crawl under the table to find my shoes, I would, or I'd just leave them there. When I got there, everyone was eating their dinner like normal. I was still nauseous, and I couldn't even think of food, let alone take another bite.

"You okay, Sienna?" Kellen asked with his mouth full.

"What do *you* think?" My hair was a mess and my eyes were still watering.

"This steak is great. Have a seat." He patted my chair for me to join him.

"I'm not staying. I can't eat. I have no intention of hanging with this group of crazy people." My voice was loud as I turned to leave, but Kellen stood up and grabbed my arm.

In a low voice, as if he were my dad scolding me, he said, "Are you serious? You can't leave this party now with what we know. We are *in* this."

I stared back into his eyes, trembling.

"You're gonna do this. With all that you know now, you have an obligation," he hissed. He actually seemed really pumped up about his new so-called purpose.

My hand moved to slap and shake him, but I was paralyzed. No words even came to my lips. I turned and ran out of the room, a blister on my heel bleeding from those damn, godforsaken high-heeled shoes. I left them under the table and ran as fast as I could.

3

My feet were dirty and sore by the time I reached home. After I called for an Uber and had him drop me off three blocks from my house, I texted my mom to pick up my shoes from under my table. Our home blended in with the others in the neighborhood, one of four cookie-cutter styles. Its red brick was classic and the paint on our garage doors was chipping, but over time we had accumulated the latest technology, like most people, I supposed.

I punched in the security code on my smartphone to turn off our system. The light above our camera over the garage blinked twice then stopped as I punched in another set of numbers to open the door next to the garage. Dad said he was going to upgrade the system so we could scan our fingers or eyes to deactivate the alarms. He'd ordered the equipment since passwords were recently obsolete. They were so easily stolen, and hackers could basically get into anything with a password. Even the temporary PINs only worked for so long. Mom and Dad probably wouldn't notice I was gone at the event until I was called for my award. They'd accept, thank the presenters, and tell everyone how hard I had worked for it, even though they really had no idea. Eventually they'd come home after debating how their own achievements would solve the world's problems.

I tried to be quiet since it was late, and Willow was

sleeping. The stillness of the house felt different than it had before tonight. Hell, I guess I was the one who was different—I knew I was a freak now. I placed my phone on the kitchen counter and stood, listening to the house breathe rhythmically like a sleeping old dog without a care in the world.

My stomach churned and grumbled, but the thought of food still revolted me. The void went beyond my empty stomach. I squirmed and scratched my hips where my dress was tight, then unzipped the back and pulled it down. Ah, a little free again, if only physically for a moment.

I felt like a fraud. I didn't even know my parents. Did they even love each other or me? I was an experiment my whole life—their whole lives—to be a part of the bigger picture. I'd probably never know for sure, since they were so screwed up.

The thought of my bed, pillow, and blankets lulled me upstairs in a trance. I longed to get under the blanket and pull it over my head for a few hours to hide. But instead, I fought my urge and crept into Willow's room while she was in her bathroom. Her favorite books with worn bindings lined her shelves, and her computer sat on her desk like a friend, always there. Her bean-bag chair was even neat, the shape of her butt neatly molded into it. Not a thing cluttered her floor, as usual. Her skin was so pale and fragile that I wanted to give her all of my strength and stamina. Well, at least what I had left after tonight.

I imagined her able to run outside and ride her bike, then return home an hour later with pink, sunkissed cheeks. I was so tired of seeing her weak—her immune system compromised. She visited the doctor's office monthly getting immunotherapy; it was endless. I wanted to hang out with her like a real sister. Go for runs, shopping, then lunch.

Too many days I'd gone to school, leaving her behind to rest all day, and I still had energy to win a lacrosse game, come home and do homework, and stay up late talking to friends.

She always told me, "Sienna, go. Do it for us, the Yardley sisters. Win the science award, play the game, have fun at the party. Just tell me everything." She made me promise to tell her all the crazy details.

I dreamed of the day she told me details.

Oh, sweet Willow, I don't want to tell you all the details about tonight. You wouldn't be proud.

She came out of her bathroom. "Sienna...you're back so early?" she said faintly. "Tell me how it went." She gasped a bit for more air before going on, "Did you get a cool award?"

"I did. I sure did." I gently rubbed her arm.

"So why are you home already?"

"I'll tell you more about it later. It's all OK," I reassured her. "You look tired."

"Yeah, I want the full story tomorrow." She patted my arm. "I think you look exhausted! And why are your feet so dirty?"

"Oh, yeah. My heels hurt, so I took them off. I need to go clean them, they are so gross!" I left her room and closed her door. I'd tell her only good parts about the evening—the music, the flowers, the surf and turf, and of course the champagne.

In my room, I brushed my hair and changed into my pajamas. The security system beeped three times, and I jumped, my brush flying out of my hands into the sink, as if it was possessed.

I found Mom in the kitchen, alone, getting a glass of water in the dark. She stood at the sink in her bare feet, as she always did, and mumbled something to herself before she took a sip. She must've heard my footsteps because she turned toward me. Her jaw dropped and she nearly dropped her glass of water.

"Sienna! How could you just leave like that?" she burst out with little regard to Willow sleeping. She walked over to the counter where the elegant, glass statue with my name carved into it sat next to the bowl of fruit, then picked it up and handed it to me. She held it so long her arm began to shake, but I didn't reach out to take it. She carefully set it back down.

"Are you kidding me, Mom?"

"Well, I just can't understand..."

"What can't you understand? That I'm fine with the bomb they dropped? That I am genetically engineered?"

"You embarrassed Dad and I by leaving. We were waiting for you to come up to collect your award, and you weren't there. This is a big deal, Sienna. You just left."

"Didn't you guys think about how I'd feel? And what, Dad's not here? Went to his house?" I asked in a monotone voice, arms crossed. Dad had moved out two months ago, trying to get some space and deal with Mom's anxieties.

"Yes. He'll be over tomorrow." She downed her whole glass of water.

"He didn't have the guts to face me tonight?" I took a step closer to her and unfolded my arms across my chest. I wasn't going away, and she seemed to finally realize this fact.

"Sienna, I get that you're upset, that you didn't see this coming, but you don't know the whole story." She sat down at the kitchen table. Her tone was flat and affirming, as if she'd done nothing wrong and had prepared for this moment years ago.

"Whole story? Really, Mom? Really?"

"We wanted to tell you, we just didn't know when would be a good time. Everything had been going as we had hoped. You're smart, talented, funny, athletic, and most important, healthy. You're *healthy*, Sienna."

"Yeah...go on..." This wasn't enough for me right now. I knew a lot of healthy people. Freakin' big deal.

"At the lab at work, we were testing genetic engineering, under the radar. My boss at the time was doing a privately-funded study, and he asked if your dad and I wanted to be a part of it. We were planning to start a family. He told us all the details, and after we discussed and researched it, we decided to try. We didn't know what would happen—if it would all work. It was the cutting edge of medicine back then, and we were all thinking of the future and the possibilities. We dreamt big. We didn't find out until about five years ago that the study was so widespread and that there was a bigger agenda." The excitement in her tired voice seeped through. She swallowed hard and looked out the window into the night.

"So, we were an experiment? Are you kidding me?" I hated the idea of all of this, hearing it all again and from my mother this time.

"It didn't really start out that way, sweetie. Honestly."

"Honestly, you want me to believe you didn't know all of this, Mom? I'm weird—not normal, not natural. That's how I feel. Being started in a hellish petri dish. In a lab."

"It's not like that. No matter how you were conceived —you're my daughter. We are a family. And look at you, just look how healthy and smart you are. You're smarter than Dad and I ever were."

"Seriously, Mom? That's what you care about? We're not a family in the true sense of the word." I held back tears.

"No. I didn't mean it that way. Yes, you are different, but in an amazing way. You've already done amazing things in your life and you're only seventeen. You've made discoveries that will change your future, and with your incredible talent, you can do so much more. The world needs you. In fact, we need the entire designer baby generation."

She reached for my hand across the table. I stiffened, feeling like I had to heave again. I wanted nothing to do with her hand.

"Why? Why is it so important?"

"Sienna, you know this world is in trouble and certain situations are escalating. I talk about medical catastrophes and health organizations not able to handle deadly diseases that get out of control. There's one on the cusp of getting out of control, in fact."

"There's always something. Always. What now, and what do you expect a designer generation to do?"

"There's a superbug called EBEX that's gaining ground. We anticipate your generation's abilities to help carry us through if and when we have gridlock with solutions."

Light footsteps echoed in the hallway, and Willow appeared at the door to the kitchen. "Why are you guys still up?" she asked.

"Sorry, sweetie. We were just talking about the ceremony."

"Didn't mean to wake you! We're heading up to bed now." I stumbled over the chair leg and landed on the table, my hair falling into my face. A wave of exhaustion came over me.

"I wasn't in a deep sleep, anyway." Willow took a glass out of the cupboard and got some water.

"Well, I'm heading up to bed. It's been a long evening and my feet hurt. I'll tuck you in, Willow." Mom skimmed her fingers over my award and paused.

I got the feeling my whole life was already carefully planned.

"Whatever happened in the past, Sienna, we're still sisters," Willow said, then fainted, falling to the floor. Her glass shattered into tiny pieces.

4

We got a hold of Willow and took her upstairs to her bed. Her fragile body was limp under the covers.

In my room again I flopped on my bed, unable to get my thoughts fully around what had happened. My parents had played God. And they loved the driver's seat. They were reinventing Eden. What's done was done. I gazed straight up at the sky as I looked out the window.

No wonder I didn't fit in and my parents left me on my own most of the time. I was just an experiment to them, born in a petri dish. Just one of their many *freakin'* experiments. Science playing around with nature. We couldn't just make people to fix the world's problems, when we *were* the problem!

My sock felt wet. I must've stepped on a piece of glass. Sure enough, a small pool of blood was forming on my carpet. I hopped to the bathroom on my other foot to grab a towel.

I got my bleeding under control and bandaged it up, then scrubbed off my thick makeup until my skin was raw. I looked closer at my features. My skin was clear and even-toned, no acne, no freckles; my eyes were round and wide, cheek bones high, small, button nose but distinct. My ears were small, my eyebrows thick, lips heart shaped and full. My body was contoured and athletic, tall and slender, with a gently round rump. I turned away from looking too long at my fingernails; they were chomped down and raw. Always raw.

I glanced at my lacrosse stuff in the corner of my room —the trophies, the medals, the stack of certificates I'd received over the past ten years. Such a steady stream that none of them had much meaning anymore. They sat there, barely appreciated. I couldn't tell you what half of them were for anyway. Sports teams and academic challenges. Life had been so predictable and driven by success that came easily to me. I gave more than half of them to Willow.

So, the scientists' experiment had evolved, and now they'd handed me their ultimate task. The one I was destined to conquer, they said. Their most significant contribution to society, they said. I blinked hard and buried my face in my hands.

Lifting my eyes toward the mirror, I took a deep breath. No, no, no! They created me this way, and I was smarter than them.

Blood seeped through the bandage on my foot. I pressed my hand to it to stop the bleeding when my phone buzzed. It was my best friend, Avery. We'd met playing lacrosse together freshman year. We were both just standing next to each other at our first team meeting and started talking. I knew we'd get along right away. She was athletic and funny, with warm green eyes that seemed trusting. She was someone who didn't BS anyone and always had my back. We played offense the first year and worked well together, learning to anticipate each other's thoughts and moves. We became a force on the team and were best friends ever since. I'd told her about the award ceremony and, of course, she texted me.

A: how was your night?

S: weird night. hey, you're up late

A: *yeah, working on a project for STEM why weird?*
S: *yeah, still figuring it out myself*
A: *that weird? was the entire night weird? and I know you must've you won something? scholarship? $$?*
S: *yeah, won something and more I'll fill you in sometime*
S: *cool! OK you better... pissed at my project partner he won't write the conclusion so I'm doing it—why I'm up late*
S: *he knows you will and will do a better job than him! always happens*
A: *yeah, but it's still a PIA, see you at LAX tomorrow AM*
S: *yep, need to rest getting sleepy*
A: *me 2 gnight!*
S: *gnight! xo*
A: *xo*

5

Sunday morning my head was in a fog. When I pulled on my lacrosse shorts, the same ones I'd been wearing all year, I realized that basically I was screwed. I was on a trajectory that was out of my control and had been from the day I was born. I was on a perpetual roller coaster—like "The Magnificent" that traveled 200 miles per hour —and there was no getting off. Too late. You die if you try. *Hang on for the long haul,* the operator's voice boomed in my head.

Ten minutes later, I slammed the door to the garage. I had to be at school for a lacrosse practice, then a game, so I threw my bag into the trunk of my car. A breeze gusted in my face when I opened the garage. The weather had spiked back to its more typical May temperatures and winds.

I grabbed my hefty team jacket and put it on. It was bulky and protective, a kind of shield in a way. It provided comfort, assurance, and force. I was a lacrosse player. It's what I did, and it made me feel alive. I was unstoppable with my team. I took my stick and rocked it back and forth in my hand, imagining running with my team, attacking the ball and our opponents.

After I arrived to the field, I jogged out to meet my teammates. Avery, Blue, Tansy, Afra, and Jazz were my closest friends on the team. Avery, Blue, and I were defenders, while Jazz was a midfielder and Afra the main goalie.

"Hey, you recover from last night?" asked Avery as we did some high knee jogging across the field.

"Physically, sure."

"Good, 'cuz we need you today. This team is tough. And what do you mean? You said it was weird last night."

"Yeah, it was. I'll tell you later." I paused, then asked, "What do you know about data file sharing for specific software programs?"

"Um, I know a lot. Like, for what?"

"Well, a scientific based data program."

Avery stopped and looked at me. "I know something about it, but not a ton."

"How about data encryption? You do that, right?" We reached the other side of the field, then turned around.

"Oh yeah. I love that stuff. I just figured out some new ciphertex for my chat history." She skipped a little as she transitioned to lunges.

"Awesome." I smiled and winked at her.

"Does this have to do with your weird night last night?"

"Ah, yeah. I've got some intellectual property that'll need some encryption. I've done some, but I know you're more up on this stuff. Let's talk more later. Right now, I want to beat this team."

"Good, let's do it!" Avery moved from a lunge to standing as the coach motioned us toward the bench to stretch and discuss strategy.

We had played this team a couple of weeks ago and lost by two goals. We knew they played rough and had an incredible goalie, so we had to stay focused on our mission to get the job done.

"Let's be aggressive, fast and smart with our plays

today," Coach said. "Protect Afra and the goal, ladies! All in!"

We gathered in a chanted, "Let's GO!" before we broke off into our field positions.

I focused on each motion, blocking out any thoughts about what had happened in the last fifteen hours. I was out to play my hardest for the team. I stayed in the moment and literally didn't want to leave.

I waved to Avery's and Tansy's parents, smiling and clapping on the sidelines, which was filled with parents and siblings. Mom and Dad didn't show up as usual. I didn't even want to see them anyway. I was content to be around my friends who didn't know anything about The Eden Project.

~~~~~~~~

By Monday, I was drained when I sat down to eat breakfast.

Slowly and deliberately, I studied the honey I dripped into my tea. Five minutes later, a ping on my phone and tablet broke my stare. Simultaneous pings drove me crazy, and it happened all the time. I hoped it was my friend Greyson telling he was coming to school. He said he'd been sleeping all day yesterday, which wasn't like him. I thought he'd text me to ask me about lacrosse. We didn't have any classes together but had met up jogging out the lacrosse fields. I was faster than him, and he joked about not being able to keep up with me.

I chewed then swallowed my quinoa, flax, and oatmeal with nuts and clicked on my messages. I checked them every few seconds, something Mom bugged me about when she was around. No matter how hard I tried, I couldn't stop myself from looking. Not that I read every single message. I just needed to know who was sending me stuff, who was really thinking of me.

The note was from Dr. Stevenson with the subject line: *CONFIDENTIAL: Task 0008977X S. Yardley.*

Damn, I wished she wasn't bothering me so early and right now. I set my phone aside and kept eating. I took a few more bites of my oatmeal and sipped my tea, but before too long, my thoughts wandered back to Stevenson. I gazed out the window, but her squeaky voice echoed in my head. Ignoring it would drive me crazy all day, wondering what my job for the contest would be. I started to imagine the possibilities and finally clicked on her message:

CONFIDENTIAL

"Good morning, Sienna. I hope you rested well this weekend. By now you've received your letter explaining our contest. We hope your parents filled you in with more details, too. The next six months will require all of your energy and more. This contest will shape the rest of your life and the people around you. You are capable of accomplishing unimaginable feats of discoveries in medicine. We have extreme faith in you and your abilities; you have proven yourself this past year.

Your project is to find a new and progressive treatment for EBEX, aka *ethicillin-bacteria resistant ether xtaphylococcus*. Superbugs aren't new, but the problem of this recent virus is escalating and has caused serious havoc, threatening to wipe out colonies of people abroad in impoverished countries and in the U.S., due to over-treatment of antibiotics and genetic manipulation. If this disease mutates, it will cause millions of people to die. It's been a widespread concern in the medical community and your discoveries could potentially save millions of lives."

I stopped reading. I felt another flutter in my stomach. Mom and Dad had talked about superbugs countless times, fearful that taking antibiotics like candy for every staph bacterial infection could end up wiping out our species, making us resistant.

Stevenson went on:

"Your mentor will be Ximena, a widely published Ph.D., and MD who's been immersed in the issue of drug-resistant superbugs for the past ten years, with a focus on community associated outbreaks. EBEX could become a new pandemic, spreading rapidly among the vulnerable, including young teen athletes. Ximena is an expert on the topic and has completed trials in the initial stages just weeks ago for early new drugs that were found to potentially be effective. She is still searching for the most effective medicine for carriers as well. She's looking forward to working with you on this project and will be in touch with you this week to meet.

Your assignment is secret. You must not share any details of your project with anyone else. If you tell any outsiders, we'll use our discretion and remove you from the project. Again, this email and your task are strictly CONFIDENTIAL.

Sienna—you can make a difference—stop this debilitating disease that has gripped the world, leading to the point of desperation. Your help and wisdom are needed as we look forward to a secure and healthy future for all.

Good luck and please reach out to me if you need anything. I look forward to learning of your progress and hearing your final presentation. **This message will destruct once you close it.**

Best regards,

J.M Stevenson, M.D., Ph.D."

I didn't close the message immediately, instead rereading it three more times. I shifted in my seat, holding my tablet and staring at her message. Her note was so personal. She had so much confidence, and this health issue was real. What if my mentor and I could really develop a new drug to stop a deadly infection?

Willow was at risk; she'd had staph infections and a consistently weak immune system. She'd fought infections before but barely. It would be phenomenal. She'd been in and out of doctor's offices all week and in the hospital more times than I could count. She could so easily become resistant to antibiotics that fought unknown, rapidly mutating viruses. I remembered Mom and Dad panicking that she had to have IV's since her toddler years and could have died.

To think I could do this would be amazing—to help Willow and so many other people. It would take everything I had. Six months was not nearly enough time to get this task done, unless Ximena was way ahead of the game.

6

As I settled in for biology class, Kellen spotted me and sat down next to me. His breath was hot and heavy.

"I ran to class to get a seat next to you. You know it's rarely available." He pulled out his tablet. *Whatever.* I ignored him and took out my tablet, too.

He leaned in, breathing in my ear. "Did you get your email?"

I was silent while I clicked on the class notes.

"Oh, come on, Sienna. I know you got an email from Stevenson," he said.

The teacher asked us to stop talking and launched into the lesson. "Instructions for building all living things, like insects, people, or bacteria, are found in DNA molecules. DNA molecules have two strands joined together through complimentary base pairing. Does anyone know what these four building blocks that function together in larger units are called?"

I knew but waited to see if anyone else raised their hand.

Ms. Choi looked around the room, paused, then locked eyes with me. I offered, "They are called genes."

"Yes, that's right, Sienna. You guys should know this already. Sienna, can you explain what a gene is, so we are all on the same page here?" She turned her back to the class waiting for me to answer. Stella, who sat a few rows away, rolled her eyes, then looked at her phone. This was an advanced class, and I didn't know why some kids were in here.

"Each gene is a set of instructions for building a specific protein. A complete set of genes is called a genome. Every person's genome has the same genes arranged in the same order, but small differences in the sequence of bases in our genes make each person unique. Manipulating someone's genes can potentially lead to eliminating disease and choosing the characteristics of your child, but of course this complicates things." I sat on the edge of my chair and sighed.

My attention wavered when I saw Stella sit up and hold her cell phone under the desk. She nudged the student next to her and showed her a picture. I saw a red, swollen joint, maybe an elbow or a knee, I wasn't sure. It looked horrible and painful.

"Correct," said Ms. Choi, bringing my focus back to her. "We have three billion letters of the human genome containing 21,000 genes. On average, a human gene will have one to three bases that differ from one person to another. And you bring up a valid point, Sienna, about gene editing. It can be crucial to long term survival, but has its pitfalls, too."

"Yep, like the child isn't given a choice." I wanted to go on, but Ms. Choi clicked on her computer to bring up a power point presentation.

She dimmed the lights and I sat back in my chair, fired up. I wanted to stand up and debate, but as I looked around, students yawned and shifted in their chairs. I knew this stuff; it helped that Mom had talked about DNA since I was born. Honestly, it went back to when I was in the womb.

Choi started speaking fast and flipping through the

slide show. Lilly, sitting on my other side, looked down at her phone and scrunched up her face, then leaned over to show me the photo. It was the red, swollen joint. Now that I saw it up closer, I realized it was an elbow. Underneath the photo, text read, "Some kid on the lacrosse team. Maybe Anish or Jackson."

I shuddered and felt Kellen's eyes on me. I assumed he was pissed off at me for bringing up the gene editing thing. He probably thought I should have stayed quiet, but I didn't care what he thought anyway.

Choi finished the power point and turned on the lights. "For next class, read the section about genetic variation. With global changes and a population boom, you'll find this information extremely relevant. Be ready to discuss."

Then she dismissed us. I gathered my stuff, shaken by the nasty photo. I wanted to talk to Greyson and Avery to ask what they knew about the lacrosse player. Kellen probably knew something, but I didn't want to deal with him. I grabbed my backpack and got up. Kellen raised his eyebrows and blocked my exit. "What's your project?"

"I'm not telling you; it's a secret, right?"

"I'll tell you mine. We can help each other. That's how this will all work anyway. Eventually."

"You can do what you want, but I'm not saying. Now move out of my way."

Kellen stayed in front of me and blurted in a whisper, "I'm going to protect the atmosphere. Stop the holes from burning us alive."

Interesting. He may have been lying, but I liked my project better and wouldn't tell him a thing. His was good, though. We could use a safety net around the earth.

"Good luck with that." I pushed past him and out into

the crowded hall. Normal girls would die to be Kellen's lab partner—smart, tall, handsome, funny (only to some people), and a star lacrosse player with a huge ego. He had everything and anyone he wanted, any girl, too—except for me. Now he was taking this angle.

I lost him easily in the sea of our classmates.

~~~~~~~~

After school and practice, I grabbed my regular clothes from my locker, stuffed them in my bag and headed out to my car. I looked down at my slow feet as I crossed the parking lot. My life felt upside down. Last week, my future was mine, an empty road ahead, but today I didn't know what to think. My life was planned for me and I felt its grip. Like a vice clamping down on my whole body. I took a deep breath and looked up to find my car when I saw Greyson.

"Hey Grey, wait up!" I launched into a light jog.

"Hey, Sienna." He smiled back, his left dimple deeper than ever. He tossed his lacrosse ball to me, but I missed the scoop. The ball rolled under a car in the lot.

"Wasn't ready for that!" I said, looking down for the ball to roll out.

"When aren't you ready?" Grey asked, jokingly.

"Huh?" I grabbed the ball, then lost it again as I stood up. I felt my face flush. "How are you feeling? You scared me with your message."

"Yeah, I passed out. Had a fever for a couple of days. Crazy, but I think I'm okay. Benched for a few games but no big deal. I can still practice if I'm up for it."

"Is it serious?"

"The doc isn't sure. Wants me to keep an eye on this thing that's been bugging me."

"Oh, really? Anything to do with the photo going

around of some kid's swollen elbow?"

"Don't think so. I saw that photo, too. Kids are saying it's Anish, and he wasn't feeling good a few days ago. He's being checked out."

"Just watch yourself, Grey. You guys are all so close to each other in the locker room and on the field."

When I stood up, my head rushed. I squinted, letting the blood flow back up to my head. My thoughts flew elsewhere. I'd love to tell Grey what was going on. It'd be a release, and he could no doubt keep a secret. I wasn't totally on board with this whole contest thing anyway. Stevenson clearly stated it was all confidential though, and that we'd be kicked out of the contest if we said anything to anyone. She didn't seem the type to bluff.

"Did you have a tough practice?" Grey asked. As I handed him the ball back, a flight of butterflies seemed to take off somewhere inside of me. We locked eyes, and I had no intention of looking away. His boyish good looks and rugged athleticism caught my attention, and I knew he saw me as a challenge—one to "catch" up with on the field.

"Not too bad. Lots of running as usual."

"Typical. I hate being sidelined. Coach got mad at one guy who was being lazy, then made everyone run extra laps."

I felt dizzy again and leaned against his car.

"You okay, Sienna? Here, drink some water." He offered his water bottle to me.

"Thanks. Ya know, I think I'm dehydrated. I wasn't feeling great this weekend." I squeezed the water into my mouth without touching my lips to the top of the bottle. The water, cold and refreshing, slid down my throat. I craved more.

He frowned. "Just take the bottle. It's an extra I don't need. Drink up."

"Thanks!" With my lips fully on the bottle, I gulped. The water hit my empty, churning stomach with a cool feeling.

Grey looked at my hands and my nails with a quizzical look on his face, and his brow tightened. He went to open his car door, then stopped and turned back to me. "Hey, Sienna...do you have a game on Friday?"

"Yeah, pretty much every Friday we have a game. You guys?" I lifted my equipment bag, ready to head to my car. I was feeling much better and searched his eyes again to sense if he was feeling the same excitement.

"Yep. Wanna grab some food after?" he asked, biting his lip.

"That should work," I blurted out. "Let me check and I'll let you know."

I needed to figure out my new schedule and meet with my mentor before I could commit. I'd make it all work. Grey and I had been out a few times with other friends, but never just the two of us. I always spent any free time I had with Willow, since Mom and Dad were never around. But Grey was a longtime friend—we'd been friends since the age of seven—and I didn't want to ruin that, either. We were older now, but we shared some growing moments from when we were kids that kept us connected. We knew each other's favorites: our favorite hiding place, our favorite ice cream flavor, and our favorite song. We'd blast our music while swinging on our friend's swing set for hours. I saw his soft side as a young boy, his edge of fear of the neighborhood bully or the gentleness in his touch helping me with a Band-aid when I fell and scraped my knee.

My heart raced with the thought of just the two of us going out.

He shot back a killer smile. "Great. Check with you later." He pushed back his curly, jet black hair out of his green eyes and leapt into in his mud splattered Jeep truck.

We'd grown apart over the years, but lately his smile made me melt, and I found that I wanted to get to know him better now, as the more grown up and complicated Greyson. My eyes tended to linger on him when he was running out on the fields. I got in my car and threw my bag in the backseat, then slammed the door. My stomach growled, and I heard a ping on my phone.

"Hello, Sienna, this is your mentor, Ximena," the message read. "Dr. S told you about me, I presume. We have a lot to discuss. I will see you Friday at the party. After that, we will meet at the University of Chicago science lab in the basement. I want to brief you on a few things before we get started."

Ximena got straight to the point. What party was she talking about? She assumed I'd be available whenever she wanted me, but I had a life, too. I clicked off my phone and drove away.

7

I sat down at my usual lunch table with my lacrosse friends, though Jazz wasn't around. Avery looked up at me with her large brown eyes and patted the seat next to her. She had saved me a seat. Her shoulder length, thick brown hair was tucked behind her long ears. She scrunched up her button nose and pressed her lips together, glancing at her phone.

"Hey, Sienna, what's going on?" Her usual baggy, hooded sweatshirt hid her slim figure.

"I'm so hungry. What are you looking at?" I asked as they laughed out loud.

"Have you not seen the pictures?" Afra asked me as they looked down at their phones and laughed again.

"I've seen a few before school but not since. Let me see."

"It's sick," Avery said. She flipped her phone to show me more pictures of a red and swollen elbow. Pus oozed from a hole in the skin.

"That *is* sick. Let me guess, it's Anish's elbow." Grey had said he was sick and there had been some rumors going around. He still wasn't in school.

"Yeah. Some people are saying he got this while changing in the locker room. Now a bunch of guys think they're going to get it," said Afra.

"And some think it's some kind of STD. That's the other rumor. Any idea what it is?" asked Tansy.

"Some of the lacrosse guys think it's a bug or something he got from his dirty locker," said Blue.

"You mean an actual bug, like a tick or something?" Avery asked. "I've heard stuff like this can happen when you share things."

"I think more of a virus or something like it. Someone said his dad visited the Middle East and came back with this," said Blue, showing us some different pictures, closer up and at different angles. We passed her phone around and looked, pulling the photos in larger to see the pus. His whole arm was swollen.

"Try to help out your hairy teammate dry off by tossing him a towel and look what can happen!" laughed Tansy.

"I heard Anish saying he got it from another lacrosse player, maybe Greyson. You heard about his pimple, right?"

"No way he got this from Grey. He was fine yesterday when I saw him," I said, my heart jumping.

"Well, that's good. Everyone has to watch out and be careful not to get this horrible thing. I hope it doesn't spread any further. So many kids are in that locker room," said Avery, as she tapped away on her tablet, looking up rashes, viruses, and bacterial infections. "Wow, look at this, guys!" She showed us some pictures she found. Nasty!

Glancing up, I saw Kellen sitting at the table across from us. He stared at me, then came over. He leaned in and put his hand on my leg. "Did you get the invite?" he asked quietly.

"What invite?"

"Open your email and check. It'll be one helluva party." He brushed past me, almost knocking me off my seat.

"Who was that, Sienna?" Blue asked, taking a sip of her drink. "He's cute and hot for you."

"A guy I know from bio class. He's not into me. He asked me if I thought you'd go out with him." I smiled, and we all laughed.

I stayed seated while the others cleared their trays. After lunch, I opened my tablet and checked my mail. There was a new message from J.M. Stevenson, with the subject: *You're Invited.*

"You're invited to a pool party! Music, food & fun. RSVP by tomorrow. BTW, attendance is mandatory. Where & When: The Morton's Home, 18001 Thistle Ave. Friday, 7 pm - Midnight. Bring a swimsuit & towel."

The party was Friday, and it was Tuesday—short notice for a mandatory party. If Dr. Stevenson was going to be there, the party wouldn't be that fun. There were many other things I'd rather do than go to a party with a bunch of genetically engineered kids I didn't know. Besides, Grey had asked me out, and I knew I'd have much more fun with him. Honestly, this was still surreal—like someone else's life. This new project and Greyson. A pit in my stomach arrived again, and I swallowed hard to keep down my lunch.

"What's up, Sienna?" asked Tansy circling back to me. We usually walked to class together after lunch.

I stood up slowly. "Just pissed off at an email I got. I'll deal with it."

"What's it about?"

"A party." She followed me as I took my tray and dumped my trash in the recycling bin. I shook my head, staring at the cups and plates in the can. I'd plan to show up late to the party and leave early and pretend to be sick again. I'd probably really feel nauseous, anyway.

"That's not a bad thing, right?"

"Usually, but this isn't a typical party." We were separated by a bunch of kids all rushing to get to their next class before I could say more.

Rounding the corner out of the cafeteria, I bumped into someone, my face at his waist. Kellen was right in front of me. It was like he was waiting for me, spying on me the whole lunch hour. Under my breath I muttered, "Little *stalker.*"

I tried going around him, but he started walking with me. I sped up, trying to lose him and searched for Tansy. She was close by, so I reached to tug at her elbow. Instead, Kellen grabbed mine.

"Sienna, wait," he said, grabbing my arm. "Did you get the invite?"

I was silent, but he pulled me closer as we were squeezed by other students in the crowded hallway. His breath reeked of chips.

"Well?" he asked again. I wanted him to shut up, so I thought about sprinting away from him, but was trapped. If I answered, he'd go away.

"Yeah, I did. Now let go of me."

"It'll be awesome. We can find out what everyone's project is, and we can get to know the others who are like us." He was clearly more excited about this than me.

Meeting other designer kids might be a disaster and chaos at the same time.

"You know the mentors will be watching and listening to us—all the time. Cameras are probably on us right now." I looked up at the corners of the hallway and walked into our classroom.

"It'll be impossible to keep our projects secret from

everyone," Kellen argued.

He tried to find a seat near me, but nothing was available, so he sat next to Avery and touched her shoulder. She smiled and looked at me, then shrugged.

He leaned toward her and I read his lips. "Hey, did you do the homework?"

"Leave her alone," I mouthed.

~~~~~~

Mom and Dad forced me go to the party. They told me all about the Mortons and their Onyx Pharmaceutical company, but I zoned out for fifteen minutes of their speech. I knew most of the history of the company and about each of them already.

Duncan Morton, the great-great-great-grandfather of Catrina Morton was a small-town pharmacist who mid-career discovered a compound medicine to help slow down the growth of lung cancer tumors. His own father was suffering from the cancer and his tumor started to shrink. He was recruited to join a pharmaceutical company to develop it further. He eventually spun off to create his own pharmaceutical company, Onyx Pharma, with his son and daughter.

They hit it big with the discovery of a drug for pancreatic cancer, but the son got greedy and stole a patented medication for Alzheimer's and sold it to another company. His drug backfired on him, causing brain bleeds and a string of lawsuits. He was banished from the family. Onyx eventually was passed down to Catrina who pursued her career in business, so she could focus on the company's future and continued growth. She met Zach, the son of entrepreneurs, at graduate school. A dynamic couple. They married during their last year of school, and they'd have been leading Onyx for the past ten years, making it one of the largest drug manufacturers in the world.

I arrived at the Morton's house forty-five minutes late because I couldn't decide whether to wear a dress or skirt and which bathing suit to bring—my black bikini with white trim, a one piece, or nothing at all. I didn't know these kids but if I decided to swim, I'd have a choice of suits. I chose a short black skirt with a scoop neck white shirt and put on my favorite necklace, which had three tiny blue stones.

After the valet took my car, I stepped up to the large front door of the mansion. Two tall security guards with rifles stood at the front door while another without a gun reviewed our invitations, asking our names and dates of birth, and scanning us up and down with a metal detector wand. He raised his eyebrows and motioned for me to open my bag. He rifled through it, unzipping my cosmetic bag, then nodded for me to go inside.

I followed a few other kids inside the double wooden doors to the grand entrance. The floor was white marble, and when we looked up, we saw a cathedral ceiling overhead. An elegant crystal chandelier hung above us. I could see a large stone patio surrounding a pristine in-ground pool with a waterfall in the backyard. There must've been fifty kids milling around outside. It was balmy with a gentle breeze. The wind had died down from the day before, and the temperatures had finally warmed up another twenty degrees. Snow one day, then swimsuits the next.

Servers walked around with trays of food while a band played by the pool. The other kids kept walking through the house toward the back. I found myself standing alone, my shoulder bag with my suit and towel still flung over my shoulder.

"Welcome, please do come on in!" A woman with short, sleek blond hair and large framed red glasses greeted our group at the door. Her lips were puffy and covered in dark red lipstick. She was wearing a super short, tight-fitted blue and white striped dress and high black heels.

Before I knew it, she'd extended her hand to shake mine. "Well, hello, I'm Mrs. Morton. And you are?" Behind her were two bodyguards wearing dark suits, looking around, earpieces in place.

"Sienna." I shook her hand and noticed a huge diamond ring with some kind of dark blue stone, surrounded by countless little diamonds. Other bangles with more precious stones lined her wrist and clinked together, making a wind chime sound.

"Wonderful, welcome, Sienna! I've heard so much about you! How's your sister and parents? I just adore Skylar and Langdon. They both are so kind and have some amazing ideas. Look, make yourself at home and have some appetizers. Most of the kids are out back at the pool. There is a cabana out there if you want to change into your swimsuit." She pointed her polished fingernails toward the back of the house.

"Nice to meet you. Thank you very much." I didn't know how the hell she knew me and my family so well. Maybe she'd studied the guest list and had an incredible photographic memory. I knew I made an impression, but usually not on strangers.

I slung my tote bag over my shoulder and hugged it tight, then went to the backyard and grabbed something edible on a little stick that a waiter offered me. Yum. I was hungrier than I thought. But before my lips touched the grilled chicken, the skewer flew out of my hand; someone had hit my elbow as they ran by.

I lost my balance and fell, while he ran to the back yelling, "Onyx is a killer and price gouger!"

The security guards chased him to the backyard and pinned the skinny kid down on the ground. "They killed my grandfather!"

The crowd stood back and watched. Mouths gaped, but the music still played, loudly, the musicians probably unaware of what was happening. The guards quickly picked up the boy and marched him off the property. Oh yeah, I *had* read about Onyx jacking up their prices on some of their drugs a few months ago and patients complaining that they couldn't afford them.

I got to my feet while others stood around, not knowing what to do. Finally, Mr. Morton appeared by the pool and signaled the band to stop. He spoke in a deep, booming voice. "I apologize for the interruption, my friends. There seems to be some confusion. We are working it out. In the meantime, please enjoy yourselves. We have plenty to eat and drink."

Then the band started up again. I walked over toward the bar to get a lemonade and saw Kellen talking to a group of people. I turned the other direction, but it was too late.

"Hey, Sienna! Over here!" He waved to me. I sighed. I supposed meeting a few more kids wouldn't necessarily be a bad thing.

"Hi, Kellen," I said hugging my bag and tightening my fingers around my lemonade. I noticed some kids were wearing swimsuits and others were already splashing around in the pool.

"That was stupid, right? Who was that kid?"

"Who knows, but he obviously has a problem with Onyx. I don't think he's the only one."

"Whatever. Can't make everyone happy. Hey, I just met these guys, Tyler, Olivia, and Oceana. Guys, this is Sienna." Kellen placed his hand on my shoulder and gave me a gentle squeeze.

Tyler looked me up and down. "Hey, Sienna, all my friends call me Ty." He patted me on the back.

"Hi, Sienna, you can call me Liv," said Olivia, giving me a little wink.

"Okay, done with introductions! Now, go get your suit on and let's go swimming!" Ty tugged at the corner of his suit and headed in the direction of the pool.

"Well, I just got here..." I held up my glass, but his back was already to me.

"What? No excuse. Let's get wet!" He ran and jumped into the water.

"We're gonna eat, then go in the pool. Isn't it awesome?" Liv took a sip of her drink and pushed her long hair back over her shoulder. We all nodded at the same time.

I was hungry and very thirsty. Draining my lemonade, I was ready for another. "I'm going to get another drink and will be right back."

Professors stood around by the bar, hovering around Mr. Morton. "And Ximena, I heard your research is going well," I heard him say. "Please fill me in on your advancements."

His attention turned to a short woman, with a bold, short haircut and large, dark eyes lined with make-up. When she stopped talking, I stepped toward her.

"Ximena, is that you?" I asked, tapping her on the shoulder. I was butchering her name for sure.

"Yes, and who are you?"

"I'm Sienna."

"Ah, hello! You look just like your profile bio picture. I'm glad you made it." She turned to me, holding her hand out for me to shake. Her voice was deep and monotone. "By the way, it's 'he-mena.' My name is Spanish, so the X is pronounced like 'he.'"

"Sorry about that. I should have known. I hardly noticed from your picture, but your red hair stands out for sure. You look so different without your lab jacket on." An awkward silence hung over us. "Hey, how are Mr. and Mrs. Morton involved with Onyx Pharmaceuticals?" I blurted out not knowing what to say.

"You don't know?" she asked with an edge in her voice, as if I was stupid and the only person on earth who hadn't heard of them.

"Well, my parents told me a little bit about them— they're the owners and business side of it, and I've read a few not-so-good things."

"Well, Catrina is the CEO of Onyx Pharmaceuticals. Zach is the CFO, and of course a multi-millionaire entrepreneur."

"Our projects' bank rollers I suppose," I said under my breath but obviously too loud because Ximena heard me.

"Well, yes." She dropped her chin and drew out the "s." Then she looked out over the pool deck, sipping her drink. "Are you getting to know some of the other kids here? They're all so brilliant! You'll have much to talk about."

"Yes, slowly meeting some—"

She cut me off. "There's Dr. Stevenson, I want to speak with her. Excuse me. I'll see you tomorrow at the lab."

"Sure, what time? Where?"

I wasn't sure if she heard me since she was off so quickly to find Stevenson, almost twisting her ankle in her shoes.

I took my lemonade and found Kellen with the other kids. The food was delicious, catered, of course, by the best. Chicken, filet mignon, chilled oysters, fancy French cheeses, and about ten different kinds of salads and vegetables all displayed around an ice sculpture. I had never seen anything like it before.

We chewed in silence before Oceana started, "I'm not sure how you guys feel, but I think it's sick that I'm genetically engineered. My parents always treated me like I was special, but I thought I was just gifted, you know a natural thing."

"Yeah, it's sick," Tyler agreed. "I figured I was just lucky to be really good looking, smart, and athletic, since my older sister, Maya, is severely autistic. I thought I got all the good genes just by luck when I was growing up."

Wow, I hated this guy.

"Now that I know about the Eden Project, it all makes sense," he continued. "I don't blame my parents one bit. It'd be tough to handle two special-needs kids, no doubt. And we have our own way of communicating. I'm always telling my parents what she wants or needs. Some say I'm telepathic, but it can be exhausting. My parents admitted they hoped I'd go into medicine to help stop autism someday. It did cross my mind."

Oceana lit up. "That would be incredible! I'm like you. My parents want me to find a cure for multiple sclerosis. My mom's been battling it for two years now, and it's only going to get worse. I guess it's been the whole purpose of my life, now that I think about it. My parents pressured me all the time to do great things. Kind of annoying, really. They pushed me into STEM programs, creating engineering projects, designing new machines and technology to make things more functional. I liked all that stuff, but wished I had some more free time." She took a big bite of some salad.

"I consider playing lacrosse my free time," I said.

"Agree. I love soccer and tennis, but the pressure of getting to and winning at States was always there. But then again, it seems that I thrive on pressure and competition. Who doesn't like a good ass-kicking!" Oceana raised her fork in the air as she jumped out of her seat.

"Hey, Liv, what do you like to do?" I asked.

"Well, I was declared a genius at age three and absorbed everything I could at school and after school. I'm a concert pianist, singer, and spelling bee winner." Liv perched on the edge of her chair. "After taking an advanced environmental class, I became passionate about abating global warming by making our cars more efficient and became an advocate for veganism. I'm making big plans to help save the world from global warming, you know. I guess I knew from a very young age that I was destined for greatness." She smiled, looking smug.

"That's awesome! Anyone speak multiple languages?" asked Kellen.

Oceana piped up, smiling. "I speak fluent Mandarin. It helps that I have a photographic memory, too."

"You look beautiful today," Kellen said in Mandarin.

"I agree," said Ty, in the same language.

Oceana preened and blushed a little.

"What about me?" asked Liv, chiming in.

I looked at them, confused at what they were saying and at their excitement. I seemed like the only one who had gotten sick over the news. I kept silent for as long as I could until Oceana asked me what I thought.

"Well, to tell you the truth, I ran to the bathroom and threw up."

Oceana's eyes widened. "But why?"

"I was just shocked, I guess."

"Well, yeah, it's shocking news, but just think about it. We have an opportunity to use our talents to stop our self-destruction. What's scary about that?" Tyler asked, winking at me.

I paused. He had a point. "True. But the thought of being conceived in a petri dish in a lab made me want to heave. I mean, it's like my parents went through a check list to order me. Seriously, no surprises. They knew what they were getting."

Ty, Oceana, Liv, and Kellen just sat listening to my rant, staring at me as if I was a freak, which I was. We all were. Nothing I hadn't experienced before.

Kids would sometimes taunt me for being so smart that I'd pretend I didn't know the answer, or I'd just be quiet. My parents never made me feel special and weren't around much. They were always working, so I ended up taking care of Willow ninety percent of the time.

"I see what you're saying, Sienna, but you should feel fortunate," said Olivia after a long silence. "Not everyone is as lucky as us."

"She's right, you know," said Tyler. "And wait until you hear what I have to say later. We can turn this whole thing around. Liv, didn't you say your dad had skin cancer a few years ago?"

"Yeah, but he came through surgery and has been doing well. He has a few more lesions that they're keeping an eye on."

Then Ty realized Kellen had been quiet. "Kellen, how'd

you feel when you found out you were genetically engineered?" he asked.

"Me? Well, I was psyched to win the award and be at the amazing ceremony with all of you. I thought it was cool, and looking at my life, it seemed to make sense. And as I thought about it more, I realized I have a new purpose in this life. Since my parents split up and Dad died of throat cancer five years ago, I've been lost. A loose cannon, you could say. But I knew I'd go into some type of bioengineering program, like my dad did, in college. Now I have more direction. And then there's the fact that we can weed out the bad people and eradicate disease, right?"

"So, no one was pissed off at their parents but me?" I asked.

"Maybe just a little, for a tiny amount of time, but really, Sienna, there's nothing we can do about it now but go forward. We've been given a gift, a powerful gift," said Oceana. "Let's do what we can with who we are and where we are."

"Okay, enough of this serious talk, guys. Let's get wet!" Tyler jumped up and dashed to the poolside and started to push kids in.

A bunch were already splashing in the water. Some climbed on top of others' shoulders and were falling off. The music blared. I got up to go to the cabana and changed into my one-piece. Putting on a wrap, I stood at the edge of the pool.

Ty swam up and looked me up and down. "Whoa, Sienna. You look great in that suit. Too much coverage, though. You got a smaller suit in your bag?"

He jumped out of the water and hung on my shoulder, dripping on me, before he slipped his hand around my waist. I backed away. "You jackass! Stay away from me!"

I threw off my wrap and dropped it onto a nearby chair, pushing Tyler away from me. "I'm going in!" I jumped and splashed around for a couple of minutes, then hung out by the waterfall with some people.

As it got close to 11 p.m., Zach Morton called all of the mentors and adults to go inside for coffee, after-dinner drinks, and a meeting to talk about their roles, while the kids stayed, talking, eating, and then dancing.

After one really loud rock song, the band took a break and most of the kids got out of the pool to dry off and get some more drinks and dessert. The huge platters of cake, candy, and ice cream didn't stay full for long. I found Oceana and Liv sitting by the fire pit, roasting marshmallows. I never got tired of s'mores.

"Mind if I join you?"

"Nope. Plenty here," said Liv, handing me a stick.

"Thanks." I reached for a marshmallow to roast.

"I love that song the band just played. What's it called, 'Hangin' On' or something like that?" Liv began to hum, then sing the chorus of the last song the band played. Her voice was smooth and mesmerizing.

"Wow, you sound amazing, Liv!" said Oceana.

"Yeah, I like that song, too. 'Hangin' On' sounds right." I twirled my marshmallow so it would brown just right and not burn. The three of us began to hum the song.

"Hey, Sienna, I saw Ty checking you out. You have all the right curves in the right places," said Oceana matter-of-factly as she rolled her stick over the fire.

"Yeah, he was pretty forward about it. But I saw Kellen looking at you." I pointed my stick toward Oceana.

Speaking of Ty, I spotted him on stage next to the band with the microphone in hand, stumbling around with the amplifier. He was uncoordinated or else tipsy. I guessed the latter.

Holding the mic a little bit away from his mouth, Ty said, "You got the cameras and security, right Kellen?"

Kellen nodded back.

"Ladies and gentlemen!" Ty spoke firmly into the mic as it squeaked from feedback. "Can I have your attention?" After two minutes, the crowd quieted down.

"There, thank you! Now. I know most of you were shocked to hear about our conception. I know I was. Shocked. Not the traditional Mom and Pop thing, ya know." He swung his hips back and forth. "But now that it's all sunk in, I have a proposal for my new friends that I want to throw out to you, right guys?"

He opened his arms to the group of guys standing next to him. They all nodded and raised their cups. A celebratory drink, but likely not their first.

"We believe we are ready and destined to take over The Eden Project. When we look at the core of our existence and why our parents created us as they did—virtually flawless inside and out, brilliant, athletic, exceptional leaders—we got to thinking, it is our destiny that *we* are the ones who will save the world. *We are superior.* Since we are the chosen ones to develop solutions to major world health and environmental programs, then it's our duty and responsibility to keep our medical advancements and achievements to ourselves. With our talents, we should be responsible for taking our advancements forth into the world in ways we deem worthy. We are the designers and the only ones here on earth."

He raised his cup and the other guys did too, all shouting, "Cheers!"

"What's he talking about?" I asked my new friends.

"Is he drunk?" asked Liv.

"For sure," said Oceana.

Ty continued, "Hear me out. If *everyone* has access to our medical advancements and life expectancy creeps well into the one-hundreds, there will be overcrowding and too many people will lead to other, more serious problems and epidemics beyond our immediate control. For example, we'll experience severe food shortages, city crowding, and homelessness, more disease and epidemics, and joblessness which will lead to horrific violence. Violence is already out of control in our major cities. Do you get the picture? It's not pleasant, and it's certainly not cool."

"I hadn't thought about any of this," said Olivia in a deep, concerned voice.

My jaw dropped. Was he serious? Not tell anyone about our research? Keep our findings for potential lifesaving treatments to ourselves? I wasn't buying into his argument. Businesses would create jobs to accommodate the population explosion. We'd find a way to accommodate.

Ty went on, as if he could hear my thoughts, "I know you might be thinking we're crazy, but we're not. Think about it. We can control our destiny and our world. We can band together and continue our cycle of designer babies—perfect genetic people—IF we stay within our circle. We can eradicate disease altogether. It'll just be a matter of time. If you think about it, most of us probably are already privileged with having the best of the best, like access to supplements and organic foods. Not everyone is as fortunate. For this reason, we demand that you keep your scientific projects and discoveries to yourselves, within our group only. We are warning you not to let any of your contest information leak to outsiders."

Ty looked at his phone and typed something. Kellen stepped in and with his own microphone in hand, added, "Ty just airdropped a link to your phones to a secure private message group so we can communicate with you. Set up an account, and we'll be in touch on a regular basis. We'll share project status updates and future meetings. The Morgans already are talking about another pool party in a month. If you are not willing and choose to step out of these boundaries, then you will be asked to leave the group immediately. If you can't handle this responsibility, then it's best you let us know now before you even get started." His voice dropped low. His feet were planted, with his hands on his hips. "Believe us when we tell you that we will know. We have our ways."

Ty nodded at Kellen.

Whatever the hell they were saying was crazy. And Kellen had jumped into the fray with these delusional, egotistical bastards.

I looked at Oceana and Liv. "They're not going to get away with this. There's no way we're all going to do these projects for these selfish brats."

But the look in their eyes made me think otherwise. Quietly, they kept eating their s'mores and looking toward Ty, Kellen, and the other kids, listening for more. People like Willow would need these treatments, even if they weren't available for years to come. Their families would also need them. The engineered kids' families, too. I shifted in my seat and bit my nails.

Kellen strutted around the stage with the mic in his hand and his chest puffed up. "You'll be invited to our members'-only message board too, which I encourage you all to accept. If you decide not to, then you're basically done with us. Or shall I say, we're done with you." His smile was crooked.

I looked around the room to see the dumbfounded looks on the other kids' faces. No one was moving.

I jumped up. "You expect us to keep quiet, seriously?" I looked right at Kellen, who I knew was already inconsiderate of others, though this seemed extreme.

"Sienna. I'm glad you asked. It's really our duty. I realize your concern if you haven't thought through all of the ramifications. I mean, things are happening fast, and we just met our mentors, so it's hard to see the big picture right now. You can bet your ass Tyler and the others on the stage have spent some time discussing our future."

Tyler grabbed another microphone. "Sienna, first of all, I want to thank you for speaking up. Really, it's important we address everyone's concerns here tonight. We are extremely serious when we say we need to all be quiet about The Eden Project and our new projects. Someone with the wrong intentions could get ahold of the power and knowledge that we possess and turn it all around, using our solutions for the wrong purpose. Just imagine what havoc would erupt! So, with this in mind, we need to be protective of our intellectual property. Extremely protective and confidential."

"I get that to a point, Tyler. But we have to think outside of ourselves. I know most of us have family and friends who can benefit from our advancements and millions of people, too. I know you do. I can't see us being so selfish and self-centered as to exclude them from our ultimate findings." I raised my voice, since I didn't have a microphone. I was ready to jump up on stage any moment.

A few people mumbled, "Yeah, she's right!"

"Look, right now we are establishing our priorities and

that is to protect our intellectual property," said Tyler. "Again, I can't stress it enough that we are considering the future and keeping things under our control. We feel securing our information is the best possible solution to the long-term health of the world—both the physical actual earth and the future of humans." He paced the stage, looking toward the house to be certain no adults were emerging. The band began tuning their instruments and doing a sound check.

"But there's a lot more we need to discuss as a genetically engineered generation!" I shouted, trying to raise my voice above the band's disorganized chaos. Tyler directed his attention to the electric guitar player.

A security guy started to walk toward him, and Ty abruptly turned off his mic, said something to the guitarist, and almost bumped into the amp near his feet. He clicked his mic back on. "Now, let's get back to the party! Music please!"

He handed the microphone back to the lead singer of the band and the music started back up, louder than before. Everyone was sitting, staring, processing what was said, or "handed down" to us. Again, I felt like I was on a ride, with a driver in control of my life. The speed was picking up and all I want to do was put on the brakes.

Liv and Oceana gave me a look of "Seriously, you're gonna ruin this awesome party?" then screamed and jumped out of their seats to head to the dance floor. The party reached another level and the energy was palpable. It was like all these smart kids were blind to being led around on a leash. Seriously. I couldn't believe no one else stood up to question power hungry Kellen and Tyler. It was like they were smashed in the head with a rock and lost consciousness, and now these real-life geniuses couldn't think for themselves. I was suddenly exhausted. These kids, inflated with power, had yet to realize the gravity of their decision. They lived in an implicit bubble, and it was growing larger as it was launched into the air, floating further and further away from reality.

Suddenly my feet were swept off the ground and I was horizontal, staring up at the starlit, black velvet sky. It was strangely wondrous, and I felt so tiny floating up toward the darkness. *Please send me out of this world!* I begged.

Hands were all over my body, and I was taken deeper into the pool. I grabbed someone's forearm trying to find some balance. Before I knew it, I was thrown high into the air toward the deep end, then fell quickly into the water. I held my breath, but some water still entered into my nose. I hit the bottom of the pool quickly and used my feet and legs to push myself back up for air. Everyone cheered and laughed as I reached the surface of the water and gasped for air, my nose stinging as I coughed up water.

8

Soaking and shivering at the edge of the pool, I pulled at my wet ponytail as it dripped down my back. I breathed deep and hard as I gradually regained my normal rhythm. Grabbing a striped towel on the lounge chair next to me, I threw it over my shoulders, wiping my nose. Too bad if I got snot on someone's towel. They shouldn't have thrown me in like that. Stupid kids. My heart pounded as I closed my eyes. I was one of them.

In the pool, Oceana was being tossed around to the beat of the music and thrown just as Liv was being picked up. They high-fived each other as they passed one another. This was some sort of initiation, I guessed. They were all freakin' so excited. I was still in shock, and they were partying like they won the lottery or something. It was like we were being baptized.

I hugged the towel tightly around my shoulders and planned my escape. I'd go to the changing room and then sneak out the back. I felt a sudden urge to get away.

On the way to the bath house, Kellen walked toward me. He sauntered like he'd just scored with the hottest girl in the school, like he was untouchable. He was on a euphoric high. There was no way to avoid him, so I lifted my shoulders and chin and wrapped the towel around my waist and headed straight for him.

"So, you think you've got this all figured out," I stated, looking him right in the eye. My bravado rose from deep within, and I was ready to roar.

"Well, yeah, we kinda do," he sneered. Then he smiled, placing his arm around my shoulder. "We'll be an amazing team. You and I and the entire class here."

"What the hell are you thinking?"

"We know what we're doing. It's genius, you must admit!" He threw his head back and laughed.

"Stealing is not genius, you dumb shit." I pushed his arm off my shoulder.

"C'mon Sienna, you can't possibly think that we're stealing. It's our own knowledge and information. If it's ours, we can't really steal it, you know?" He put his arm back on my shoulder and squeezed, turning me to start walking with him.

"But we can't just abandon the mentors and other people who need help," I argued.

"Okay, I get you care, you're awesome. But they can figure it out on their own. If they can."

"But it's our obligation to help..."

Just then Oceana bumped into my shoulder as she was walking to the changing room. "Oh, sorry, Sienna!" She laughed loudly, almost tripping over her towel. "Isn't this a blast? Come to the changing room with me. I have to tell you something."

"Sure. I'm headed that way, too."

"Wait, you're not leaving already, right? The party is just getting started," Kellen protested, avoiding my earlier comment.

"I'm putting on my clothes, then leaving."

Kellen put his arm around my shoulder, but not in a comforting way. "You're in with us, Sienna, because if you have any doubts and plan to go out on your own, you'll regret it. You'll be lost and a total waste of a life.

It'd be a shame. Think of the potential you have—that we all have—in making a difference. That's what you want to do, right? Make a difference in this world?"

I swallowed hard. I wanted to leave, to run and hide for a little while. I brushed his arm off of me and ran to the bath house, but he followed me, leaning in for a hug. Damn him. He hung his arms around my neck, so tight that I was trapped. I held my breath.

"Think long and hard about this, Sienna. Long and hard. You're one of us from the Eden Project. There's no changing you or us," he whispered into my ear. A chill danced down my spine, long and cool.

"You have no idea what you're doing!" I yelled, gasping for air. "Get off of me!"

Just then Oceana came out of the shower, wrapped in a towel, long hair dripping. "What are you doing?" she screamed at Kellen.

"Just having a little talk here, Oceana. We're fine," Kellen said as he backed off and gave me a peck on the check. "Fun party, right?"

"Don't you dare touch me again!" I screamed.

"It's all good, all good," he said, walking toward the door. "See you two beauties, heading back to the party. It's raging." He winked as he walked out.

"Are you okay, Sienna?" Oceana asked.

"I'll be fine. Thanks for that!" My hands shook as I tightened my towel around my waist.

"Yeah, anytime. He was pushing his limits, I could tell. Are you going home now?"

"Yeah, I'm done for the night." I sighed and threw down my bag on the bench before walking over to the sink. I leaned over the sink and splashed my face with water, my eyes red and burning. Not knowing what to do next,

I combed my wet hair, arms shaking. He'd been so in my face, strong and determined. I hadn't ever seen that side of Kellen. It was like he was trying to control me, while at the same time flirting with me in a way that was confusing. Ugh! He, Tyler, and the others were taking on more than they could handle. They didn't know what they were up against. They were talking about controlling an entire generation and excluding people who needed help. I pulled my wet hair up into a bun, threw my bag over my shoulder and was out of there. I knew what I had to do.

9

In my car, I looked at my phone. Greyson had called and texted wondering if I was meeting him. Shit, I screwed up. I forgot to call him to let him know I couldn't meet him for dinner tonight. I wanted to see him, his sweet, innocent, normal face, right at that moment. It wasn't too late to text.

S: sorry Grey...I screwed up...just got your msgs. can you meet me now? sooo sorry I missed your msgs!

I waited to hear his reply. It was just after 11:00 p.m. I'd be awake most of the night anyway. I started my car and sat there. He was probably already out with friends, pissed at me. No reply. Come on, it'd been like one minute. But I was a jackass for not texting him sooner to let him know I was busy. Two minutes and nothing. Then three. Finally, after ten minutes of me just sitting and staring out the window with my phone on my lap, I felt and heard a ping.

G: thought you forgot. i made plans. want to come to Jack's and hang out?

Ah, phew! My hand shook as I typed back.

S: yep be there in 20 min he's in Deer Valley right?

G: yea :)

I'd race there, and there wouldn't be much traffic this late. I started the car and put Deer Valley into my navigation. I didn't know Jack well, but if Grey was willing to forgive me for being absentminded, I could care less.

When I pulled onto Jack's street, I noticed only a few cars parked in front of his house. The street was dark and the houses small and brick. It'd be very toned down and chill compared to the party I just came from. I parked a few houses down from Jack's and stepped out again into the cool, calm night. It felt like I was another world away. With my hair still wet and pulled back tight into a loose bun, I tied my jacket around my waist and jammed my hands into my pockets. I texted Grey that I was out front and asked him if I should just walk in or wait for him to let me in the front door. He said he'd come and meet me at the door. I stood alone in the quiet, looking around the house and at the same black sky dotted with stars. Taking a deep breath, my shoulders relaxed. I jammed my hands deeper into my pockets, fingers scrunched up. Peeking in the window next to the front door, I saw Grey walking toward me. A butterfly fluttered in my stomach. His jeans hung loosely around his thin hips and he moved like an athlete, with purpose. His smile assured me he wasn't upset.

"Sienna. Come on in…" Grey opened the door and squeezed my elbow.

"Hey, Grey. I'm so sorry I didn't text you earlier. I had to be somewhere. Last minute, ya know."

"Stuff happens. Glad you were able to come. Everyone's downstairs."

I took off my shoes and followed him downstairs. His shoulders were broad and his hair thick and wavy, curls bouncing as he went down the stairs. My stomach flipped, and I resisted putting my hand in his hair.

About ten other kids were hanging out, eating, drinking, and making out. Music blared. Grey led me toward a couch where a few other kids sat. We walked past a garbage can full of empty beer bottles and sat down, our legs touching. He leaned forward to grab some chips from the bowl on the table in front of us.

"Want something to drink or eat?" he asked. His breath faintly smelled of beer. As he reached, his shirt sleeve pulled up, and I noticed a red spot on his forearm, one I hadn't seen before.

"I'm good, thanks. You been here awhile?" I was still full from eating at the Morton's.

"I dunno, a few hours maybe? Hey Jack, Sienna made it! You know Sienna?"

"Uh, I think so, hey Sienna...what'z up?" Jack slurred.

"Thanks for having me over last minute." I wanted a beer, just to keep my hands busy.

"Sure, no problem!" Jack jumped up to change the music.

"So, what did you have that came up last minute?" Grey asked with a mouth full of chips.

I responeded, "Oh, well, ya know, it was uh, something to do with a project I'm doing. I just found out about it a few days ago. I'm so sorry I forgot to text you."

"That sucks." He pushed his leg against mine when he sat back on the couch, and my heart skipped a beat.

"I'll have to tell you more about it later. Kinda loud in here!"

"Did you say you want to hang out tomorrow?" He read my mind.

"Yeah, sure, after our lacrosse games? We'll be starving as usual." I moved my leg against his as I leaned in to hear him better.

"Okay. For sure you have nothing going on after?"
If anything came up with the project it'd have to wait.
"Yep, for sure. Hey, what's that on your arm?" I pointed to

the red area.

He must not have heard what I asked him because all he said was, "Great. Hell, yeah!" His smile melted me. "Whoever is done first with their game, meet at the other's game. Both home games, right?"

"Yep, perfect!" Relief flooded over me; he wasn't mad.

"Hey, your hair's wet." Grey reached over.

"Oh, yeah. I just didn't have time to dry it before heading over. I already screwed up and didn't want to be super late getting here."

"Glad you made it. Sure you don't want a beer or something to drink?" He stood up. "I'm getting another."

I got up, too. "Sure, I guess, thanks. Hey, what's that on your arm?" I repeated, as we walked toward the bucket of beers.

"What? Oh that. I think I just bumped my arm on something."

One of the girls put her arm around his neck as he passed and whispered into his ear. "Hey Grey...did ya see that gross pic of Anish?" she asked laughing.

He jumped back and turned to look for a drink, as if he didn't hear her. Everyone knew about Anish, and for sure all of the lacrosse players did.

"Well, did you?" She released her arm but nudged his side, clearly not giving up.

"Yeah, I've talked to him. He's really sick and in pain. He seemed kinda scared, too. All the guys on the team are worried about him and getting sick. The coach talked to us about not sharing stuff and to let him or our parents know if we don't feel well."

"Wow. It sounds serious," she said as she backed away. "I'm going to get another drink. Want anything?"

"No, thanks," we both said.

Grey saw a friend at the tap. "I'm going to say hi to Jack and fill up. You good?"

"Yeah, thanks. I see someone I want to say hi to also." I noticed a girl from one of my classes, so we started talking. Just two girls at a party. Normal teenagers. I'd never liked beer much, but right then it tasted amazing. I'd talk to anyone at this point. My first sip went down smoothly and hit my nervous stomach like a cool ice cube. Slowly, thoughts of the pool party drifted away and felt like it was all a dream, literally.

I lost Grey for a while. I overheard a couple of the guys say something about Anish, that he was still sick and would be out from school for a few more weeks at least. It was serious.

My eyes locked with Grey from across the room. His glassy blue eyes pierced mine and we started walking towards each other through the small crowd. I tried looking down but literally couldn't pull my eyes away from him. I was focused on him and only him. He was laughing, relaxed and happy.

"What's so funny? I know I'm super awkward, but really, you're laughing at my face?" I faked a laugh.

"I've never seen you drink beer, and you're loosening up," he said, smiling.

"Yeah well, if you had my kinda night, you'd understand why this is going down so fast."

"Well, you shouldn't drive home. Can you stay here?"

"I haven't had too much. I'll stop now, so in a few hours I'll be fine. Give me water." I put my arm around his shoulder so he would hold me up, putting my acting skills to full use.

"Okay, let's both chug some water and then get outta here." Grey grabbed my hand, and together we found

some bottled water in a nearby cooler.
  My buzz from being with him lasted all night.

10

With a two-fold buzz, a slight one from the beer and a major one from spending time with Grey, I slept probably two hours. My head spun with thoughts of Grey, Kellen, and the unreal pool party. Then there was the "baptism," Oceana and Olivia, and then Grey again. Ximena, the lab, Tyler delivering his ultimate plan to "his people." We had a responsibility. My head hurt and I couldn't stop the calamity inside. The sun was barely up when I slipped downstairs to get a bite to eat and find the biggest cup I could for coffee. A lacrosse game would surely clear my head and set me straight. And then I'd be with Grey again.

~~~~~

Our game ended before Grey's. We crushed our opponents, which was great, but I noticed Jazz had a burn on her neck. And then late in the game, a girl on the other team fell on her. She totally flopped on Jazz since we were winning by so much. It was so obvious, the ref even called her on it. When I asked Jazz about her neck, she said she thought she'd burned it the other day when she was outside for too long. Damn ozone holes. We were all warned to slather our entire bodies in SPF 50 sunscreen with zinc oxide anytime we were outside for more than ten minutes, no matter what time of year.

I cleaned up quickly and headed over to the guys' game with Jazz, Avery, and Blue. The fields were a mess from the recent rainstorms. They were ahead by one. Grey was feeling better and in the game. Soon after I got there, Grey flipped the ball into the goal and scored! He celebrated by jumping up and down, and high-fiving his teammates.

I yelled, "Way to go, Grey!" and he looked over, then pumped his fist. Even though I'd seen him only hours ago, I missed him. We locked eyes briefly before he was back to playing. Even his sweat looked good to me.

Avery nudged me, noticing our interactions. "Hey, what's up with that?"

"Oh, it's nothing."

"Really, is it? Doesn't look that way," Jazz teased. Blue laughed as we watched the game restart.

After they won and he cleaned up, we jumped in his car and headed to a small sandwich shop nearby. We settled into a booth and once we got our food, we were barely able to speak until we swallowed a few bites.

Finally, Grey blurted out, "Coach yelled at us for some of our plays, but hey, we won. Sometimes he's never happy."

"Ours, too." I took a long sip of my drink.

"What are you doing the rest of the day?" Grey coughed between bites.

"Homework and hanging out with Willow. You?" I took a bite of my sandwich, but Grey was still coughing and covered his mouth with his arm. "You want some water?"

He nodded, took a little sip, then coughed some more.

"Work, too," I continued. "Then some stuff my mom wants me to do around the house. But I'm not happy with her right now."

"Oh, why?" he asked.

"It has to do with the project. It's too long and boring

of a story to go into right now."

"Hmmm...okay. Whatever. What are you doing around the house?"

"Mostly work in the greenhouse. Taking some old stuff out to plant some things for the spring."

Grey coughed again at the same time my phone pinged. A message from Ximena: *see you at the lab today, have important things to go over and work to do. X*

The lab. Right. A daily thing now.

I also saw that Ty and Kellen had sent a reminder to set up an account for the private group. They resent the link. Resigned, I clicked the link and set one up. No matter how disturbed I felt, I had to stay in the loop to know what they were planning. Next, I texted Ximena, *yes, see you later, like about an hour.*

"You good?" Grey asked.

"Me? Just Willow asking when I'll be home."

I was not a good liar and wanted to tell Grey everything, but I didn't feel like dealing with the consequences until I knew more of Ty's plan. "Hey, what's new with Anish? I heard rumors and saw some pictures. Looks nasty."

"Yeah, the boils got worse on his elbow. And now he's on some serious antibiotics and at home until the open sores go away. He's got a fever and the shits. That's what his brother told me."

"Oh wow, that's not good."

"No, not at all, and now I'm hoping I don't have what he has." Grey coughed and scratched his leg. The spot on his arm wasn't worse but also not any better than 24 hours ago.

"I noticed that spot on your arm last night. You should get that checked out."

"I'm fine, really."

"And your locker is near Anish's." I paused, then looked at my phone when it pinged again. "Look, I gotta get going. Let's pay the bill and get outta here."

Grey held my elbow and we walked close together to pay with our tablets.

"I'll drop you off at your car. Let's do this again, soon," he said and put his arm around my shoulder.

Driving home, I couldn't stop thinking of Grey—us out last night and then today together at lunch. He made me feel good, an unfamiliar feeling lately. Spending more time with him meant less with everything else. My chest was tight. I stepped on the gas pedal and hauled home.

11

Ximena had texted me after the party that I was to meet her the next afternoon for a briefing. The U wasn't far from home. I'd eat, shower, and zip over there. I couldn't imagine her project briefing would be short, so it'd be a long night.

I found my way to the building where the lab was located. After taking an elevator down two levels to the basement, then getting lost in the concrete halls for fifteen minutes, I finally ran into a man wearing thick black-rimmed glasses who told me I was on the wrong side of the building. He escorted me to the hall that connected the two sides and I thought he'd turned back. Instead, I heard his footsteps trail behind me. I wanted to bolt into a run, but thought again, and turned around. "No need to follow me. I've got it from here."

"Just making sure." His voice echoed in the hall. "It's not easy to navigate down here. Why'd you say you were going to the lab?"

"Oh, I don't think I said."

"Hmm...good luck then!" This guy gave me goosebumps and I started jogging.

Showing up late for my first meeting at the lab to go over my project with my mentor was not cool, but then again, I wasn't even one hundred percent sure I was all in on this project.

I had broken into a sweat when I finally found Ximena's

research and lab room. There were keypads with letters and numbers on the outside of the door along with what looked like a face and iris scanner (aka CFAIRS, Combined Face and Iris Recognition System). I had seen one only once before at Dad's office. The door was propped open, so I stepped inside.

Microscopes of all sizes adorned the long tables, sinks were spotless on the side of the room, and glass jars and beakers of all sizes were laid out on various counters. The chemical smell cleared my sinuses as I stepped further into the room, my shoes squeaking on the clean floor.

Ximena peered into a large microscope, wearing a white lab coat, as she mumbled, "The cells appear to be white and multiplying, while the cell walls..." She stopped and I cleared my throat. I noticed the tips of her toes barely touched the bottom of her stool.

"Um, hi, are you...?"

"Ah, Sienna, you finally found your way here." She pulled back from her instrument and glared at me with her dark eyes. This was going to be interesting.

"Yeah, sorry, it's very confusing down here." I felt stupid saying this, but felt lame not being there on time and didn't know what else to say.

She waited for me to come over to her. "Good to see you again." She stood and stuck out her hand. She was several inches shorter than me, so now that she was standing, I was looking down at her. Her voice was edgy and loud to compensate for her lack of height.

My hand was sweaty and a bead of sweat crawled its way down the middle of my chest. I scratched my shirt to stop it while I looked her up and down before shaking her hand.

Not to stereotype or anything, but she was your typical science geek. Her skin was pale from being inside a lab all the time, her fingers were bony, and her eyes beady. Her red hair was no doubt a bad dye job, hurried and uneven. It was growing out and her roots were peppered with some gray. Her eyes were like shiny marbles. She took all of me in, her lids widening like a cartoon character.

"Can I see what you're looking at?" I asked as I sat next to her. I was hoping to feel a little more comfortable at an equal level.

"Sure." She sat back down.

I peered into the microscope at her prepared slide. The instrument was wicked powerful! The cells were active, dividing fast.

"This is amazing! These cells are dividing like crazy." I couldn't believe what I saw.

"I'm glad you find this fascinating," Ximena said, her voice calm. I noticed that her tone was always authoritative. I stared into the scope for at least five more minutes, watching the cells on the slide until finally Ximena interrupted.

"Sienna, I'd like to get you up to speed on this project."

"Of course, sorry about that." I pulled back, feeling dizzy trying to focus on her. Not a hair was out of place on her little head.

"I've been doing this type of work for close to twenty years. I was about your age when I started. I'm looking forward to your insight on this and to finish this up so people can benefit from a new form of treatment." She pulled up a spreadsheet on her computer. I sat hunched on my stool, in awe and silence.

"You see, these are some of the tests I've done on various antimicrobials that have developed over the years.

Not very effective, can you tell?" She pointed to some graphs on her computer.

I nodded.

"And here, see this? This one is the closest I've gotten to a possible intervention to this current strain. See this here?" She pointed to a blip in the graph. "Five years ago, we did a trial on this next-generation medication and it worked for a few people, but not others. It was back to the drawing board. We need a long-term solution to the drug resistant superbug. A new antibiotic that bacteria can't resist. Something that will continue to work like a slow-release medication, I believe. There's the vaccine path, too. But I've been focusing on a next-gen drug. Then to make things more complicated, some people are carriers, we just don't know who."

"So, you'd like me to take more samples to test?" I wasn't quite sure where she was in the process, since she'd been working on this for so long. She must be close to a final drug. From what I could tell, it looked like she was on the right path.

"I'd like for you to help me test this new drug combination that I think has potential. I want you to help me develop this and take it to the next level."

"Ah, okay," I said, smiling. This would be huge. My heart raced and my hands began to sweat.

"I need a fresh young mind like yours on this to take a different spin on my ideas. Sometimes when you work on something so long, you get stale. Mental blocks happen and I need a fresh perspective. I saw what you've done with your other projects and the Powell Award you received. You're brilliant, Sienna," she said definitively and looked at me like a proud mom. A look I literally hadn't ever seen before.

"Thanks. It's just what I like to do," I said, shrugging.

"Well, I'm glad to have you on board. Together we can make a significant impact on lives and our world."

"You really think so? I've known a lot of sick people." I was surprised how my throat clenched when I said this.

"Here, let me show you some of my recent tests and findings." She pulled up another file. "It's going to be a lot of work, though; a lot of hours in this lab in order to meet our deadline. Countless. But I believe we can do this. Don't expect to have much of a social life for the next few months." She looked me up and down, her eyes stopping on my bruised knee.

"I figured," I said, biting my fingernails.

"What's that bruise from?" she asked.

"Lacrosse game yesterday."

"Ah, hmmm…you may have to stop that. Don't expect much free time." She scanned her computer.

Yeah, right, like I'd give up lacrosse for *anything*. I wouldn't cut back on practice and games; I'd just work late nights and sacrifice sleep. Our team was kicking butt and we were favored to win regionals, even States.

"You have the potential to win this contest and save lives, Sienna. This is very serious business."

I sat quietly for a minute. It felt like a good time to take a deep breath and say, "I get that. I really do. You'd be amazed at what I can accomplish in 24 hours. I don't need much sleep. You'd be surprised."

"I've got a timeline for us to follow, and I expect you to stick to it." She tightened her thin lips. She was more of a tight ass than I first thought.

"Sure, whatever you need." I decided to play her game for now. She was almost certainly feeling the pressure from her billionaire funders, right? Fair prize for me, but she probably got a huge pay off if we won this contest. She came across as cutthroat—willing to do whatever it took to win and win big, to finally finish her decade long project that she'd poured her life into.

"There's a lot of oversight with this project from mentors. That's why we're here. And my superiors want weekly progress updates, maybe daily. No exceptions."

"Got it," I said, shifting in my seat. The picture became a little clearer to me now. These geeks were going to be looking over my shoulder every minute. They could probably hack into the lab computer and track all of our work right this second. I heard that's how these billion-dollar projects worked. I read a lot about the pharmaceutical industry, keeping up with any new trends on drugs that might help Willow. They knew when you got up to go to the bathroom and how long you were gone.

Luckily, I had workarounds. Dad and I knew about hackers, maybe too much about them. I'd find a way to hold onto a bit of my normal life, too, see my friends, and play lacrosse.

I stayed another hour in the lab reviewing the protocols with Ximena. She briefed me about her progress and what I was to do next. I took mental notes and notes on my tablet. When she was done, my head was spinning with all the data Ximena had unloaded on me.

As I suspected, the lab had tight security. Before I left, Ximena registered my fingerprint and iris map so that I could access it on my own at any time, day or night. There was a keyless entry and I could only enter it with my fingerprint and iris. I had to place them on the scanner to log out and lock the lab, too. There were lot of lights and beeps and an automated woman speaking instructions. Cameras were all over the room and people were watching constantly. The walls felt like they were closing in, and I had to leave.

Finally, I found my way out of the lab. Anxious for some fresh air, I rushed toward the door and burst out. The sun was just about down, and the cool air slapped me in the face as I took a long, deep breath. Gazing up, I saw that a few stars were beginning to sparkle high in the sky.

I screamed, releasing the suffocated feeling that had wrapped around my body from the intensity of the past two hours. Scanning the building, I saw more cameras on corners, a bright light shining directly on me.

12

It was almost midnight when I walked into my house, famished. I breathed in the smell of fresh blueberry pie, which made my mouth instantly water. I thought of Willow. I was always thinking of my sister. Willow's favorite pie was blueberry and Mom made it as often as she could pick fresh berries from our indoor garden. She'd go on and on about the antioxidant properties. If we didn't have them, she'd order them months in advance from the best markets, so we'd have the freshest. They were big and juicy. Perfect GMO berries, ha! Ironic.

Here I was, a genetically engineered girl eating genetically modified organisms, resistant to disease and able to handle stresses from the environment. We'd both been altered. I held a spoonful on my fork and studied their perfection. Mom and Dad had been eating these berries for at least seventeen years, I guessed.

After I ate a big piece, slowly chewing and savoring each sweet, guilty bite, I headed upstairs and saw that Willow's light was still on. I knocked on her door and peeked in.

"You're still up?"

"Yeah, it's late but I can't sleep," Willow said, getting out of bed.

"Did you have some blueberry pie? I just did. Yum." I licked my lips.

"I had a small piece. I got to watch a movie today about

the apocalypse, so my infusion wasn't too boring. Those stories really scare me because I know it can happen and probably will before we know it. I haven't done much to be tired. You have some blueberry stuck on your tooth." She smiled and steadied herself as she stood, then walked toward the bathroom.

"Oh, thanks. I could eat the entire pie, but I know you want more tomorrow." I picked out the blueberry skin. I heard her flush in the other room. "You know, you shouldn't be scared too much about the apocalypse. People are doing what they can to stop it. If it's possible to stop." I wanted to believe this in my heart of hearts, but so much was out of our control.

"Why are you home so late tonight?" Willow asked.

"I've got a new project. I can't say much about it, but it'll take any extra time I have."

"*All* your extra time?" She sat down on her bed next to me and grabbed a corner of her blanket, twisting it in her fingers.

"Yeah, but it could help a ton of people." I rubbed her thin arm, feeling bad now about eating any of her pie.

"Well, if they need you for the project, then they have the best and smartest woman in the world," she said, forcing a little smile.

"I don't know about that. I hate that I won't be around much."

"Me, too. Can we still have girls' night and hang out? Please?" She brightened up again.

"Of course! I'll always make time for girls' night. Always." I'd find a night soon and put it on my calendar. It was always our special time. "Okay, now time to get some sleep. I've still got some homework to do."

It seemed to never end, but the pie gave me a second

wind and I was awake again. The sweet taste of blueberry lingered in my mouth. I gave her a kiss on the cheek and pulled her covers up to her shoulders. She snuggled in.

"Good night. Remember, believe and you can do anything," we said in unison.

We said things at the same time a lot; reading each other's minds became a habit from spending so much time together during her monthly antibody infusions. We would read, sing, watch movies, shows, and play games together during her one to two-hour long sessions. We knew each other better than anyone else.

More than once she'd caught something that her body couldn't fight, and she had to stay in the hospital. I was scared but never let her think I was. We'd Skype and always talk about what we'd do when she got home.

In my room I sat on my bed and pulled out my tablet to check my assignments for the next day. Luckily, I'd been able to get a lot of work done at school today. I speed read so that helped. Next, I read my text messages. One from Greyson.

hey, r u ok?

He'd sent this over two hours ago.

I typed back, *yeah, fine, u?*

It was a few minutes until I saw his response.

G: *fine. Ur headache gone?*

S: *oh, that, yeah.*

G: *u never miss a ball! Couldn't believe it…*

S: *no big deal…I'm human 2, ya know…it happens* ☺

G: *guess so. Wanna grab some food after ur game on Fri?*

S: *hmmm…maybe…still not sure if I have time. Will let u know asap…*

I had no idea what Ximena would want me to do but I had to eat, especially if I was to work all the time. I needed the energy and I was getting tired of my natural energy bars all the time.

G: *k...hope so..lmk. c u tmrw.*

S: *k. thx, g-night.*

I wanted to hang out with Grey, but if I led him on and then didn't have much time to be with him once this project got going, it wouldn't be fair. But the project wouldn't last forever. A deadline loomed. On the other hand, his black curls and his deep dimple were outrageously cute and irresistible. Instantly I felt warm all over. I had to find some time on Friday to be with him. In reality, we'd been together all these years, but now things were different. We *looked* at each other differently. I read his text again and rolled over onto my stomach.

I opened my tablet to get back to work. It was late and I had at least another hour of homework to do.

Mom's footsteps came down the hall. "You're still awake?"

"Yes, long day and still have a few more things to do for school."

"Long day for me, too." She sat down on the bed, her eyes red, her hair a mess. "Look, I've been meaning to tell you something since you learned of the Eden Project." Mom took a deep breath and looked me in the eyes. "Dad and I want to have another baby like you." Her mouth curled into a smile.

I turned and faced the window. "Wow, Mom. You guys are crazy. Literally." I choked back tears. She was slamming me with all kinds of crazy shit right now. She couldn't stop herself. It was just how she was.

"We've been talking about it for a while now. Actually, for years, but we finally feel like the time is right. Dad and I feel like we owe it to our community to have a boy this time, who will carry on your work, Sienna. Who will lead his generation to do great things and not continue on our path of self-destruction. Another project recently launched, and we want to be a part of it." Her statement was definitive. They had made up their minds.

"But Mom, you're getting old, and Dad's even older. Besides, Willow needs your help more than ever now. What about Willow?" I shouted her name a little too loud. I didn't want her to ever, ever hear this conversation in a million years, and I could think of a million reasons that second for them not to have another child. They were so freakin' selfish.

"Willow's doing fine. I mean, she has her ups and downs, but more ups now than anything else. A baby will be good for her, too…" Mom's voice trailed off.

"What do you know about her ups and downs? You're never there for her, or for me, for that matter. Besides, a baby will just complicate things. There's no way I'm taking care of this baby, too."

"C'mon on, Sienna, calm down. You know that's not all true. Of course, you won't take care of the baby. You've got your work and school to focus on. You're grown up and we all get older and take on new responsibilities in our lives. We all know our age doesn't matter. This is the *future,* Sienna. Besides, I had my first attempt last month. I could be pregnant and will know soon. I'm probably not, since statistically these things take several months. We'll see. But we wanted you to know."

She pressed her hands firmly on the table and got up, turning for the kitchen to get more water. I felt a deep chill in the air.

This was it. There was no changing her mind. I had tried before.

13

On Monday, Greyson wasn't around at lunch and I didn't see him while passing between third and fourth block as usual. I figured he was caught talking to a friend or his teacher. As I started to jog toward to the lacrosse field, I looked for him, as we often met up and ran out together. My head was in full throb mode, so jogging was only making the pain stronger. I pushed through it and hurried out to meet my team. Humming, I found the beat, and took my stride down to a walk. I slugged some water down my throat, hoping that would help. Grey was nowhere to be seen. Some of his buddies walked out to the field but he wasn't with them.

I caught up with his teammates. "Hey guys, have you seen Greyson today?"

"No, we were looking for him in the locker room. Maybe he's out at the field already," one kid said.

"He wasn't in my math class," another offered as we picked up the pace together.

"Hey, weren't you at Jack's party on Friday?" another asked, throwing his ball up and catching it in his net. "With Greyson, right?"

My mouth was crazy dry, and I swallowed hard. "Yeah. I was."

"Fun party. Anyway, I thought I overheard someone say he's sick. I usually eat lunch with him, but he wasn't there."

"Okay thanks, guys. I'll check in on him later. Have a good practice," I said, rubbing my forehead as I ran ahead of them. My head still hurt and hoped I wasn't getting sick, too. Grey may have seen the doctor after I left him on Saturday.

I arrived at the field ten minutes early and called him to check in quickly but got his voicemail. "Hey, Grey. I haven't seen you today. I hope you're feeling okay. I had a fun time this weekend...uh, call or text when you can to let me know you are okay. Thanks, see ya, bye!"

I hung up, hating my message, but it was too late to erase it. I was so awkward and stupid when it came to guys. Having no experience didn't help.

I ran a warm-up lap around the field, sucked down a few gulps of water, and snuck out my phone to check my text messages, just in case I missed one from him. Nothing. Shit. I'd made a fool of myself at the party.

My stomach was jumpy and my headache raged. I drank more and stretched while my teammates straggled onto the field. Coach hated when we were late, and she was ugly when she yelled.

After everyone warmed up, we stretched some more. I looked for Jazz but didn't see her.

"Blue, where's Jazz?" I asked. "I hope that girl who landed on her didn't hurt her last game."

"Haven't seen or heard from her since Saturday. I tried calling her and she hasn't called me back." Blue reached for her toes. "I'm getting worried. Seriously."

I stood up, reaching for my toes too, still looking around for Jazz. "Me too. She already missed a ton of practice from who knows what."

"Yeah, and I noticed a burn on the back of her neck. I can tell Coach is pissed, too. Well, maybe concerned."

I switched positions, reaching over my head to stretch my side. "And she's missed a ton of classes, so no doubt her grades suck. She's missed so much school. Maybe her classes are too hard. She's taking a bunch of advanced classes and you know how her parents are. Seriously, they ride her."

Blue stood too. "It sucks. And she has piano and lacrosse. Too much. I thought she said a while ago that her parents want her to play at a concert in New York and she didn't want to. They had a huge argument."

"Poor Jazz. I miss her. Let's keep trying to check in on her. I'm worried about her neck burn, too. I'll call her on my way home, and you try too. Let me know if you get in touch." I took my stick as Coach told us to get in our lines to start some drills.

Our practice was rough with some extra sprints at the end—just when we were most tired. My headache stopped sometime midway into practice, and I dripped with sweat as I walked to my car. Checking my phone, I saw a voice message from Grey.

His voice was weak. "Hey Sienna, sorry I missed your call. I'm really sick. I have a headache, fever, and gross stuff coming out both ends. I'll spare you the details. I slept all day Sunday and most of today. Hope you're fine. I had fun on Friday and Saturday, too. Talk later."

He coughed throughout his message and barely sounded like himself, poor guy. I rubbed the back of my neck. I seriously could not get sick. There's no freakin' way I could sleep all day. I revved up my car and steered toward my favorite pizza place. I grabbed a couple of slices of pizza then headed to the lab. Before I got out of my car, I loaded on my deodorant; there was absolutely no time for a shower.

At the lab, Ximena was talking on the phone when I showed up. I peeked at her computer file open at her workstation. The file showed some kind of assay, or analysis, to detect mutations in specific genes in bacteria, which would help in treatment decisions for some new targeted therapies.

Ximena raised her voice. "I asked you to test these therapies months ago!" She paused and listened, then cut off the person on the other end. "I don't want to hear any more excuses, Gene!" She abruptly ended the call.

"I'll be damned. No one wants to take responsibility for screwing up," she spewed, slamming an open palm on top of the table. "Now we're behind. I was all set to launch this susceptibility testing protocol and now it's not ready." She clenched her jaw so tight I thought for sure a vein would pop.

"Look, I'll do the testing. I've done this kind of stuff before." I strummed my fingers on the desktop, suddenly anxious to dig into this project.

"Yes, let's get you going on this. You know, I was expecting you in the lab more this weekend, at least a few hours on Sunday. Where were you?" She turned and glared up at me.

"Oh, sorry, I didn't realize. I had family stuff to do and a game," I mumbled as she stiffened.

"Excuses, again!" She threw up her hands.

"I'm a fast worker, so let's stop talking and get working." I was determined to move on.

"Yes, yes. Good. Let me see...this may just work out after all." She pulled up her stool and showed me the details of the assay and what this Gene person was supposed to do. She took me through the steps, and I got working on the susceptibility testing. I was prepared to work into the night to get us caught up. If we tested this new therapeutic combo medication on that adapted gene, we'd be golden. If the drug didn't work, then we'd be back at the drawing board but with more information for the next round.

A few hours later Ximena left the lab to meet with Dr. Stevenson and some other mentors. I continued to do the preanalytical steps, sample processing, pipetting, and used the centrifuge. I read and re-read the laboratory informatics system and plugged in my processing results. My eyes became so dry and tired I had to lay my head down on the desk. I figured just a few minutes of rest and I'd be able to keep working.

Hours later, I woke up with my arm asleep, tingling underneath my head. I tried moving my arm, but it slipped off the desk like a rubber snake. I shook it out to get the blood flowing again. A small pool of drool had formed at the corner of my mouth. I lifted my head. Where the heck was my bag and phone? Disoriented, I fumbled around the room a few minutes and then suddenly remembered I put my bag on the floor by the door. I pulled out my phone to see it was 5 am! Crap! I had been there all night. I wondered if Mom even realized I wasn't home. She'd texted me once just after midnight.

A message from the designer kids message group also popped up.

"Hey guys, submit your weekly project updates by the end of the day today. Outline format, highlight your progress, findings and any results. Party at Morton's place! Let's get together this Saturday night. RSVP at the following link. See you there!"

Ah, another party. I'd feed them something about my project so they'd think I was in on their game.

Next, I called Mom.

"Sienna? Are you OK?" She seemed genuinely happy to hear from me. Crazy, right?

"I'm fine, Mom. I fell asleep at the lab. I figured you'd track my phone anyway," I said groggily.

"Yes, thankfully, I did, so I knew you were at the lab, safely locked in. When I didn't hear after calling, I figured you fell asleep. I need to get Ximena's number just in case."

"I'll get you her number. I worked all night and dozed off, I guess." I wiped my eyes and shook out my hand, still a little tingly.

"You're coming home now, right? I need to talk to you and then get to work, of course."

"I'm getting my stuff now and will be home soon. I literally stink and can't stand myself right now. I desperately need a shower." I sniffed the air. Yes, I really smelled bad.

"See you at home, then. Let's have a cup of coffee together. We have lots to discuss and catch up."

"Everything okay?" I slipped my bag onto my shoulder.

"Yes, sure is. Oh, darn it, I can't wait to tell you until you get home!" There was a long pause, then she blurted out, "I'm pregnant! I just found out last night. I could barely sleep. The artificial insemination took last month; we're going to have a boy who's just like you. You're having a brother!"

"Seriously, Mom? I know you told me you were going through this, but already, on the first try? A baby in the house..."

A crying, stinking baby who I'd probably be taking care of while Mom and Dad worked non-stop. They could at least have waited until I was at college. I rolled my dry, burning eyes. Screw her and Dad and their new project. I wasn't going to be a part of it and their control-freakish lives. She'd have to find someone else to take care of their new "project." I wasn't going to be the one responsible for raising their child. I had taken on more than my share with Willow.

"What were you guys thinking? Again? You're seriously engineering another perfect child to live in this stressed-out world we've created?" I slammed the lab door behind me, hoping she'd hear.

Who really knew what this baby's future would be and what his world would look like—if this world was even still around when he grew up.

14

It was two in the afternoon and my eyelids were heavy. I struggled to focus in advanced literature class. The teacher's monotone voice hammered on, and I couldn't make out any words. One eyelid drooped shut, then the other. I had been alert all morning, buzzed by the caffeine from a specialty organic double caffeine coffee, with a splash of cream to deaden the bitterness. Mom brewed it, then realized she shouldn't drink it. I took my time getting home that morning, so I'd miss her. I knew she had to go to work and wouldn't wait for me to drink coffee together.

After only being able to focus on the assay work at the lab, all I could think of now was a baby boy crying in the house. Noisy and smelly with poopy diapers. And even though I'd be off to university soon after he was born, crying was crying. Gradually the caffeine effect wore off. The doctors hadn't figured out a way to change my sleep cycle when they messed with my genes. I could get so much more done if I only needed three or four hours of sleep! I leaned forward on my desk and laid my head on my forearms.

Fifteen minutes later class was over, and everyone was getting up. My next class wouldn't be any better. I started stumbling toward the student center to hide and get a nap. I'd watch the class online. When I got there, I checked my messages on my tablet. One from Willow and one from Grey sent a few hours ago. I read his first: *not getting better. worse fast. doc soon.*

Poor Grey. I'd never known him to get so sick. I texted back: *get better. Lmk what dr says.*

Willow's message was short: *home tonight? Can't believe m&d news.*

Willow must have felt terrible about this baby. He'd only keep Mom busier than she was already. Willow always made excuses for Mom and Dad's absence. When they canceled lunch dates with her, usually last minute, she wouldn't get mad, saying they had more important work to do. A few times, they took us to the theatre in Chicago, but they'd check their phones for messages and leave in the middle of the show to make calls.

I quickly texted her back: *yes. Talk then.*

I'd have to get home to eat something before going back to the lab.

Dinner together?

I replied, *yep* ☺

I settled into a quiet corner and cuddled up against my bag. My eyes were heavy again and I pulled up my knees, trying to find a comfortable position. I closed my eyes but the buzz of other students talking was distracting. I let my mind wander to Grey, imagining him walking down the hall with his slight swagger, pants hanging off his hips in a rugged, boyish manner with his backwards baseball cap. His smile would spread as he saw me down the hall walking toward him.

I'd never known Grey to be sick enough to go to the doctor. He should have snapped out of his flu or virus or whatever it was by now. I played with the zipper on my bag. Damn it, I couldn't settle down. I texted Dad to ask him to call me out of school, telling him I had some lab work to do for the project. Ten minutes later he texted back that he called the school.

The only way I'd relax was if I could see Grey to be certain he was okay. I got up, grabbed my stuff, and headed to sign out. On my way out, Dad texted again, *The woman at school asked if you were sick with a fever. She said a lot of kids are being called out for being sick. How are you feeling?*

I put the back of my hand to my forehead; no fever. I texted him back, *No fever. Headache and tired but that's from lack of sleep, I think.*

LMK if you do feel sick. Something's going around
Will do Dad

With Grey on my mind, I gradually got a second wind. I drove with the window down, cold wind in my face, and my music playing loud. *I'm coming over. Hope ur home*, I texted Grey. He sent nothing back.

I arrived at his house about twenty minutes later. The garage was open and a car inside, so I assumed he was home. His house was a split-level, probably eighty years old. The siding was pulling off in sections and paint was chipping. I walked past the front bushes, all brown and dry and a few dead. The walkway was cracked. I knocked on the door and after a few minutes, his mom arrived.

"Hi, Mrs. Halloway. I heard Grey's not feeling well."

"Hi, Sienna. Yeah, he's pretty bad. We just got back from seeing the doctor, and now I'm going to pick up some antibiotics. He doesn't think Greyson will get better on his own," she said through the door.

"I'm sorry he's so sick. Can I see him?" I put my hand on the door handle.

"Well, I don't want you to get sick, sweetie."

"I don't either. I brought a mask, just to be safe." Once I said this, I realized it sounded kind of weird. But with the work Mom did, she was always thinking about viruses and made us carry masks all the time. Weird, but smart.

"Oh, in that case I guess, if you really want to. You can stay with him while I go to the pharmacy." She opened the door.

"Okay, thanks. Hey, any word on Anish and how he's doing? I know he's been sick, and I worry that Grey got this from him."

"You know, I mentioned that to the doctor and he just took note. He said he'd look into it and follow up with Anish's doctor. Who knows. These doctors are so overworked today. It's just crazy and sad at the same time. No one gets their full attention anymore, it seems."

"Well, if you find anything more out, let me know. I might be able to help. In some way."

She thanked me and I walked into their living room, which had hardwood floors with a few chairs and a table in the middle.

"Grey, it's me. Can I come in?" I announced my arrival with a raised voice, just in case he had to get decent before I walked in. But I'd also be totally fine if he wasn't.

"Sienna?" a weak voice responded from a back room. It didn't even sound like him, but like a young child, afraid.

"Yes, it's me." I took a few more steps into the house. "Can I come in?"

"Sure, but be careful."

I pulled out my mask from my bag and secured it around my nose and mouth before turning the corner into Grey's room. He lay in a ball on his bed, sheets and blankets off, just in his boxers. He was sweating; his hair slicked back and wet, and both of his eyes were shut.

"Grey, your mom is getting the medicine. You should feel better in 48 hours, hopefully."

He opened one eye, which was red and a little swollen. "Good, good," was all he could say and that even seemed to make him breathless. I guess he didn't care how little he was covered, he was so uncomfortable and sick.

I stood in the doorway taking in his pale, weak body. A small raised patch of red was on his lower leg. His other leg looked fine. Goosebumps appeared all over his body and he began shivering. I found my gloves in my bag, pulled them on, and walked over. He moved to slip on his covers and reached to scratch the red patch. I held his hand to stop him. His arm looked more swollen than the last time I saw it.

"I know it itches, but try not to scratch," I said quietly and pulled up the covers for him. "Let me get a cold towel to put on your head."

"Thanks. My head hurts so bad," he moaned.In the bathroom I ran cold water over a washcloth. In the small room, I noticed the tile was chipped in spots. At least the sink was clean. I went back to him and placed the washcloth on his forehead. It was burning hot. "Here you go. What did the doc say?"

It took a while before he spoke in broken sentences. "That feels better...he said...I have...a ...virus. Gave me... anti...biotics ...said to sleep...drink fluids ...will be better... few days...everything...hurts."

His voice was strained and weak and his skin was clammy and pale, his sheet soaked through. I closed my eyes, hoping it'd all go away when I opened them. Another weird, bad dream, gone. But, no, nothing had changed when I opened my eyes. I stood up to get him a cold glass of water and a straw, holding the glass up to his pale lips so he could take some sips. Thankfully he kept it down.

I left his room to see if his mom was back from the pharmacy. It sounded like she had shut the door and was in the house.

"I got his pills. I hope he can swallow them." Mrs. Halloway opened the pharmacy bag and took them out. "His doctor said to give him this right away. Grey's bloodwork wasn't at all normal."

"Okay, let's do it. He just took a few sips of water." I filled up his cup with more.

We both walked into his room and helped him swallow the pills. He was slow and deliberate but got them down.

"Does Grey normally take vitamins and organic supplements?" I asked his mom. I always took mine daily and so did the rest of my family. It's what we did to keep viruses and colds away, since just about everyone was becoming resistant to antibiotics. Grey needed a boost, especially if the antibiotics didn't work. We had special weekly deliveries of GMO foods to boost our immune systems. At first, I thought it was just because of Willow, and maybe it was, but it wasn't long before all of us took them. Mom insisted that we did to stay healthy.

"No. We've only been offered the chance to sign up once. I tried, but we were rejected." She dropped her chin and looked at her knobby, arthritic hands.

"Well, no worries, we have plenty. I'll bring some over to you. Grey needs more vitamins and minerals in case these meds aren't quick enough to take effect." I was shocked that they didn't have access to these vitamins. I thought we were all sent unique passwords to grant us access to the websites so we could order our monthly supplies.

"I'll be back later, if that's okay with you."

She faced the kitchen sink, her back turned to me. "Yes, that'd be great. So thoughtful of you, Sienna. We'll be here." She fussed with a few dishes, one slipping out of her hands and banging against the sink.

As I drove home, it occurred to me that not everyone could buy the foods and supplements we had. Mom probably got special approval because of the Eden Project and was given access to only the best quality stuff. We were always getting packages of mixes and supplements.

I rolled down my window and heard a noise overhead. Above me, a drone approached from behind. Not too unusual—it was probably delivering food or a package. I turned right toward my house, then stopped at a stop sign. The humming was still overhead. Another left turn down my street and my heartbeat quickened; I looked in the rearview mirror to see the drone still on my tail and getting closer. I cut right and darted down a back alleyway.

Drones weren't allowed down the alleys because kids hung out there. It was too dangerous, and accidents had happened with drones banking into kids. No back-door deliveries were allowed, ever. Regardless of the law, this one followed me. I made a quick turn, circling back to head home.

Down my street, I sped up and floored it into my driveway. The camera on the side of the garage moved and locked on my vehicle. Opening the garage door, I closed it behind me as fast as I could. I clicked on my tablet and hit "home connect" on my device. An extra camera flicked on in the front of the house. Just as the garage door touched the ground, there was a quick thud, followed by a dull flipping sound. I jumped and ran inside to look out the front window. The drone rammed right into the garage door and was flying over the house across the street, cockeyed. Good, it was damaged. I would have cornered that thing in my garage and beaten it to a pulp if it had flown inside. My heart pounded out of my chest as I watched the drone until it was far out of sight.

Staring out the window, I felt dizzy. It was mid-afternoon and no one was home. Willow was with her tutor every afternoon and Mom was at work. The silence was uncomfortable and eerie. I studied my tablet, checking and re-checking the alarm system. Everything was on and armed. I took a deep breath, closed my eyes, and an image of Grey appeared: his pale, weak, shaking body wrapped underneath his thin blanket.

I tore through our closet of recycled paper bags, then walked into the kitchen pantry to raid our shelves. Our pantry was 200 square feet—not your typical pantry. Mom and Dad were ready for the apocalypse any day now. But, seriously, if the world did end, we'd all be dead anyway, so we wouldn't need any of this stuff. If a huge ice cap melted and the ocean rose and we were flooded, then we could possibly survive for a little while. That was the latest fear these days. I grabbed ten containers filled with antioxidants, organic nutrients, essential oils, exotic truffles, and more, and stuffed them into the bags. Something in there had to help Greyson.

I was slipping on my shoes to leave when my phone rang. Mom had probably found out that I left school, but I doubt she really cared. To my surprise, it was Kellen. Now? Seriously? I let it ring and it went to my voicemail. In a matter of seconds, my phone rang again. I answered but didn't say a thing.

"Missed you in class today. Skipping out on school?" Kellen's voice was deeper than usual. I was quiet.

"I hear you breathing…" He drawled out the "e," giving me the chills.

"None of your business."

"Ah, yeah, it's my business when you leave school to hang out with your boyfriend Greyson," he whispered, louder.

"What?" *The drone.* "What do you care if he's my boyfriend."

"He'll be fine. His mommy is taking care of him. And you know you shouldn't be hanging out, let alone kissing, anyone who's not on our project." Kellen took a deep breath.

"What do you know, anyway? I can do what I want." I balanced my bags and started walking to the garage, arms full.

"I'm telling you, you better back off. I care, and you can't help him. Keep your supplements for you and your family. He's sick and it can spread—it *will* spread. You'll need the supplements more than you know, Sienna. Please listen to me." Kellen hung up.

The tone of his voice softened, as if he really did care. His hardened exterior had slightly slipped. If he was really a genius, and cared, Kellen had better stay away from Grey.

I looked out the window to be sure no one and nothing was around before I drove back over to Grey's. I kept looking in my rearview mirror all the way to his house. What the hell was Kellen saying, that I'd need the supplements more than I knew? We had so many! Halfway there, my phone rang again. It was a text from Ximena. I couldn't read it while driving, and she'd think I was in class anyway. She could wait; I'd see her soon enough at the lab.

When I arrived at Grey's house, the front door was open. "Hello!" I said quietly but firmly. I couldn't help but breathe in the damp, moldy smell that permeated the air. The curtains were drawn, and the house was dark.

"Mrs. Halloway, I'm back," I whispered, trying not to wake Greyson.

"Come in," she said in a hushed voice. I walked to his room, trying to keep my bags quiet, but they rustled loudly when they banged into each other in the narrow hallway. He was resting but restless. Both eyes were crusted shut and a little more swollen. I had only been gone about two hours, and he was worse. I tried not to look shocked in case he opened his eyes.

Quickly, I put on another mask to cover my nose and mouth and slipped on some gloves. Taking out the containers, I laid them out on his desk. I twisted off the lids and started scooping out the dry powder and mixing them as I did every day. I'd brought one of my special tumblers. I grabbed a straw from one of my bags and took the mix over to his bedside.

"Grey, can you hear me?" I leaned into him. He was faintly breathing. "Grey." I rubbed the side of his arm. He tried opening one of his crusty eyes but couldn't.

I took the washcloth on his bedside table to the sink and ran it under warm water, then gently rubbed his eyes and cleared away the crust. Eventually, he opened one eye. His gem-like blue iris shone through the redness. He was in there.

"Here drink some of this. It'll help you, I promise." I wasn't certain, but hopeful it would make him stronger.

He could barely hold up his head to lean toward me and take a sip. I helped him sit up. He took the tiniest sip, but it was something. A start. I sat with him for a good half hour as he slowly sipped the drink. Finally, tired from drinking, he laid his head back down and closed his eyes again.

"Thanks, you're the best," he said, then drifted off to sleep.

His stomach full, I took a clean cloth and wiped his face and forehead, and pulled the sheets and blankets over him, patting him on his hand. He was so angelic. I leaned over and gave him a quick kiss on his forehead. His fever hadn't let up; it was still raging. He'd have to keep the super fluids flowing all night. I washed my hands for three minutes in their kitchen sink and organized the supplements.

Before leaving, I instructed Mrs. Halloway on what to give him every couple of hours, even through the night, then told her I'd call her to be sure he drank everything. It was going to be a long night. I bit my nails, then crossed my fingers behind my back.

15

When I walked up to the Morton's house, the thud of alternative music rumbled. I counted the stone steps as I walked to their front door where a woman stood and welcomed me by my first name. She then politely directed me through the main room to the back yard. Round tables were set up with flowers as centerpieces, with a large buffet of food lining the perimeter of the pool deck. Kids were hanging out eating and drinking. I didn't have any intention of swimming this evening, so I didn't bring my swimsuit. Hunger gripped me, and my stomach roiled with the smell of grilled food. My body clung to the need to be fulfilled while my mind was on high alert, looking out for Tyler and Kellen.

I helped myself to a large plate of mixed green salad, some artisan cheese, organic chicken and rice, then looked around for a seat. There were a few empty ones, including one by Oceana.

"Hi, is anyone sitting here?" I asked, going over.

She wore a blue sleeveless top with a short skirt and high platform heels. We were wearing similar skirts, colorfully striped with a little flare.

"Hi, Sienna! Nope, go ahead," she said with a smile. "How are you?"

"I'm okay. How are you?" I took a bite of orange cheese.

"This project has me stressed out. So much to do with schoolwork, too." She took a drink of water, then wiped her mouth with a napkin.

"I agree. All of that, and I have lacrosse too. So, what are you working on for your project?" I asked, taking a bite of chicken.

"Not sure if I should say, ya know. Ty said he and Kellen are the only ones who know about all of the projects right now."

"I won't tell anyone."

"How do I know for sure?"

"I don't know if anyone cares outside of our group anyway."

"You're probably right. I'm working on long term battery storage options, you?"

"Sounds cool! We need better options. Mine is in medicine. Kinda an extension of what I did for my project that won the Powell Award."

"That's good. I don't remember what that was..."

"Well, it's too much to go into right now. Hey, look, Tyler is over there with the mic again, over by the band."

There was a thud and then some squeaking feedback on the audio system. Tyler wore fitting blue pants, a crisp blue and white plaid button-down with dark brown laced shoes. Not a hair was out of place.

"Good evening, guys! I know you're enjoying an amazing meal, so please finish up, and I'll be back at the mic to give you an update in a few minutes."

Everyone slowly quieted down and finished eating. One guy at our table pushed back his plate and chair. "That was awesome! I'm so full now. Wonder what Tyler's hot topic is tonight?"

"Did you guys send him your research outlines? He was pushing for mine last week. I've been busting my ass to get this done," said a second guy at the table.

"No kidding!" a girl chimed in, dropping her fork on her plate.

"I sent something to him, but not my full outline," said the first guy.

"I sent him my stuff. I think Ty's right, that we should share our stuff so we can band together," said Oceana.

Ty reappeared at the mic. "Hey, guys, again, thanks for coming here. Thanks to the Mortons for graciously hosting this phenomenal group of young people! Let's give the Mortons and ourselves a round of applause," said Ty. A loud roar of applause and a few whistles erupted.

Catrina and Zach Morton stood next to Tyler, who handed her the mic. "Thank you, thank you all for joining us this evening to relax a bit and spend some time together! You all look wonderful! We are so pleased to hear of the progress of your projects. We've been communicating with the mentors on a regular basis and are thrilled to know you are all working so hard. School work, sports, and friends are also big parts of your lives, so we want to show our appreciation for your sacrifice to this project. In turn, we've decided to award scholarship money to the top three outstanding projects in the next two weeks. Zach and I will judge the status of your projects and contact the winners in two weeks. Keep up the wonderful work and enjoy the evening. And thank you all for your dedication and outstanding abilities!"

Catrina stretched out her arms, her bangle bracelets clicking together. Her bright white smile shone from between her deep red lips.

Zach stood and leaned into the mic. "I couldn't agree more, Catrina. Well said! Just know that we are here for you, to support you and your projects one hundred percent. We get that you are stretched to the max but know that what you are doing right now is contributing to the whole of society. We need you, and the world needs you now. So, thank you!"

He handed the mic back to Tyler. "Another round of applause to the Mortons! And for offering their home tonight to us."

We applauded and some stood up. When things quieted down, Ty took to the mic again and said, "Now, Mr. and Mrs. Morton, I hope you'll understand, do you mind excusing us so that we may talk in private? As designer kids on a mission, we'd like a few moments to ourselves, only if you don't mind, of course." He was pouring on his charm, beaming a wide smile at Catrina. He was hard for her to refuse.

"Oh, certainly! Not a problem at all. I understand, kids. By all means, take your time. Zach, all good with you, as well?"

"Of course, of course!" Zach said, shaking Tyler's hand then clasping Catrina's in his and raising them together, before they walked off into the house.

Once the door closed behind them, Kellen joined Tyler, standing next to him and spoke into the mic, this time a little quieter.

"I hope you are all enjoying our message board and sharing some of your project statuses with the group. By now I've received almost all of your outlines and see the trajectory of where your projects are going. It's all so fascinating, so thank you. I know your mentors are staying on top of your work, and you guys are digging in with full conviction. This is exciting, my friends! Very exciting!"

He paused and paced, taking a deep breath before continuing. "So now that you've established yourselves and bonded with your mentors, we must take over from here.

By that, I mean, in order for us to stick together and take control of our intellectual property, we need each of you to send us your progress. Let's work together, my friends. Let's share amongst ourselves to ensure we and our future are taken care of. We *are* the future."

"So, you guys will basically store all of our data and go from there?" shouted out a girl from another table.

"Yep, you got it. Let's do this together, you guys. We are more powerful together than apart," Kellen explained.

The guy at my table shifted in his seat and stood up. "Yeah, I get that. My mentor's kind of an ass anyway. I'm in!"

"Me, too!" said several others, and then more chimed in, until there was a clear majority standing united. A few sat with arms crossed, unsure yet of their decision to join in.

"Hey, no! We can't do this! What about..." I stood up and shouted but was cut off quickly.

"Wonderful! We all think alike. Let's do this," said Tyler.

"We'll be sending you guys more messages on our group board, so please respond. If you have any questions, please post them there or reach out to one of us," added Kellen. He found me in the crowd, and we locked eyes as he walked toward me. He smiled as he quickly approached and reached out to give me a hug. I stepped back, but his arm took hold around my waist. "Sienna, you look beautiful!"

"Hey, Kellen, thanks, I guess." My shoulders stayed tense as I stood between three other kids, unable to move. Kellen was bumped by someone and knocked into me.

"Are you having a good time?"

"Sure. I suppose, but I'm..."

"Want a drink?" he asked.

"Well, I was going to say I'm ready to leave. The show seems to be over, ya know." I looked around for Oceana or someone I could pretend to know to get away from Kellen.

"Look, Sienna. Don't run off so fast. Let's have a drink. I mean, we kind of know each other, but I'd like to get to know you better in a different way." Kellen saw a waiter and motioned him over. "Hey, yeah, can we get a couple of drinks? Something cold, please."

The waiter nodded. "Sure, of course. Sparkling water?" Kellen gave him the thumbs up.

"Kellen, you know I don't agree with all that you and Tyler are doing. You won't win me over."

He wasn't about to give up easily. "You know, Sienna, more than your amazing looks, you are incredibly astute. Your brain is really what I'm interested in. I want to get to know the real Sienna Yardley. Like, what makes you tick? What makes you come alive? What literally *moves* you?"

He so surprised me with these questions, that I was speechless for a minute. Why was he wanting to know me this way? Just then the waiter arrived with our waters and I gladly took one. The cool bubbly water soothed my dry throat. "Thank you, very much." Then finally I said, "Kellen, there are so many things, you cannot imagine!"

"Well, I'd love to get inside your mind and know. The more I get to know you, the more intriguing you are."

"Hmmm, flattery again. What is it that you really want, Kellen? My gut says it's not me directly."

"Believe or not, it is," he whispered close to my ear.

I started to sweat and again looked for Oceana and saw her walking in toward us. "Oh look, there's Oceana. I told her I'd find her before I left. Gotta go."

I headed her direction, but not before Kellen said, "I really want to know, Sienna! And I'm not giving up!"

16

When I walked into the kitchen, Willow was behind the refrigerator door. She turned around holding a bag of carrots, lettuce, and some shredded cheese.

"Hi! Oh good, you made it home in time for dinner. I'm about to make a salad for us." She shuffled over to the island and plopped the items down. I stood staring at her.

"Is everything okay? You look like you're in shock or something," she said, reaching for a cutting board and knife. I methodically opened the bag of carrots and brought one to my lips.

"I really look that freaked out?" I took a bite.

"Yes."

"Wait, I should wash my hands. Scrub my hands, I meant to say." Going to the kitchen sink, I pumped some soap on my hands, ran the hot water, and then sang the Happy Birthday song, with an extra verse, before I shut the water off.

"I was thinking we'd do salad and also make a few gooey pizzas. Want something to drink?" Willow focused on washing the lettuce.

"Sounds great. I'll get us some water. I'm thirsty." I reached for the container of mega-multivitamins and handed her one.

"So, what's up?"

While I took a long gulp of water to wash down the vitamin, I debated on how much I should tell Willow about my afternoon. "Well, I'm worried. Greyson is very sick."

"Like stomach sick or cold sick?"

"A weird sick. His mom took him to the doctor, and he's on antibiotics so he should get better in a few days. It's just that a kid on his lacrosse team had a weird virus thing, and I'm hoping he doesn't have that. But I also think it's spreading in the school. Lots of kids are out sick with fevers."

"Well, stuff goes around school. We all know that. As long as he's on antibiotics, he'll be fine, right?"

"That scares me, too. We all take so many antibiotics that we're building immunity to them and then we can't resist bacteria. Do we have more blueberries?" I peeked in the fridge and saw we had a small container left. I felt panic rise inside of me as my eyes darted around the inside of the fridge, looking for a savior, a panacea of some sort.

"Yeah, I got some from the greenhouse this morning. Hey, did you raid the pantry?"

"No hiding anything from you! I took some stuff over to Grey. His family doesn't get all the supplements that we do. I guess it's not unusual. We're lucky Mom's a doctor and that Dad's got a great job so we can afford monthly supplies. I also noticed Grey had a red spot on his arm the other night and it got swollen."

"Red spot? Like a rash?"

"Kind of, but nothing like I'd seen before. I mean, it was getting pus under the skin, like a zit." I shuddered, thinking of how much a huge pimple on your arm would hurt.

"Ew! Can you pop it?"

"Willow!"

"Well?" Willow laid out pizza toppings. "Anyway,

what do you want on your pizza?"

I scanned the counter. "A little bit of everything you have there. Hey, not to change the subject or anything, but what do you make of Mom being pregnant?"

"I don't know what to think right now." Willow lowered her chin as she cut the tomatoes.

"Shocking, right?"

"I guess. I mean, I understand why they want to have another child; they've always wanted a boy. They've made that clear since I was little, and we all know I'm not perfect."

"No one's perfect, Willow."

"You're as close as someone gets to perfect."

"Well, that's debatable!" I scattered some of the chopped vegetables on top of my crust.

"I just don't know, why now?" She threw the lettuce into a bowl.

"Who knows. Maybe because I'll be going to college soon, and they don't want to be empty-nesters? And you're more independent now. You know Mom and Dad are needy, right? Need to have a project all the time."

"Well, I've been their major project, right?" She laughed and we both worked on creating our pizza masterpieces.

After we ate and talked about everything else besides the baby and Greyson, we cleaned up quickly. She was growing up and had all the same, real teenage dreams I did at thirteen. I secretly hoped they would all come true. I gave Willow a huge hug before getting my things to go to the lab and mixing a high-powered antioxidant smoothie for later, in case I had another all-nighter at the lab.

I was late to the lab. This would be a perfect time to

confirm that my genetically engineered body was resistant to disease. I took another mega vitamin, for security's sake. I hoped that Ximena would be gone for the day and I wouldn't have to deal with her whining that I wasn't working hard enough. I'd probably be there all night, again. There was a lot to cover and I had to do it as fast as I could.

At the workstation there was a note by the computer, along with a folder. It was from Ximena:

Sienna, sorry I missed you. Long day but some progress. Take a look at the documents in this folder and in the file on the computer labeled, "Antimicrobial susceptibility testing (AST) data." Please continue to test the sample drug with these mutations and record your findings. I've completed the next phase of two for clinical effectiveness. I will discuss more with you later and will look at your work tomorrow. I need a report filed of your work immediately.

It was cool that she had completed two phases. I scanned the room and walked over to my favorite computer. This was a room full of drugs and very potent medicine. Maybe even something that could help Grey.

I scurried around the room, looking through cabinets. Most of the medicines were labeled. Standing on a step stool, I reached up high into one of the cabinets. The slight buzz of a motorized camera tickled my ear. Of course, there was surveillance in the room. I'd be kidding myself if I thought anyone would be left alone in the lab without cameras watching their every move. I pretended to search for something innocently, then looking perplexed, stepped off the stool, empty-handed. I'd have to hack into the system and reset the cameras, so they'd be off a few seconds to miss me completely. Resetting the timer might work, too.

Sitting back at my workstation, I clicked to open Ximena's folders. She was getting closer to finding a drug that worked against the mutated genes. That was the missing link—finding the additional gene mutation that was resistant to the current drugs and attacking it. Sometimes the drugs worked for people, other times they were unsuccessful. If we could find the gene and the drugs, it'd be a huge breakthrough. We could even alter the current antibiotics to make them better, so they were less adaptable.

Ximena labeled a few slides she was monitoring with the *mec*A gene, the gene related to resistance to the antimicrobial agents. I took a look into the microscope. Amazing! Even with the *mec*A under stress and repressed, the drug appeared to boost the level of and prevent atrophy of the gene over time. This was huge. I tested and retested and recorded my findings of her samples. Ximena was brilliant. It really was possible to develop new drugs to help alter genes.

I pulled my tablet out from under my shirt to keep it out of the range of the cameras and synced it up with the computer to download all the files in the folder. Back-up to a back-up was critical in these types of situations.

I made a duplicate slide, leaving the original in its box and put the duplicate in another box, then slipped it under my shirt, tucking it into the edge of my pants so I could feel it at all times. I had left my jacket on to give me some extra bulk. The lab was secured, but I wouldn't put it past any of these genius Eden kids to get their dirty hands on our stuff.

Several hours passed while I worked. Around 10 p.m., I clocked myself out of the lab, using my finger and eye print.

~ ~ ~ ~

It was late, but that didn't stop me from driving over to Greyson's for a short visit. I texted Mom that I'd be home in half an hour. Grey's window was open a crack, and I slipped in as quietly as I could. A fan was blowing, making some perfect white noise. He was asleep, so I put my stuff down and dug in my bag for a mask. I had accumulated so much stuff that afternoon between lacrosse, school, the project and now Greyson, that my bag was bulging. I didn't see a mask. I must've used my last one today. I kept my distance as I walked over to the bags of supplies that I'd left in his room. Before midnight was a good time for some kale and carrot fortified broth. It'd help him sleep through the night. I took the compact cubes of the vegetables out of the container and tiptoed down the hall to the kitchen to heat up some water in a big bowl. Seconds later, the cubes were dissolved, and I was again by Greyson's bedside.

He must have sensed me next to him. One crusty eye cracked open. The other stayed shut. "Hi," he managed to whisper.

"Hey, glad to see you awake, finally." I wanted to touch him but knew better. His face was less ashen, and his blue eyes were more vibrant.

"How'd you get here?" he asked, confused.

"Well, I drove, then let myself in." I stirred the broth, trying to even out the floating chunks. I plugged in a small heating plate and soon the steam rose, coating my nostrils in vapor. The vegetable broth reminded me of soothing my past colds and stomachaches. My stomach growled.

"Figured so." Greyson tried to prop himself up on his elbows. "What day is it?"

"It's Wednesday. I've got some broth for you to sip. It'll help you get stronger." I dipped the tip of my little finger into the broth and pulled it out quickly. Still too hot.

"Sure, I'm hungry. But gotta go to the bathroom first." He sat up. "Ugh, my head hurts," he said, falling back on his pillow and splashing the hot broth onto my face and into my eye.

"Ow!" I cupped my burning eye with my hand.

"Ugh! I'm so sorry!"

"Crap, my eye's burning! Hand me an ice cube, fast!" I didn't want to rub my eye with my exposed hand, if it wasn't too late already.

"Here, here's an ice cube. Want a towel, too?" Luckily there was a bowl of ice on his nightstand.

"Sure. Clean one. Wait, I'll get one."

"There are some clean ones in the hall closest."

I got up slowly and with one eye open found my way to the hall closet, while I held ice on my other eye. I grabbed a soft brown hand towel and walked back to Grey's room.

"You okay?"

"I'll be fine. Just give me a few minutes to catch my breath." My eye was slowly swelling. "Hey, you still have to go to the bathroom, right? You haven't sat up in a long time. Take it slow. Let me help you." I cradled his elbow as he slowly stood. "I can take you so far, but then you're on your own to pee." I said laughing and he managed a curl of his lip.

He was weak, but by shuffling slowly, he made it to the bathroom across the hall. He closed the door slightly, and I heard a short stream of liquid hit the toilet bowl water, before it stopped and slowed to a dribble. He'd barely had anything to eat or drink. He sneezed.

"Ow!" he mumbled and shuffled slowly back to his bed,

holding his side.

"You okay?"

"Not really. Do I look okay to you?" he shot back.

"Sorry. Dumb question. Here, sip this broth. It should be cool by now. It'll give you some strength." I held the straw and bowl up to his mouth. His chapped lips, with flakes of loose skin, cracked at the corners as he opened them to sip the broth. It was a perfect temperature.

"Ew. Bitter," he said as a little dribbled down his front.

"Yeah, just drink." I lifted the bowl to give him some more. My eye was feeling better. I kept icing it. I wondered if the swelling would affect the eye scan at the lab.

Greyson sipped again and sat back. "So, I heard my parents talking. Can't remember when, but I heard Dad telling Mom that there are others in the neighborhood getting sick. Like Anish and his dad." He paused and licked his lips.

"Really?"

"Yeah. They were saying they still think Anish's dad traveled over to Saudi Arabia and brought something back. He picked up a terrible, atypical superbug maybe. It's a really weird strain. You know, one of those we're resistant to but that they've never seen before. They said Anish's dad is pretty sick and the docs are trying everything they possibly can to fight this."

"Did they say any other cases have been reported?"

"It's been under wraps, but I'm pretty sure there are a lot more cases. They don't want people to panic."

He spoke slowly and with an edge in his voice. In the last few years, the majority of the population had become resistant to antibiotics. Terrible outbreaks had happened overseas, even with kids and their sports teams. Antibiotics were totally overused and now were something like five percent effective or maybe even less, depending on the person and situation. We had been getting regular shipments to keep our immune systems healthy and, of course, we all thought our own organic immunity-boosting foods should help. But it seemed that people were getting sicker before getting better. And they were dying.

"Dad said he heard that the government is in hyper mode and the CDC is working 24/7 on this. They aren't even sure what the bacteria is, if it's a new virus or something else. Or they're not telling anyone. Can you find anything out?" Grey closed his eyes again. He reached for the broth, then scratched his leg and arm.

"Geez! Don't touch those sores! It's worse than it was a few days ago. Has your mom seen this today?"

"Man, it does look bad," he exclaimed, examining the puffy red sore on his leg and his red arm. "Mom!" he yelled. "Sienna's here—can you come take a look at something?"

About ten minutes later, Grey's mom appeared bleary-eyed and in her sweatpants and nightshirt. She looked at his sore and ran from the room to call the doctor. A few minutes later, she came back to tell Grey the doctor was on his way over to the house and should be there in an hour.

"He said there's been an outbreak of people with high fevers and sores, so he wants to see you right away."

"Ok, good. I'll see what I can find out about Anish and his dad," I told them. "You just focus on getting better. Be sure to take some supplements every couple of hours."

"If I can stay awake, I will." He swallowed hard. "This sucks."

"It does. Be tough. I know you can." I went to itch my

nose, then stopped myself. I forgot I didn't have my mask on.

"I'm sorry about your eye, Sienna. It doesn't look bad, really."

I smiled. "I'll be fine. I'll call you tomorrow!"

I doused my hands in the hand sanitizer I kept in my pocket before opening my car door. Looking at the bottle, I shook my head. This stuff was part of the problem.

~~~~~~~

At home in the garage, I stripped off my clothes and left them in a pile behind some tools. I'd torch them later. I trotted up the steps in my bra and underwear.

I rubbed my nose—for all I knew, a deadly virus could be in there. Sick. Literally. I took a hot shower, scrubbing my whole body, cleaning out my nose and under my nails. I brushed my teeth for at least five minutes, maybe longer. Clean and dry, I sprawled out on my bed, my body tired, but my mind racing. Grey could *not* get any worse. He couldn't end up in the hospital, the last place he should be, where viruses spread rampant.

I read my emails on my tablet to catch up on messages and to see my assignments for tomorrow. There was a note from Avery. I'd forgotten to check in on Jazz. Avery said in her note that she hadn't heard from Jazz and was going to her house tomorrow to check in. She asked if I could go with her. I wrote back, "not sure, but will try. Talk tmrw." I really wanted to be there for her. I missed her.

The image of Grey's oval face surrounded by his dark hair, bright eyes and killer smile, dimple, and athletic swagger, popped into my mind. I felt a surge of excitement in my belly. We'd fight this.

I Googled EBEX and clicked on the news items. One

report in the *Wall Street Journal* said there was a severe case of a man in Chicago who possibly had EBEX, an unusual strain that experts thought could be the result of a virus he had picked up while visiting the Middle East. He was in the ICU and may lose one of his limbs. There was a video of a reporter standing outside of the hospital telling the latest on his condition. The man's name was withheld, but I was ninety-nine percent sure it was Anish's dad. Shit, this was bad. Very bad.

I read a few more headlines, all with dire news but saying that infectious disease experts were investigating the situation, and that anyone with symptoms was instructed to see their doctor or go to the emergency room as soon as possible. I closed my tablet, shocked. I opened it again to pull up my physics assignment and saw a secure message from Ty to the designer kids.

"Project updates: Keep sending! They are incredible, but we need continual data to stay ahead in this game. Love to get anything you have by the end of the day. Get in touch if you have questions or concerns. Let's do this!"

I could barely make out the words on the page. It had been a long day and my eye was scratchy and sore, so I held more ice on it until it was practically numb. Ty was all over these projects. Time to chill but also figure out what Ty and Kellen were planning next.

I was extremely tired and clicked off my tablet, getting under my covers. The quiet settled in me, and I turned off my light. Just as I was about to drift off, I heard a stifled noise. A soft, distant moaning. I sat up to listen. Again, a soft moan.

I got out of bed and walked down the hall, pausing in front of Willow's door and heard her muffled moan again. Opening her door, I saw her laying on her side with the pillow over her mouth, breathing through her nose. She moaned again.

I sat next to her and moved my hand in a slow circle over her back. I knew Mom had done this for years when she was tiny, but she'd been absent as Willow grew. And now, Mom was exhausted and pregnant. I still had a hard time believing she was going to have a baby at her age.

Willow shifted onto her stomach, propping the pillow under her head. I lay down next to her, putting my arm tight around her. She moaned again, and I rubbed her back.

I woke up a few hours later in the same position. There was no room in her bed for us both, and I practically fell off when I moved. I didn't want to wake her, so I quietly slipped back to my own bed. It was 3:30 a.m. A few more hours of sleep and I'd be up, leaving for the lab again.

At 5:30, my alarm played an old Coldplay song. Slowly, I dressed and drank a pre-mixed energy-immune boosting smoothie before putting on my gloves. I stepped out into the garage and picked up the bag that held my clothes from the day before. I added it to the pile of kindling for the weekend bonfire we sometimes built in the backyard. I tucked it under a few other bags and other piles of wood we'd been gathering for the fire.

On my way back from the garage, I heard footsteps— Dad. He must've slept here last night.

"Dad! I didn't know you were here!" I gave him a hug. "I've missed you."

We held onto each other tightly until we relaxed. He smelled of fresh soap and cologne. I backed away.

"And I, you. I'm sorry." He looked at me with pleading eyes and a pout.

"Well, I've been busy anyway," I said, placing my hands

on my hips, before slipping one into my pocket of my jeans. I had no intention of going into my entire back-story with him this early in the morning. I had no energy to explain all the details.

"What's wrong with your eye?"

"Oh, got bumped at lacrosse. Not a big deal."

"Hope you bumped her back." He nudged my shoulder.

"So? Why were you here last night?"

"Mom wasn't feeling good last night. The bottom line is that I'll be over here more. With the baby coming and all." He put his hands into his pockets too, mirroring me.

"Great." I slung my bag over my shoulder and headed toward my car. It'd be good to have him back, to feel like a family again.

"You off to school this early, Sienna?"

"Have to go to the lab before class. This project is eating up all my time." I half-smiled.

He smiled back. "Yeah, congrats. Right up your alley. Hope it's going well. I want to know as much as you can tell me about this thing you're working on. Let's talk over dinner?"

"Yeah, sure," I mumbled. "I'll try to make it tonight, but no promises."

"Great. Have a wonderful day discovering lots of cool stuff!" He was trying to sound like a teenager, but it wasn't cutting it. I looked up with my good eye into the sky. No drone. Good. Too early for drone noise. I got into my car and backed out of our driveway.

All I could think about on my way to the lab was that I was going to need to disable the cameras so I could search it for Greyson's meds. Pulling up to a red light, I looked both ways. No one was around. I tapped my brakes and ran it, but checked my rearview mirror to be sure no one, especially a police officer, had seen.

Suddenly, a black car came flying around the corner and appeared right behind me. Who the hell was this? I stepped on it and prayed it wasn't an undercover cop. They were everywhere, deterring crime at all hours of the day and night. Things had gotten so bad with gangs in the city and suburbs the last six months that a whole neighborhood killed themselves off.

I swerved, making a quick turn to lose the car and then darted down an alley. The lab was just a half a mile away. A few more cars were on the road and one cut in front of the guy chasing me. I flew down the alley and into the lab's entrance, tapping my finger at the gate until it opened. I was in. It closed behind me, and I took a deep breath.

Thankfully, no one else could get past security without credentials. I looked over my shoulder and saw the black car stop by the gate. All I could make out was a man wearing a hat. He thumped the palm of his hand on the steering wheel, then sped away.

17

It took a few tries to unlock the security pad with my swollen eye. I didn't want to exhaust my attempts to get in and then get locked out. I'd have to lie to Ximena about what had happened to my eye, and she was the type that could see past any bullshit.

On the third attempt, I got in. I didn't have much time, so I worked quickly on the lab's security system. As a little kid, Dad taught me everything about our home security system, including how to engage and disable it when I was home alone. As the system became more complex and I grew more curious, I studied its security pathways on my own. Later, I figured out that he was paranoid and that was the real reason he wanted me to know how to lock myself in the house.

Early on in my parents' marriage, they had been hacked and had their identities stolen. Identity theft had become the next black plague—it was rampant and crippling. From then on, my parents had been obsessive-compulsive about securing their life together, and their power struggle worsened.

As a little kid, I spent a lot of my free time on computers. I thought their fear of being "stolen" again had pushed them away from each other. Mom became obsessive-compulsive with almost everything, from washing her hands, installing cameras everywhere in the house, and setting up multiple bank accounts.

Her levels of anxiety rose to the point that Dad couldn't deal with her anymore and decided to move out temporarily. I got used to it, which surprised me. I loved seeing them when they did "couple" again every so often. Maybe with the baby on the way, they'd be coupled more often, or else he'd move back in.

I remembered seeing them stare into each other's eyes, probably like they did when they had first met. I always hoped I'd find the love of my life. When my parents separated, they missed each other too at times, or so Dad told me. But somehow, I think they found some comfort in not having their lives completely intertwined, so they couldn't be vulnerable if they were hacked again.

After the theft, their arguments were raw, a controlled strain. Neither of them was willing to give in to the other.

As I worked on Ximena's computer, I navigated my way around and was able to change the time clock on the cameras. With the cameras paused, I rifled through the cabinets looking for vials of drugs that could possibly help Grey. I took a few samples that I figured probably wouldn't be missed and moved around some other bottles on the shelf so as not to leave an empty space. I also saw some IV bags that might help, since he was so low on fluids. I took two. After checking through the entire lab, I engaged the security system and sat at my workstation. Essentially, it was as if no time had passed.

Ximena would have to check my progress before I could move forward with more analysis. I looked at my tablet and checked the real time again. I had to be at school and prep for a test, and I couldn't miss more classes that morning.

Gathering my things, I checked out with my finger and

eye print. It accepted both eyes this time. The one that was "boiled" was much better and not as swollen. When the door opened, Ximena was just lifting her finger from the finger pad.

"Oh, Sienna. Surprised to see you here already." She pushed her glasses up her nose.

"Hey, Doc, just had to finish a couple of notes for you before school." I took a step forward to get past her, hiding my hurt eye.

"Great. I'll take a look."

"I think you'll be impressed what I found. Can we talk later? I'm late for school already." I wrapped my fingers tightly around my bag's shoulder strap.

"Sure, sure. Get going," Ximena said, stepping into the lab.

I hesitated. "Hey, Ximena, have you heard anything about a virus from overseas? I read something it about the other day." I tried to sound as clueless as possible.

"I did get a call from the CDC and a memo. There's something wicked going around. I can tell you that they are extremely concerned. The number of cases is climbing, quicker than they had thought." She held the door open as we stood in the doorway, too close to each other.

Cornered, I broke into a sweat. "Really?"

"Yes. They want us to report any incidents. Anyone who's sick who may be resistant to treatment," she said, her voice low and quiet.

"Oh?" My mouth dried instantly.

"Yes. For obvious reasons." I was silent. "You know, to prevent a panic and a pandemic, of course. There's a possibility it could be EBEX, and they'd be interested in our testing."

I blurted out, "I read it was a guy who went to the

Middle East and maybe came back with some kind of foreign bug."

"CNN, right?"

"*Wall Street Journal*, actually. Doesn't matter, just scary that it came from so far and it's so serious. The current antibiotics don't seem to be working."

"Guess the word's out. Well, some of it, anyway. You know reporters don't always get all the facts correct."

"What more should we know?" I prodded.

"Well, that's for the CDC to release. I'm not surprised to see something this serious come overseas. The physicians are doing all the testing and bloodwork as we speak, so we'll know more soon." Then she changed the subject. "So, you're making progress here?"

I blinked hard. "Oh, yes. I think we're on to something." My eyes widened as Greyson's face popped into my mind.

"I must send progress notes to Dr. Stevenson today. I'm also trying to stay ahead of the others. I think we can nail this contest if we're a step or two ahead." She was cut-throat in a weird way, but I liked that about her.

"You know about the others' projects?" I asked. I was never against having an edge.

"Just between you and me... I have my ways." Her smile was a lingering one.

"Great." She was sneaky, and I sensed she knew a lot more about our competition than she'd ever tell me. She only knew a sliver of what I was capable of doing. I looked at the time on my tablet.

"I really gotta go!" I almost put my hand up to give her a high-five but stopped myself.

~ ~ ~ ~ ~

"It's supposed to rain, again, guys. Bring your pon-

132

chos," Avery said, looking at her weather app and the radar on her phone. We suited up in the locker room for our lacrosse game after school. A loud moan echoed against the metal lockers.

"Yeah, it sucks, but we gotta deal with it. It is what it is," she added as we slammed our locker doors, pissed off. "Hey, Jazz just texted that she'll be at the game. She's on her way now."

"Yay! That's cool!" Blue and I said in unison.

We'd had plenty of rain this spring season and running on the fields for two hours when they were a wet, sloppy mud pit was not a lot of fun—muscles got pulled, ankles rolled, and sprains and other crap happened. It seemed as if at least one player was out each game with an injury.

A rumble of thunder made us move a bit faster, unable to postpone the inevitable.

"Let's go. Time to get out to the field before Coach gets mad." I grabbed my lacrosse stick and we headed out of the locker room.

The sky was dark and clouds thick in the west. The winds picked up and gusted so hard we actually couldn't move. Avery and Blue jogged ahead. I saw them chatting while Blue cracked the slightest smile. Jazz was still a no-show. I'd check in on her later to be sure her burn wasn't worse and that she wasn't sick.

I kept jogging and looked across toward our field. Someone was moving toward me in the distance, first walking, then jogging. As we got closer, I could tell it was a girl and one of the guys I met at the party—the party that changed everything. They picked up the pace, heading directly toward me. As they got closer, I saw that it was Liv—thanks to her swagger—and Tyler.

"Hey, Sienna, wait up!" Tyler yelled through the wind,

while Liv nodded.

"Oh, hi, Tyler." My tone said I wasn't enthusiastic. I flipped my lacrosse stick around in my hands, holding it in front of me. It could be an ideal weapon if I needed it to be. I'd used it once before to defend Willow, and it wasn't pretty.

Tyler was all smiles with his perfectly straight, white teeth shining back at me.

I felt my gag reflex rise. "I really have to get out to the field, or Coach will be royally pissed," I said, keeping a slight jog.

"Got your project update. Very interesting. Are you telling us everything?" he demanded.

"Oh, that. Yeah, sure."

"We're surprised you haven't gotten too far with it."

"Well, it's been slow, I have to admit."

"Really? I'm not buying it," Ty said directly.

"It's not like I'm not trying."

"You gotta give me more. I know your mentor must have some stuff. Can't you send me some of her data?"

"Uh, she's really protective of her data, Ty. It's not like she's given me total access to the years of research she's collected. Be realistic here," I said flatly.

"Push her for more. I need more."

"I'll try, but no promises," I lied.

"Also, we just want to make sure you're keeping your project discoveries to yourself and your mentor," said Liv, standing with her legs firmly planted.

"You know, what we talked about at the party?" Ty added, frowning when he saw my eye.

"Yeah, I got it," I said. Staying in the loop on everyone's project would only be to the other designers' benefit.

"Well, we need you to stick with our plan," Ty said

calmly as he caught up to me, and wrapped his arm around my shoulder, slowing me down. He started walking with me to the field. A drop of rain hit my nose, and I looked up.

Despite the wind whipping around us, I felt Liv's breath on my neck behind me. "We have a plan and we need you. You're a valuable team player, if you know what I mean."

I stopped and looked deep into her eyes, swallowing hard. She held my gaze. Her breath was warm on my neck and a chill crept down my spine. "Seriously? I don't know what you mean," I said sarcastically. "And I don't need your flattery."

Ty smiled and squeezed my shoulder tighter.

"You're crazy," I said, trying to shrug out of his grasp.

"No, I'm genius. And so are you and all of us. Like I said, we gotta stick together."

"You're in over your head. The mentors will see through you."

"Well, they haven't so far. I've got the wheels in motion and they're only speeding up," Ty said, laughing.

"Look, thanks for the visit, but I gotta go. Like I said, my coach is pissed already, and it's gonna downpour any second, so get outta here." Honestly, I didn't really care if Coach was pissed, and running extra laps made me faster anyway, but I wanted them to go away.

Ty leaned in closer and whispered in my ear, "Listen to me, Sienna. You stay away from Greyson. Leave him the hell alone. He'll be fine with his mom and dad's help and their doctor feeding him medication. Just imagine if his infection spreads to us. It can't and it won't. I won't let it. Don't go around helping his kind, you got it?"

More chills crept up and down my back, and I pushed

him away, hard. "Leave me alone, you ass. I'll do whatever I want."

"No. No you won't. This is about the designer kids, The Eden Project, Sienna. You don't seem to get it, do you? The weak will only get weaker and are of no help to any of us in the future. We can secure our destiny. It's time you focus on why you're here and why we as a group were created. It's about saving the world, and we're here to get the job done. Get your act together."

Ty came back hard, his face close to mine and his eyes big with his hands balled into fists. Like he was really gonna hit a girl? Right here at the school? On the lacrosse fields in front of Liv? Large raindrops poured steadily onto us, and the wind gusted and swirled again.

I took my lacrosse stick and pushed him harder, until he slipped and fell. I was ready to slash him, but he bounced back up and pushed me hard in the side, making me tumble and hit my rear hard on the ground, rain pelting in my eyes. The shock reverberated from my tailbone up to my spine. I couldn't breathe for a second, and with my eyes closed, I took a quick gasp of air, before rolling over and pushing myself up. With my stick still in my hand, I jabbed it at Ty's knees, but he was too quick and dodged away.

"She's whooping you!" Liv crowed to Ty.

Pissed she wasn't helping me at all, I dug deep within myself and found some impossible strength. I jabbed harder, but Ty was faster, and darted out of the way again, reaching for my shoulder.

"Don't kill her, you idiot!" Liv yelled as she finally tried to pull him off of me. She was weak though and his grip tightened. I swung my right arm around and hit his elbow to break his grasp. Then I stepped back to hit the back of his knee. Once he was on the ground, I jumped on his back, but he threw me off into the mud.

Finally standing back up, I got in his face, breathing heavily. I spoke slowly and clearly into his dirty ear. "You have it all wrong, sly Ty. Yeah, I want to save the world from self-destruction, but you think you're really going to destroy the weak while doing it? Let them die off, so we can be heroes? You're crazy. That's not how it's going to be happen," I hissed.

"C'mon, Sienna..." said Liv from the sideline, with a nervous laugh.

"Really, Liv? After this kid just pushed me around? You know I'm not stupid. You're smarter than this jerk, too, and you know it. You guys better stay away from me, or you'll regret it."

Ty stood tall, dripping in mud and from the rain as thunder clapped in the distance. "Think long and hard about all of this, Sienna. You think long and hard."

I found my lacrosse stick on the ground and ran hard and fast past them, kicking up more mud. A few tears merged with the rain. By the time I got to the field and turned around, Ty and Liv were still standing there, stunned, before they took off.

~~~~~~

The start of our game was delayed until the thunder stopped, but the rain and wind still raged. I was on fire, literally. The first half of our game I scored three times, still fuming and full of adrenaline. No one was stopping me, not even their best half-back. I envisioned Ty and Liv behind each of our opponents' masks, and I kept coming at them and running past them with an unknown force within me. I focused on playing hard and getting goals.

At half-time, I drank my electrolyte drink on the

bench. I couldn't get enough; it tasted so good. I rubbed my neck, still feeling Ty's fingers clamped around it, fury in his eyes. I shook off the disbelief of what actually had happened and tried to focus on my team.

With a momentary break in the rain, we huddled in the wind. Avery sat down next to me. "Holy cow, Sienna, you're playing awesome. Way to go. Keep it up and we'll crush these guys." She took a swig from her water bottle.

"Thanks. I'm a little jacked up." I took another gulp and used a towel to wipe the sweat from my forehead.

"I'd say. What's up?"

"Some kids really pissed me off before the game. I was literally picking them off one by one on the field." I sat my drink between us on the bench. "Felt good."

"They must've really made you mad. It's a good thing!" Avery said, reaching for her towel. Jazz joined us on the bench.

"I'm so glad you made it to cheer us on, Jazz. And in this horrific weather!" Avery said through another gust of wind. "It's so awesome to have you back on the field with us even if you can't play right now."

She put up her hand, and they high-fived. It was so cool to have Jazz back, but she didn't look like herself. She dragged her feet, moving slowly, and spoke quietly.

"Yeah, I'm not feeling great, but I had to get out of the house. You guys are doing incredible."

"Thanks. We've missed you, Jazz." I gave her knee a little squeeze. "How's your burn?"

"It got worse before it got better. It still hurts."

Avery nudged her shoulder. "Still going out tonight, just us girls?"

"Sure, I guess," Jazz said, looking down.

"Yeah, 'cuz were gonna win! Let's get 'em!" I leapt off

the bench, re-energized and ready to kick some more butt.

~~~~~~

We ended up making three more goals, while the other team scored two more before the game was finally called because of the flooding on the field. We took it as a win, 6 to 4—we were all drenched, tired, and hungry. After we changed and dried off, Jazz and Avery piled into my car to go get something to eat. When we finally sat down, I was ravenous.

"I'm so hungry! I could eat this whole thing of salt." I shook some salt from the shaker into my hand and licked it.

"Me too," Avery agreed. "This weather is so crazy, right?" She chugged the water the waitress placed on our table.

"Yeah, it's stormed just about every game this season. Sick of it, but you know they say it's because of global warming. People were such idiots to let this happen. Anyway, what are you guys getting to eat?" I asked.

"I think a vegan burger or pasta. It's gotta be big, though." Avery patted her stomach.

The waitress brought some bread, and Avery and I devoured it right away.

"So why did those kids make you so mad today, Sienna?" she asked between bites of bread.

"I'm working on a project and they want me to do something I don't want to do." I ripped into a piece of crusty bread.

"Then don't. They can't push you around," said Jazz, rubbing the side of her neck.

"True. I actually literally pushed them around. Hey, can I see your neck?"

"Sure, I guess," said Jazz, pushing her hair away. I stood to look. It was red, and the skin was tight with pus starting to press underneath a spot.

"Have you seen a doctor?"

"I tried, but she was too busy, so my mom wanted to wait a few more days to see if it got worse. She thinks it's a burn from the sun a few weeks ago. I had my hair up."

"You need to get that checked out before it gets any worse. Promise you will," I said.

"Yeah, listen to Sienna, Jazz. Before it gets serious. Stuff is going around," said Avery. "So, Sienna, what's the project?"

"I'd love to tell you guys, but..." I hesitated, then plowed ahead. "Hey, why not just a teaser? It's just you two, my best friends."

"We won't say a thing," said Avery and Jazz at the same time.

"I know you won't. If you guys do, I'll have to hurt you." I smiled. "Okay, this may sound weird and sci-fi and all, but...I found out that I'm genetically engineered."

They were silent, as if waiting for more.

"So...that explains why you're super smart and pretty," Jazz said flatly.

"Well...if you think that, thanks. I wasn't happy about this whole thing. The other thing that bothered me was that I was mandated to be a part of a contest."

"What type of contest?" Avery asked.

"I don't want to give too much away, but I have a mentor, and we're working on a breakthrough medicine." There, I probably said too much, but my friends wouldn't go around saying anything. They didn't do that.

"Wow, cool. Can you tell us what it's for?" Jazz asked.

I ignored that. "Hey, you guys know of many people

getting sick at school?"

"A few. Why?" Jazz chimed in.

"Greyson is super sick. He's bad. That's why I want you to get checked out, Jazz. I've been giving him some of my supplements and organic foods from our garden. He doesn't get this kind of food, ya know?"

"Hmmm...didn't know that. That sucks he's sick. You've been hanging out with him, then? I did hear something's going around, but I don't know of anyone violently ill," said Avery. "No, wait, there's one girl in my Urban Studies class who's been out all week, but I'm not sure why."

"Another one? Crap. Grey's violently ill. He's been really bad, both ends. Very weak." I wanted to see Grey tonight. Jazz shifted in her chair and rubbed her neck. A thin layer of sweat glistened on her upper lip.

"God, I hope he gets better soon. Hey, tell us more about your project, it sounds interesting," said Avery.

"I'll tell you more as things progress. Promise."

Thankfully our food arrived, and I sucked it down. I had very few manners at the table with my two friends. I wanted to eat and get over to Grey's house. I was hungry for him, too.

We finished up, and I dropped the girls off at their houses before heading over to Greyson's. On my way, my phone started going crazy. I pulled over to read a slew of messages from Grey.

G: *this sucks i feel terrible*
you there? oh prob at a game this weather sucks so i hope you play well
i miss playing
i miss everything right now i can't wait to get out of my room

141

Then ten minutes later:
G: *i really hate this i feel like crap and nothing's helping*
not even the meds i want to see you
call or text me when you get this
this sucks so bad i want to die

I read this last line five times. No, he better not do anything stupid. I called him, but he didn't answer, so I texted him.

S: *Grey, don't do anything stupid this sucks but i promise to get you better*
i will take you away from all of this
we can go into the city or something

My chest heaved up and down as I dictated my texts, making a ton of spelling mistakes. My stupid phone was defaulting to words I didn't want to say. I fixed it, then waited for a response, but five minutes went by and nothing. I texted him again.

S: *G do not do anything*
i'll be there in twenty minutes i can't wait to see you

Finally, he texted me back.

G: *i'm tired and can't take this anymore*
keep researching for me i wish i was dead no one else
should get this and deal with the pain
it'd be easier for you 6 train maybe I'll just ride it...or not
I'm so confused

18

I read Greyson's text again and again. What was he talking about? Easier for me? What did 6 train mean? I took a deep breath and set my phone on my lap. Rubbing my eyes, I leaned my head back on the headrest of my car seat. The wind whipped around my car, rocking it from side to side while the rain continued to pour down. I tried to clear my thoughts.

He was headed to the train station? Going into the city without me? That had to be it, he was leaving me a clue. He lived a two-minute walk to the train station, but in his condition he'd be more like twenty minutes. I stepped on the gas. I could be there in fifteen.

When I arrived, I sprinted out of my car at breakneck speed, my bag tight by my side. All I'd done over the past weeks with Ximena would practically mean nothing if I didn't get to Grey in time. I felt the rumbling of the train coming toward me, like looming thunder in the distant sky, threatening as it approached with the push of the wind. I fought the grip of fear on my parched throat and pumping heart and kept running until my legs were numb. The six o'clock train was on schedule. Who was I kidding when I prayed on my way to the station for Divine Intervention – for the six o'clock train to be late because of the smog, diverted by a terrorist, or derailed down the line? Maybe I'd be the Divine Intervention.

The horn sounded loud and long, followed by a deafening pause before it blared again, echoing around the station. The air was heavy, and I squinted to make out the figures of people on the platform. The faint shadow of his figure—his lean legs—caught my eye as I rounded the corner, bounding up the steps two-by-two. I turned right onto the platform in front of the tracks. Wind whipped my long ponytail into my face, strands sticking to my dripping sweat. Men and women sauntered safely at the edge, waiting for the in-bound train to slow and the doors to open. I dodged them, but one man anticipated wrongly. I bumped into him hard, both of us catching ourselves from falling, my bag hitting him in his side. My muscles seared out in pain, and lungs gasped for air. My moment of pain didn't surpass the loneliness, anger, and sadness that Grey had endured or that the others with his resistance would experience.

I was surprised by this stranger's unusually thick, black, bushy eyebrows as he reached down to pick up his tablet. When I paused, I looked up and saw Greyson's shadow again.

"Stop! Stop!" I screamed as loud as I could. As I closed in on Grey, I prayed for the train station platform to move, too. Like out of a Harry Potter story. This was painfully real as I saw him lean in toward the track. He wasn't standing straight.

"Grey, NO!" I screamed and time seemed to stop. As he fell sideways, he turned his head my way. A somber look in his crystal blue eyes locked with mine, and I saw a glimpse of regret and hope all at once. The train's brakes squeaked, and I reached for his arm as he reached for mine. The cloudy sky grew thicker, and we seemed to freeze in time. Our arms locked, and I pulled him violently back from the platform, throwing him like a baseball bat that just smacked one out of the park. The train stopped short of us. Breathless, I fell on top of Grey, hoping I didn't crush his frail, boney body. I saw his right foot exposed, toes bare. His shoe was stuck in the track. A damn shoe! I laughed out of relief.

The riders on the platform boarded the train as if nothing had happened. As its long horn sounded, it pulled away from the platform in the direction of the city. It rumbled down the track and faded away into the distance.

Grey was breathing on my neck. His sweet, sweet breath had the faint smell of a honey crisp apple. It was life that soothed my soul and parched throat. His eyes opened, one bruised and swollen on the side from falling so hard onto the platform. He stared straight ahead as if he was evaluating if he was still in the real world or not. In his eyes, I saw that for a brief moment he hoped he had been transformed into the afterlife or maybe Harry Potter's world. Instead, I laid on top of him, hugging him tightly and feeling his chest rise with air again and again, until I suddenly heard a monotonous buzzing. It grew louder as I pulled myself away from Greyson. I noticed that his pants were ripped, and his knee was bleeding steadily, a piece of his skin hanging loose. Looking up, I saw not one, but two drones flying fast our direction. They were flying toward one another, in the same path and got closer and louder. One hovered for a few minutes, while the other flew straight at it, both lowering.

"Can you get up?" I asked Grey.

He took a shallow breath. "I don't know."

"We gotta get out of here." I grabbed his arm to pull him up, but he stumbled.

We both looked up as the two drones were about

to collide. I dragged Grey behind the train station and crouched over him against the brick wall. They clipped one another, both spinning out of control, before diving toward the train tracks. A train traveling toward the station barreled down the tracks and smashed them. Pieces flew, and some shards hit passengers walking on the platform. Startled, they jumped back, confused as to what had just hit them. When the horn sounded loud and long, I covered my ears and closed my eyes, waiting for it all to pass. Grey was holding his ankle, trying not to look at his knee. His pants were soaked with blood.

After the noise stopped, Grey moaned, "I think my ankle's hurt, too."

"Are you freakin' crazy? What the hell were you doing, Grey?" I ripped off a piece of my shirt sleeve and wrapped it around his bleeding knee.

"Ugh!" He moaned in pain louder and held his ankle, leaning back against the wall.

"Look, this should help." I dug out some antibacterial ointment from my bag and spread it on his open wound, then put a band-aid on it. It was worth a try. His ankle was swollen and bruised; that would need to be immobilized. The people controlling the two drones that collided probably were viewing a live feed on their phones of the area, which meant Grey and I would appear on that feed unless we'd ducked out of their range in time. I'd tried, but those drone cameras generally had a wide angle. They'd found us, and I didn't doubt that other drones were being sent. We needed to move quickly.

"Can you get up and walk on the other leg, Grey?" I stood and tried to gently nudge him up. He didn't move, and though his bleeding had slowed, his face was ghostly white.

"Take some slow deep breaths. Don't pass out on me."

"I'll try. I'm such a pain in your ass," Greyson mumbled, shaking his head and looking down at his legs. I barely heard him. "I just needed to get out of my house. To run away and not get my family or friends sick. I was delirious. I'm so sorry to put you through all of this."

"Shut up, just shut up! How can you say that? I'm here for you. I care, Greyson." I choked back tears that formed at the corners of my eyes. Above, the sound of a small engine grew louder. I looked up and sure enough a larger black drone headed our way. I could hear the clicking of the camera and the whirling of the engine. I tugged at Grey's shirt, pulling it over his head as I did the same.

"Grey, we gotta move. That drone is watching us..." I whispered.

Finally, he was able to stand up, wincing, and took a few, tiny steps. We managed to get inside the station and rested a minute against the wall. I felt my phone move in my pocket. That was it—my phone was being tracked. I took it out and opened the security feature, enabling another level of firewall—the maximum, to stop the drones from picking up my signal and tracking me.

I had to stop anything and everything from finding me. I clicked on Avery's cell number and waited for it to ring.

"Avery, it's me... can you pick me up at the train station at Forest Drive?"

"Why are you there?" she asked, sounding confused.

"Sorry, I'll have to explain later. Just get here as quickly as you can. It's urgent, so hurry!" My voice quivered a little and I hung up. I looked at Greyson's twisted ankle and his ripped-open knee. I took a deep breath. We had to get through this.

"Hang in there, Grey. We're going to the hospital.

Avery will be here in ten minutes. You can do this." I leaned into him and squeezed his shoulder. "While we're waiting, let's ramp up our firewalls. Someone's following us."

Grey and I huddled in a corner, hiding under our hoodies and working on our tablets and phones. I kept one eye out for any suspicious activity in the station. So far, everyone seemed to be going about their business as usual. Then I noticed the man with the bushy eyebrows, the guy I bumped into earlier on the platform. He walked into the station and headed toward the bathroom across from us, holding tightly onto his tablet. I thought he had already boarded a train and was long gone into the city. I held my breath and worked quicker.

"Sorry to get you into this mess, Sienna," Grey apologized.

"Really, don't apologize. I want to help you."

"Do your parents know anything about this virus? Did you ask them?"

"I do know that the CDC is investigating. I'm trying to help, but I can't tell you everything right now, especially if someone if following us and maybe even listening. Trust me," I said a little louder. There was a commotion near the door of the station leading out to the parking lot. I peeked out from under my hood. A few people ducked inside to avoid another drone.

"What's up with these things?" a woman said, irritated.

I looked at the time on my phone. Eight minutes had passed. Avery was expected to arrive within two minutes. I tapped my fingers on the edge of my phone, as if it would help time go by quicker. *Please, please, Avery, hurry.*

I put my hand on Grey's back, and before I knew it, he quietly leaned over and puked, again and again. I found a tissue in my bag and handed it to him to wipe his mouth and nose. He peeked out from his hood and looked me in the eyes. My stomach dropped. Oh, God... oh, God, why was this all happening? Grey's face was now paler than it was ten minutes ago. We stared at each other, silent. I rubbed his back some more. It felt like an eternity.

"Hang in there, buddy. I know it sucks. I'm going to get you help. Once Avery gets here, we'll take you straight the hospital." My mouth was dry, and I swallowed hard. I wanted to get up and get water from the drinking fountain across the room, but I didn't want to blow my cover. The man hadn't come out of the bathroom yet.

Finally! Avery's little blue car appeared in the small window of the station door. I got Grey up as fast as I could and waved to her as we stepped out and off the curb to get her attention. "I'll hold you tight, Grey. We can do this!"

Suddenly, a drone swooped low, almost touching the top of Avery's car. We pulled down our hoodies and jumped in the back seat.

It was too much for Grey. He sat back in the seat and passed out.

"Avery, go!" I yelled. She stepped on the gas and floored the car out of the lot and away from the station. The car lurched forward and she made a sharp U-turn away from the drone.

"You okay?" Avery asked once she was driving straight on the main road.

"I'm fine. It's Greyson who's passed out!" I smacked his cheeks to try to revive him as I laid him down across my lap. "He hurt his ankle, his knee is bleeding, he has an infection in his leg, and he puked everywhere. We need to get him to the hospital. There's one close by."

"Nearest hospital," Avery said into her GPS on her dashboard. The automated woman responded, "Turn right at the light." The map showed that the total distance was five miles, but with all the lights and traffic, it'd take fifteen to twenty minutes.

"Step on it!" As Avery sped and crashed through yellow lights, Greyson came to and let out a barely audible moan. I put his legs up as high as I could to get some blood flowing back into his core and head. His breathing was shallow, and he was sweating, literally soaked and clammy. He looked horrible—still pale but now with dark circles under his eyes. Avery suddenly slowed a bit and made a sharp turn. I held Grey tightly as he almost fell off the seat.   "Sorry! Hang on!" yelled Avery as another car laid on their horn, and then another.

Ugh. My stomach was upset from all of the quick turns and my head started to ache. I peered out the window and saw a sign twenty feet ahead for the hospital. *God, please get us there without a crash*, I prayed.

"You're doing awesome, girl. Keep on going!" I just wanted to get Greyson there before he passed out again.

Grey leaned over the edge of the seat. "I think I'm gonna lose it. Open the window... now... ugh..." I pressed on the button to open the window, but it was too late. He dry-heaved toward the floor of the car just as Avery drove up in front of the Emergency Department and slammed on the brakes. She got out, ran to open the back door, while I tried to hold up Greyson.

"Oh, sick!" she said.

I stayed calm for Grey's sake and pointed at the doors. "Yeah, let's just get him out of here and in there."

Just then, that stupid drone came flying around the

corner, camera focused on me, as it slowed. I covered our faces as we hobbled into the building. The drone hovered, watching, until we were inside. Avery jumped back in the car to park it and shouted to me through her open window, "I'll meet you inside." I nodded.

"We need some help, here!" I called out among the hustle and bustle of the emergency room waiting area, to anyone willing to listen. Grey hobbled, blinded by the bright lights, then looked down at his leg, knee, and ankle. His eyes rolled again and his head dipped back.

A nurse ran up, taking Grey by the shoulders just as he was about to collapse.

At the same moment, the man with the bushy eyebrows reappeared. He slipped past the nurse attending to Grey and into the back area. It was chaotic and I quickly lost sight of him.

"Hey, that guy can't go back there! Send security!" I hollered, but my words were lost when paramedics rushed in with a kid on a gurney.

"Gunshot victim, sixteen-year-old girl," one paramedic said urgently to the doctor.

19

The nurse immediately put Greyson in a wheelchair and wheeled him into a bay, closing off the curtain. I tugged on it, stepping in to let her know of his dire situation. Besides being delusional, he may have EBEX or something worse, I warned her. If he had EBEX, it was messing with his head. The medical team quickly decided to quarantine him.

I went back to the waiting area and found Avery, telling her what was going on with Greyson. We both headed to the restroom to wash our hands and were careful not to touch anything after that.

A few hours later, stitched, bandaged up, and still fighting his infection, Greyson rested in the Emergency Department's recovery room. While we waited, I clicked on the news on my phone and read the headline, "Mysterious virus takes first victim in Chicago." I showed Avery. Hovering over my phone together, we silently read the article.

I held my breath as I read that an unnamed man—who I was 99% certain was Anish's dad—died this morning from a virus known as EBEX. He'd supposedly acquired it from traveling to the Middle East while on business. The article stated he had traveled to Qatar and then onto Rome before coming back to Chicago. Authorities were contacting the passengers on his flights and guests at the hotels where he stayed. I let out my breath and took a few short breaths as my heart raced. EBEX was what Grey probably was fighting. Anish was infected too, and Grey was his teammate. The whole team was at risk. I clicked off my phone and felt perspiration forming under my arms.

I started pacing and looked for a nurse. "Avery, I've got to see Grey." She nodded.

When I found one, I asked if I could see him and that I was a relative. She said I could only stay a few minutes and I'd have to wear special gown and mask. I shouldn't get too close to him. No touching at all, she said. Still, she gave me a gown and mask and took me back to the recovery area. The nurse told me that Grey's parents were on their way.

"Hey, Grey, are you hanging in there?" I asked in a whisper. His eyes were closed, and his knee and leg were elevated on the bed.

"Barely. I'm extremely tired." He opened his eyes just a slit and his dry lips stayed parted. But his complexion was pink, not pale like before.

"What were you *thinking*?" Almost immediately I regretted it. He was immobile and looked exhausted. With my face close to the window as it could possibly be, I breathed loudly through my mask. I probably shouldn't have been so upset with him; he was vulnerable and what was done was done.

"Not much at all, I guess." His eyes scanned down his body.

"It's been tough. I know. Remember, I've been with you." I gently tapped his arm. "You're not alone in this, my friend."

"Yeah, you're right. I feel so stupid. I wasn't thinking straight." Grey dropped his chin further. "I was running away from the pain—like trying to physically run and get away from everyone, too. I don't want anyone else to get this. I just couldn't take it anymore. Feeling like crap. Being stuck in my room. Not seeing friends and getting behind in school. Not able to do anything—it's been unbearable." His eyes welled up with tears.

"I should have been there more for you."

"Naw, you were there when you could be. I'm grateful." He tried to smile, but his lips barely curled.

I took a deep breath in, loud, in my mask. It was time to tell him. "I've been keeping something from you. I'm not as nice as you think I am."

"Huh?"

"I've been working on a project no one really knows about. It has to do with what you might be dealing with." I swallowed hard. "This infection is deadly, and your body can't fight it off like usual. I'm certain of it. I'm working on a new drug that will fight it. Well, that would stop it. One that your body won't resist."

"You are?" Grey sat up in his bed, his heavy eyes wide.

"It's top secret. I shouldn't be telling you this, but you need to know there's hope. I'm close, Grey, very close... *we* are close, I should say."

"Secret project? That's sick."

I'd said it, there. Ty, Kellen, and Liv could strike me down, but I had to tell Greyson. His life depended on it. "It's important you know that there are people who don't want everyone to get better with new medicine. *Any* new medicine for an infection," I warned him.

"Really?" He was as baffled, as anyone would be. He closed his eyes a moment and took a deep breath. "The drone. That's what that was about?"

"Yeah. I'm pretty sure they didn't want me to get to

154

you."

"Someone was watching you? Us?"

"It's weird, I know." I lowered my voice to a whisper. "Selfish bastards," I said to myself. We were silent, and I heard voices outside the door. I wouldn't put it past Ty to show up at the hospital looking for me.

I leaned into Grey to whisper in his ear, "I'll get you a sample by tomorrow. Promise. I think you should try it. Our first patient." I smiled, wishing I could touch him and squeeze his hand or arm.

His eyes glazed over and he rested his head back onto his pillow. "Perfect."

The voices outside got louder. Beads of sweat surfaced on my hands; the gloves I was wearing were suffocating. The nurse came in and said it was time for me to leave. I was relieved to see the voices were simply Grey's parents who had arrived. I nodded and said hello to them.

"Time's up. Gotta go. I'll check in with you later, Grey. All smiles, right?"

His parents were suited up in gowns, too, but were able to go into his room, staying at the doorway. I waited at the door and slowly took off my mask and gown, straining to overhear the nurse talking to the Halloways.

I heard Mrs. Halloway gasp, then ask the nurse, "Is he going to be all right?" She put her hand on the nurse's shoulder to steady herself and began to sob.

"He's in serious condition and has an IV drip of a cocktail of antibiotics. We've consulted an infectious disease specialist and she's on her way and will see him up on the floor. She'll take a look at his leg and decide the next steps. He's also dealing with a hurt knee and ankle, so it's best he stays here awhile. We've already put in orders to admit him and get him to a room on the third floor."

Mr. Halloway started to ask a question. I backed away and hung outside of the bay area. About 20 minutes later, someone arrived with a wheelchair. Grey emerged with an IV pole and bag linked to his arm. Mrs. Halloway stayed close to him as they wheeled him toward the elevator.

"Grey, hang in there. You're strong," I said as he rolled by. I gave him a thumbs-up, and he smiled with a glimmer of hope in his eye and mouthed the numbers three-oh-five. His room number.

I headed back to the waiting area and Avery. My thoughts were jumbled, making me feel numb. It was good to lay eyes on her, a solid rock in my life. She was a friend who knew me, who could rattle off my favorite dessert (ice cream), the name of my first dog (Ginger), and my favorite band (LoKo).

"I had to grab some coffee. Want one?" Avery held up her cup and tipped it to take a sip. "Ah," she muttered as she swallowed her warm drink. "My nerves are still jacked. This may or may not help."

"Yeah, I'm jacked, too. Would love one." We walked down the hall toward the cafeteria.

"How's he doing?" Avery asked once we were halfway down the hall.

"Pretty beat up. He's been through a lot. The infectious disease doctor is coming to see him. God, I hope she can help figure this out. In the meantime, I'm going to do my best to help him."

My mind raced just thinking about getting him some of our new drugs. If they worked, he'd feel better in two days. The sooner he had them, the safer he'd be from himself and his own mind. I regretted not getting him a sample a few days ago, even if I'd had to tweak a few things.

What was I thinking? Or not thinking. We could have avoided all of this drama.

"Well, at least he's at the hospital getting help. He looked horrible when I picked you guys up. He could barely walk, let alone move. Is his ankle broken?" Avery was talking, but I only heard the end of her sentence.

"What?" I paused in deep thought. Then her words came to me. "Yeah, his ankle is fractured. He may need surgery. I'm afraid that might not be ideal for his condition." I trailed off in thought, again.

I had to be careful of any drug interactions. He might be under anesthesia for surgery. Giving him meds the day of surgery might be pretty risky. On the other hand, he needed them now so he could get better to have surgery. I'd have to know what else he was taking and cross-check any side effects. No one could find out about this new drug. Not yet.

We walked into the cafeteria and I looked for the coffee machine. I followed the strong smell and sucked it through my nose with a deep breath. *Ximena.* I'd figure out a way to ask her a few questions. She had to know more from past trials. I paid for my coffee with my smart phone then joined Avery at a table.

She put her hand on my elbow. "You like him, don't you?"

"Yeah, can you tell?" I blew on my hot drink.

"Hell yeah, girl! You were hovering all over him when I pulled up to the train station. What is all this about, anyway?" She took a sip of her coffee.

I moved over to where the creamers were, and she came with me. Putting in a splash of cream, I took a long, drawn-out sip. I figured she'd notice and ask this question.

"We've been hanging out lately. We've known each other for years. Since we were little. I guess I never looked at him as anything more than a friend, but this time it was different. I was all over him because he was hurt, and I had to protect him from the drone taking photos of us. I'd heard of things shooting out of drones before. It's really unbelievable what those things can do. Right now, it's better that you don't know too much more than this. Trust me."

Just then, my phone buzzed. It was Kellen calling me. I seriously didn't want to listen to his voice at the moment.

"My phone's been crazy, too. Mom wants to know where I am. She just needs to chill."

Avery looked down at my phone and rolled her eyes. "True! So does mine. I went as far as blocking her calls for a while, I was so pissed at her."

I listened to Kellen's voice message asking if I was okay and to call him. Why would he care if I was okay, and what did he know about me? He knew what happened, so maybe he has some information I need. He and Ty sent that drone and they'd seen the footage. If he was after me, then why did he care how I was doing? There must be something else. I texted him back. *I'll call you soon.*

I surprised myself that I even cared why Kellen was contacting me. We were still standing by the milk and cream counter. I looked up and around the cafeteria and noticed a few doctors and nurses were hanging out, but mostly it was just visitors sitting and eating. A few people were in line for drinks and food. I saw a familiar brown coat—it was the man with the bushy eyebrows and tablet.

I took Avery's elbow and quickly walked toward the

exit. This guy was following me. I had a strange sense that I'd seen him even before the train station. Maybe at one of Willow's appointments at the hospital or maybe the science awards downtown. Or maybe he worked at the hospital and I had passed him at some point. I felt his eyes on me, and my gut told me to leave, get out of there fast.

My phone rang; it was Kellen again.

"Code Silver, Code Silver, Code Silver." A calm female voice came loud and clear over the hospital's intercom.

I darted a look to Avery. Both of us were wide-eyed. "What the freak is Code Silver?" she asked as we walked faster toward the Exit door down the hallway.

"I have no idea. I'll look it up on my phone." I dictated the words and read back the response as we both bolted into a jog. "It's for a person with a weapon and/or active shooter and/or hostage situation. Shit! Could be anywhere in this huge building," I said, glad we both had running shoes on.

"Let's get out of here," Avery said running faster, but the hallways quickly got crowded as more people came out of their rooms and offices.

"Wait! What about Grey? I can't just leave him!" I shouted over the noise of the intercom and the chaos that erupted.

"Are you insane?"

"Code Silver, evacuate the building immediately," the woman's voice articulated.

Doctors and nurses ran everywhere trying to help patients. I peeked into one of the stairwells in the hallway. People were running up and down, bumping into one another. I pulled back and closed the door, then asked a someone in a lab coat what was going on.

"There's a hostage situation. Not sure where," he said

as he checked his phone for messages. "Looks like fourth floor."

"What does this mean?" My eyes were wide. Grey's room was on the third floor, thankfully.

The man grabbed my arm and looked me in the eyes. "Clear out of here, girls," he said, before running up the stairs.

"But my friend is up there!" I yelled up to him.

"We better get out of here, Sienna. Grey will be okay. They'll take care of him," Avery said, trying to reassure me. But I knew she was just as clueless as I was. I texted Grey: *be safe Avery and I are leaving the hospital. Be careful. Lmk u r ok. xo.*

Once Avery and I reached her car, we sat in it for a few minutes catching our breath. Overhead, two helicopters approached, and a few drones hovered above the hospital's rooftop.

Grey texted back: *lots of chaos up here. mom and dad here. heard a guy has a patient and nurse. making demands. don't know more. get out NOW be safe*

Suddenly, gunshots blasted and echoed, followed by the sound of shattering glass. It looked like a window had broken on the second floor. Avery and I both screamed and jumped in our seats.

We sat frozen for about five minutes, literally stuck to our seats, unable to move a muscle. Then in front of the main entrance, a big, black armored truck pulled up and a SWAT team of twenty men or so flowed out, armed and ready to take control.

"God, I hope no one was killed!" Avery was shaking and staring up at the window. "We should leave, seriously, leave."

I bit my nails and stared.

There was movement. One of the drones was similar to the one I saw following us at the train station. People were flooding out the hospital's main entrance. I stared and squinted to see more details and noticed the man with the bushy eyebrows running out, with a hat on. He looked both ways and then disappeared in the crowd. I held up my phone, zoomed in, and took a picture of him.

I put my hand across to Avery as she started the car. "Wait! I need to call Grey before we leave. I need to know if he saw this guy up there on his floor."

Grey's phone rang and rang before he answered and said he was still with his parents, on a different floor.

The SWAT team had surrounded the building near where the window was shot out. My phone rang again—it was Mom calling me. "Sienna, where are you?"

"I'm at the hospital parking lot. I'm with Avery." I did my best to sound calm, but my mind was racing, and my leg was shaking.

"What are you doing there? Get out! Now!" she barked in a voice I'd never heard before.

"Like I said, I'm with Avery. We're leaving soon. I'll explain later." I'd only tell her bits and pieces of the story. That's all she deserved.

"I'm on my way to the hospital, Willow is there."

"What? Why?" She had to be kidding me. Willow *here*, with a Code Silver going on?

"She had some trouble this morning. She was admitted, just to be careful."

"I'm not leaving, then. I'll wait for you."

"I'll be there in fifteen minutes or less. If I can get through the traffic."

"Yeah, they may not let you in the lot with this gunman in there. Police are blocking the entranceways."

More screams erupted from the crowd of employees and visitors corralled outside. Another window was blown out, this time on the third floor, where Grey had been headed. My phone dropped from my hand. What the hell was going on? I fumbled to pick it up and tapped on Mom's stored cell number. Her call had cut out.

"Mom, Mom, you there? Where is Willow's room?" I prayed it wasn't the fourth.

"She's in 273. I just left to take care of some work issues and can't believe some crazy person is in there! It's a hospital, for Chrissake!"

"Crap. I'll see what I can find out. Have you tried calling her?"

"Yes, but she's not answering. She may have been getting a scan. She was supposed to get a scan while I was gone. I should've been there..." Mom trailed off.

"Mom, you're in panic mode. We know nothing right now. Try to get in touch with her doctor?"

"I will. Keep in touch." She hung up, and I sat in Avery's car, wanting to go in and get Willow and Grey out.

I was seething. Mom, gone again from Willow's side, when she needed her. Willow should never be on her own, no matter what Mom needed to do for work. She was such a shitty mom. I would never do that. After a few minutes of my anger building, I couldn't sit there anymore. I opened the door and got out, thinking about my next move. They both had to be okay.

"What are you doing?" Avery asked.

"I can't sit here. I need to think," I said. My phone buzzed, it was Kellen again. This time I picked it up.

"Seriously, what do you want?"

"Are you alright? Where are you?" His voice quivered.

"Why should I tell you?"

"I just heard about the stuff going on at the hospital." He was so quiet I could barely hear him. "You need to get to a safe place."

"No shit. Too late now." He was silent on the other end. "There's no real safe place, anyway, right?"

Avery paralyzed, had turned off her car. We weren't driving anywhere.

"I know it was stupid of Ty to rough you up. I told him to back off. But he's not the type to listen. He's on a mission."

"If he's behind all of this, he's a dead man. He's taken this way too far."

"I'm not saying he is. I don't know. But he's capable." The call dropped.

The SWAT team had gone into the hospital. The helis were circling and one landed on the roof of the building. More armed men poured out. Then quiet.

I called Willow. No answer. "Avery, if you want or need to leave, go. My mom is on her way. I'll find her. Willow is in there. I'm not leaving her and Greyson until I know they are okay and not being held by some insane person."

Avery got out of the car, too. "I'm not leaving you. What are you going to do?"

"I can't stand here. I'm going around the back to see about getting in there. I've got to check on Willow."

"There's a guy with a gun in there. You can't."

"Watch me. Stay here in case my mom comes."

If Ty had anything to do with this, Willow could be in trouble, too. If he was after me and wanted to start some sort of crazy class war, this would be one way to do it. Go right for them at the hospital where they were trying to get help and get better. Ty was the coward, attacking people who were helpless. *Wipe them out*, was what he had said. No medical advancements for them. I ran harder and faster than I ever had. I tapped into a new level of speed I didn't even know I had in me.

Another shot echoed around the hospital campus.

20

Since the SWAT team was inside one of the medical office buildings, I ran around to the to the physician's entrance on the west side. The door was locked, but I noticed there was a key card box where you could swipe a badge to get in.

Staff and visitors were outside by this time. I had no idea what the patients were doing—if they were being held somewhere for protection or if they were being shuffled outside, if at all possible. I would think with a Code Silver, the protocol was some sort of lock down, as it would be impossible to move every patient out of the building. Plus, there was the EBEX situation. It could spread like crazy and those patients couldn't leave.

A man in a white lab coat came running around the corner, heading toward the door with his badge. "What are you doing here? You need to leave, right now!"

"I can't. My sister and friend are in there. I have to get to them. I have to," I pleaded.

"It's not safe. What are their names? I can try to find out."

"Can I go in there with you? I promise I'll be careful. I can't just leave them."

He shook his head, hand on his badge to swipe open the door. "Look, I don't have time to sit here and talk to you. This is a serious situation, and I need to get to some of my patients."

Just then his phone rang, and he picked it up. "What? Okay, I'll be right there."

He turned his back to me, swiped his badge and opened the door. My hand was quick, and I grabbed it before it could shut behind him. Not noticing, the doctor sprinted off down the hall and up the staircase. I was in!

I jumped the stairs behind him, taking two at a time up to the second floor to try to find Willow. My phone vibrated in my pocket. It was Mom. Before opening the door to the second floor, I texted her, letting her know I was on the way to Willow's room. Behind one of the workstations, a woman crouched, hiding behind the desk, watching a computer monitor and probably keeping an eye on patient vitals. I went the other way, looking at room numbers. Room 266, 267...

All was quiet until I heard the creaking of a wheelchair rolling. I flinched. Patients were still in rooms. Of course, there was nowhere for them to go. Down the hall, I saw an officer coming my way. My heart raced.

Room 273. There it was. Just in time to avoid the officer, I opened the door, expecting to see Willow safe and sound in her bed, getting better, but the bed was empty. My hands started to shake. Maybe she was getting a scan like Mom said and never made it back up to her room.

That'd be good, as she'd probably be on a lower floor and could exit easily. I left and decided to take the staircase to check to see if Grey was in his room. I wouldn't be surprised if he'd left with his parents. They'd shuffle him off somewhere as quickly as they came.

I moved swiftly up another flight of stairs, but when I opened the door to the floor, I heard a deep, blood-curdling scream and a man's voice. My body froze, but my mind couldn't get to Grey's room fast enough. I was on autopilot. My brain could only think of Willow and Grey being in trouble, so I forced myself to just keep moving.

I crouched low as I shuffled along the hallway to Grey's room, doubtful he'd be there in bed. I opened the door slowly, with my shirt covering my face.

"Hey, Grey. It's me," I warned him. Nothing. His room was empty and stale, still smelling of disinfectant. I stepped back, unsure and uneasy. I was alone. My pulse quickened and I glanced at my phone—my connection to people outside this room and hospital war zone.

The silence was broken with the sound of fresh shots being fired, close enough that they could possibly be down the hall. Still crouched, I turned around and opened the supply closet door across from his room. It was dark and quiet, and full of metal shelves with boxes of medical supplies. I stepped inside, closed the door as quietly as possible, and held my ear to it. Nothing. Eerily quiet for being a hospital normally full of people, 24/7.

Then I heard something, like someone moved. I sensed a person was in the closet. I turned slowly to look over my shoulder and saw Grey cowered, sitting in the corner, wincing in pain.

"Grey!" I whispered.

He breathed in deeply, as his held then rubbed his leg.

"Sounds like the shooter is down the hall. Let's hide here for a few minutes and then try to sneak out the back staircase. Can you do stairs?" It was the dumbest question I think I'd ever asked someone.

"I'll do what I have to do to get out of here."

"Good. Did you see the shooter?" I asked, trying to make him more comfortable and get his mind off of his pain.

Grey took a deep breath as if debating what to tell

me. "I saw a little bit of the back of him from down the hall." There was a long pause before he spoke again. "I was afraid but managed to roll off of my bed and crawl down the hall to this closet. Mom and Dad left just before the code was called to get something to eat. I don't know where they are." Dazed, he stared at his hands gripping his leg.

I heard a scuffle outside our door and put my finger up to my lips to keep him quiet. Men were talking down the hall, arguing about how they were going to get out of here alive. Then it was quiet.

We waited another five minutes, which seemed like forever. Seriously, five minutes is a long time when you are waiting in a closet and can't see what gunmen are doing or planning, if in fact those men were the gunmen. Finally, I opened the door to peek out. No activity. No one was around.

"Let's move! Follow me."

We stayed low, as low as Grey could stay given his injuries. He hobbled, softly grunting a few times. I looked back at him with wide eyes and whispered in a deep voice, "You can do this." He kept going and when we reached the stairwell, he let out a deep groan when we got inside.

"Almost there," I said. Holding the railing, he hobbled down the stairs, counting them under this breath.

"One by one. We can do this." I rushed ahead, but then slowed down, not wanting to push him. He didn't need to hurt himself further. Finally, we reached the bottom and opened the door to outside. The cool wind hit our faces. I looked left and right. The area was clear. All the commotion was on the far side of the other office building and this was a large hospital campus.

I called Avery. She was still where I had left her. I told her we were on the way.

A few minutes later, we met her at the entrance. We each grabbed Grey under his arms and lifted him as best we could to the car. Adrenaline and fear moved us.

We stayed low and got into the back seat, hoping security cameras weren't on us. I figured all eyes would be on the shooters. We were just kids.

"Take it easy out of here, will you?" pleaded Grey. He straightened his leg in the car, laying it across the back seat. I got in the front and flipped my hood up to cover my face while Grey laid his head down on my lap.

"Geez! You two. I'll do my best to get us home safely. If that's where you want to go." She stepped on the pedal and her electric car purred away. No noise was perfect. Ahead we saw an officer signaling us to stop. Avery slowed down.

"Where do you think you are going? This campus is on lockdown."

"Is it? Officer, I'm sorry, but I have a really bad stomach, GI cramps, and I gotta get home. I was visiting my friend when the code alarmed, and I just ran out of the building. I have to get home." I could imagine Avery giving him a look of desperation, holding her stomach. He shone his light in her car and deemed her harmless. "Okay, get out of here and fast."

I hadn't thought about where we'd go. Maybe Avery's house would be the best; we could hide Grey in her basement where he could chill out and heal. He needed time away from my trail.

"Your house is the best. Let's go there." I sat up and clipped in my belt buckle. "Did you see my mom at all?"

"Nope. No one is getting onto the hospital campus.

They set up a security checkpoint and only authorized vehicles are getting in. We were lucky that we got out."

"Shit. And Willow wasn't in her hospital room." I texted Mom, *Where are you? Willow's not in her room.*

"I have no idea where my parents are," Grey said. "They went to get some lunch and then all this shooting happened. I don't have my phone or tablet. Can you text them, Sienna?" His voice was tight. He looked pale and shaky. He coughed hard, so hard I thought he was going to throw up again. His shoulders were boney, too, like he needed a good meal.

Come to think of it, if I took a long look at him, I'd barely recognize him. I missed the fun, goofy guy that made me laugh. He noticed me staring at him and smiled, the right side of the edge of his mouth curling up and his dimple as deep as it always was. I could box that smile and stare at it forever. His teeth were slightly crooked, but that made him boyish. His eyes still had a little spark —he wasn't giving up. I wouldn't let him, and he knew it by now. I could tell. He was resolved. I texted Mrs. Halloway that Grey was with me and I'd reach out to them later.

Mom's call snapped me back to reality. "Mom, are you okay?"

She asked me the same. She had been turned away by the police at the hospital entrance and was hanging out by the shopping center next door. One of us had to get to Willow, who wasn't answering her phone. Mom was frantic and Dad was on his way.

"The SWAT team has this. Willow will be fine. I'm sure they moved her to a safe place." I believed this to be true. It had to be, especially since the shooters were chasing me and Grey from the train station. They were after us, but now Grey was safe with me.

"Mom, I'll be in touch later. I'm going to get away from here. Let me know if you hear from Willow," I said and hung up. I didn't want to reveal to anyone, especially not Mom, where I was going with Grey.

Avery drove fast, despite our complaints. I glanced back at Grey and gave him a look of "Oh well!"

She focused on the road and zipped around, making short stops, if any, at the stop signs. Grey just had to sit tight and hold on. She took the backroad winding around to the emergency department. An ambulance sped right towards us, but Avery dodged the truck, swerving us onto the grass. Then she swung around the roadblock. Police were focused on the building and never saw us coming. Perfect timing. Grey and I ducked down in our seats and Avery passed them.

~~~~~

We arrived at Avery's house frazzled, but in one piece. I quietly helped Grey out of the car and hustled him— as much as I could—down to her basement. I didn't have gloves or a face mask, so I was relying on my own invincible immune system to not catch his EBEX. I also figured he was past the point of contamination and he had antibiotics in his system—a strong dose. This was our last move before he could really rest and let his body heal.

He laid down on the couch, practically collapsing. I propped him up with a pillow and covered him with a blanket. He rested his head back in relief and sighed. He was sweating and his hair was wet and sticky. I found a hand towel in the bathroom and wiped his forehead, calming him. His pale face slowly became flushed with some color.

Sitting next to him, I rubbed his shoulder. "You did it,

you made it out."

I was proud he stayed strong after what he'd been through that day. It all seemed like a fantasy, some scene from a terrorist movie. He was safe for now, and the sooner I started him on my new medication the better. I'd always believed him to be strong. I kept rubbing his shoulder until he closed his eyes and his chest heaved slowly.

He swallowed long and hard. His mouth was dry and so when he spoke quietly, I could barely hear him. "Was that shooter after me?" His head remained back and his eyes, closed.

I sat in silence for a moment, because when he actually finally said those words it sounded ludicrous. Why would anyone want to hurt or even kill Greyson? He was the sweetest, coolest guy I'd ever known and hearing this, knowing there was even the possibility of a tiny hint of truth in his inquiry, tore me up inside. It literally felt like my insides were tearing, ripping apart; my gut clenched so tight that I had the sudden urge to run to the bathroom, bend over the toilet and yak out my insides. But I didn't.

I didn't let this "terrorist cell" of some sort break me down. I held on for him. I held onto the edge of the couch and dug deep into my soul. There was more for me to do and to finish. I took a quick drink of water, then got him a cup of water. When I came back, he had drifted off to sleep. Neither of us needed to answer his question aloud. We both knew that someone was after us. But we had gotten away and were safe for the time being.

I put the cup of water down next to the couch and pulled the blanket around him. I played with a few strands of his dirty, flyaway hair, ever so lightly so as not to wake him. The stray strands slid through my index and middle fingers so smoothly and innocently. I stopped and held them, then leaned in close to his cheek, as I tucked them behind his ear. Part of me wanted him to be awake, to look in his eyes and let him know I never wanted him to slip away. To think I almost lost him earlier that day seemed impossible. I wouldn't let him get those thoughts of leaving me and everything in his head ever again. I would work, day and night, to make sure that didn't happen.

Giving him the tiniest of kisses on his bruised cheek, I curled up next to him on the floor. Screw EBEX.

21

I bolted up, my heart racing, suddenly awakened from a deep sleep. Where was Willow? I must've fallen asleep on the floor. I ran my fingers through my hair and looked around. I didn't recognize anything through my blurred vision.

Then I heard footsteps coming down the stairs toward me. Thankfully, it was just Avery. Grey was asleep on the sofa. With that, the real nightmare rushed back to me.

"Hey, I was just coming to check on you guys." She crouched down on the floor next to me, hesitant to get any nearer to Grey.

"I must've fallen asleep." I rubbed my eyes and looked for my shoes. I had to go back to the hospital to find Willow.

"Yeah, and Grey's out cold, too. He can stay here. My mom's okay with that," she whispered, "as long as he stays down here."

"That's so cool of her. Fabulous, I think he should stay here for now." I found my shoes and put them on.

"Where are you going?"

"I have to figure out where Willow is. I pray I'm not too late. She could be in trouble." I started for the stairs.

"Let me know what's going on. I worry about her too, ya know."

"I will. If you can keep an eye on Grey, that'd be awesome." I didn't want to leave him right now, but I knew

Avery would take care of him. He'd be okay resting if he was well hidden. Suddenly, my stomach growled. I forgot when I last ate anything.

"Let me get you something to eat before you go. My mom made some pasta for dinner."

"Avery, you guys are amazing. I'll have a quick few bites, then have to go. You get it."

"I get it," she said as I tiptoed after her up the stairs.

While we ate, I tried calling Willow, Mom, and Dad. Their phones just rang and rang, eventually going to voicemail. Their happy mechanical greeting seemed fake, or at the very least reminded me of happier times. Like when we had all eaten a warm pancake breakfast and our bellies were full or were all sitting around the fire pit in the backyard on a warm summer evening, hanging out with neighbors. Each voice had a tone of gentle satisfaction that didn't relate to the current crisis. As if this crisis wasn't real, but in another world completely, or like I was in a bad reality TV show.

I shoveled in the pasta and looked up the local news online. The shooting situation and the EBEX infection spreading at the hospital were the headlines all over the top news outlets. It was broadcast that someone in the hospital had a rare infection that was spreading, and the shooters were somehow involved. Photos and the details were plastered all over. No names, just that the SWAT team and police didn't get the shooter or shooters. They said the shooter presumably snuck out into the woods nearby. Several patients were in critical condition. At least one man and two women were shot and in the ICU. It was all so stale, factual, and real. I had been there with real people, and very sick people were in trouble. I shook my head in disbelief.

All of a sudden, a flurry of text messages and phone messages came through my phone. I showed it to Avery. "Shit, look at this!" My phone must've been jammed or lost satellite reception for a while.

"Crazy!"

Mom and Dad were simultaneously trying to get in touch with me. Ximena, too. I called Dad back; he'd be able to tell me calmly what was going on. He was always able to keep his cool, no matter what. One time when we were on vacation—our usual camping trip out west—a bear got into our food supply and we were literally out of food for the next few days. Dad didn't panic. He made those days an adventure, teaching us how to survive on the food in the woods. It was fun, until we got lightheaded from not eating much. We ended our long weekend early and found a restaurant in a nearby town. He always turned mishaps into adventures and learning experiences.

He picked up after the first ring. "Sienna, thank God you're okay! Where are you?"

"I don't want to tell you anything over the phone. How's Willow?"

"Well, it's crazy," he began, then abruptly stopped.

"I know, I know, tell me about it!"

"Sienna, the SWAT team and the FBI are looking in every possible area and corner of the hospital to find Willow."

"What?"

"They suspect she's hiding and scared."

"No!" I screamed and suddenly felt dizzy. I braced myself, holding onto the table. "Oh, no. I can look for her. She'll talk to me. I'll find her."

"We've talked to the FBI, and in fact I'm with them

right now. They're working with the hospital team and are doing everything they can to find her."

"Dad, this can't be happening." I was breathing so hard I thought I was going to faint. Avery held onto my arm tightly.

Then Dad's tone changed. In a businesslike, stoic voice, he said, "We shouldn't be discussing this over the phone."

"Right. You're right, Dad. Sorry I wasn't there earlier. I looked for her in her room, but she was gone."

My stomach churned. I should have gone to her room first and not been with Grey, who had his parents with him. Willow was alone. Family first, right? I could have been there for her. I should have known she'd be scared. Instead, I was thinking of Grey. I hung up and told Avery I had to leave immediately. We'd move Grey to my house or back home tomorrow, maybe. Right now, my family needed me. My mind raced. I could go search the woods or drive around the area or talk to the FBI about the designer kids and Tyler.

"Sienna, are you going to be okay?" Avery saw the look on my face. Hers was as white as mine felt.

~~~~~

Willow was a tough girl, but I worried about her constantly. She was always fragile, like a delicate flower in the wind, petals clinging to the stem for dear life. Some days she was able to stay tough, others she'd wither. It was crazy to think someone might be after her, little Willow!

I could just imagine Tyler trying to get to her when she was escaping and unaware. She was innocent and had nothing to do with my project or any of the Eden projects.

I remember always fighting for her—wanting to be

right by her side at the playground, school, and choir practice, when I could. She had the most angelic voice. I begged her all the time to sing, loving the sound of it. I could never get enough.

When we were younger and it was at all possible, I wouldn't let her out of my sight; and, when we were separated, I'd worry so much I'd get a stomachache. I'd demand that my parents bring me to her. I knew she could be gone in a minute, and I'd move the earth to not let that happen. I should have gone to her room first.

At home, Mom and I reminisced about Willow, her silly comedy skits where she'd sing and dance for hours, putting on long shows on Friday nights for us and close friends. Then she'd be so tired on Saturdays that Mom had to wake her up at noon to eat. I'd find a way to get her home tonight. I imagined us in the garden this weekend. Her singing voice carried so beautifully among the glass walls, like a butterfly flitting around corner to corner, exploring the plants.

"I thought Willow was safe in the hospital," Mom finally said. This thought had clearly been nagging at her.

"I did, too, Mom. This is all so unbelievable." I shook my head, biting my thumbnail.

"She was just having a setback, and the doctor told us to bring her in. It wasn't that unusual, really, it wasn't. I expected her home in a few days, and now this." She went to the cupboard in the kitchen to make us some herbal tea.

"She'll be fine. I believe that." I wanted to be honest but couldn't. My phone buzzed.

Avery texted: *any news? keep me posted. they'll find her.*

Mom sat down at the table, rubbing her belly. Her eyes were red and swollen from crying and exhaustion. She handed me my cup.

"What's happening here, Sienna? I have dreams for my family: for you, Willow, and our new baby boy. A better life, one devoid of violence and hatred. A world with clean, pure air—no pollution hanging over our cities with unbreathable air, killing us. We need to be smart and not take earth and humankind to the brink of existence. Can you see why we joined the efforts to engineer our family? We need your and our baby's generations to save us; to help align our priorities to enable us to survive. To defeat depression and genetic mutations that haunt us and only bring about destruction to ourselves and others. It's how our lives were intended to be, I believe—one with the earth. It's nothing new; life was simpler and clean before man invented machines and things to make our lives easier. Now we are just destroying ourselves. Dad and I want nothing more than for you and the others to work on these scientific breakthroughs and keep advancing medicine. You can make a difference. It's not too late."

I sat staring at her, my fingers grasped tightly around my warm cup of tea. "What about Willow? And Greyson? They matter, too, Mom."

"They do, Sienna. They do." She shook her head and looked down, negating any emotion and truth to her statement. It was as if she'd given up on them. It wasn't too late. I honestly didn't know how she could give up. I stared at my mother, the person whom I should be closest to, who should understand me, and I felt like she was a stranger. A cold-hearted woman, someone I'd never met before, and never cared to get to know.

"You really mean that, Mom? Because I don't think you do. I believe everyone has a fair chance to live and contribute. Everyone is here for a reason. You told me that when I was a little girl." I nibbled on my nails. She really did say that once.

"Things have changed, you know."

"You're right about that. This whole genetically engineering thing has gone too far. Seriously. It's not natural. We are supposed to *all* figure out solutions to our problems. It's our duty, Mom." It was like I was the parent and she was the kid. She and Dad had stepped over the line. I was on the brink of complete madness that they engineered me and my soon-to-be brother. It wasn't for them to decide. In fact, I was alive by mistake.

Maybe something happened in my making that went wrong—I'd read it could happen—because I didn't think and feel the same way as Mom and the other engineered kids. They saw their clear path in life, but that wasn't going to stop me from making things right.

"I don't get why you did this the first time and are doing it again now. You have no right. You and Dad didn't think this all through." I raised my voice, walking over to the sink to rinse my cup. I reached for an apple. It was puny, but I took a bite anyway.

"You don't fully understand. We did, Sienna. More than you know. I was just getting started in genetics at the time, and my colleagues wanted Dad and I to be a part of this huge project—something that would save the world or the very least make a difference. We were desperate. It's much bigger than us. You're part of a bigger picture. You need to understand this."

Mom was interrupted by Ximena calling me. In her squeaky voice, she demanded to know where I'd been. I explained, leaving out a bunch of the details. She wanted to know when I'd be in because she needed me to finish up some testing. We were getting close to a non-resistant antibiotic. It might take all night, she warned me. Although I'd been doing testing on my own, bringing home some small samples of assays and antibiotics, I didn't let on to Ximena. I heard her arguing on the phone with the big drug companies who were pushing her every day for answers. Big bucks were on the line.

I'd just hung up with Ximena when my phone and Mom's pinged at the same time. We read Dad's text out loud: *better get to the police station on Lake Ave, fast.*

I followed Mom in case I got a chance to go to the lab later. Ximena meant business and even if I had an hour, she wanted me to be working. We arrived at the police station to see that Dad was a mess. His eyes were red from crying and dark circles had set in. We'd all been through a lot with Willow's health, and Dad had always remained strong. He'd been our rock. But now he paced, worn out.

He hugged us both right away. He was sweaty and his B.O. was astonishing. It literally it made me gag, and I pulled away from him. "Dad!" I said, swishing the air under my nose.

"Sorry, sweetie." His smile was pathetic and forced. A look of relief washed over his face. "Glad you guys are here."

"What's going on now?" asked Mom.

"Willow's at the hospital. The police just got a call that she showed up there. She's being triaged, and the police will take us over there right away with an escort."

"Oh, thank goodness she's there. She'll be okay, right?" Mom grabbed Dad around his neck.

"We don't know yet for sure."

"Let's go!" I said, grabbing both of them by the elbows as we followed the police officer to his car.

22

Mom and I followed Dad into the emergency department, but Mom did all the talking with the doctors. I sat in the waiting room, biting my nails.

After about an hour, Dad finally came out to find me. "Willow is hanging on. She's being evaluated by the doctor." His voice was tight and wavering.

"Those bastards. I'll literally kill them for this. She was running from them, right?"

"They're not sure what happened. Right now, they're just treating her. We'll find out eventually."

"I'll find out what happened." I twisted my hands into the bottom of my shirt.

"Well, we do know that Willow twisted her ankle when she tried to escape and somehow no one found her. She must not have gone too far. She dragged herself down to the emergency department," Dad said, choked up. I knew he was steaming up inside, harboring his hatred for now.

"Seriously?" I swallowed hard in disbelief, again.

"We're waiting to hear from the surgeon and what her prognosis is." His words drifted off with exhaustion. I clung tightly to Dad, as if the force of our love would keep little Willow alive.

"Can I see her?" I asked, my eyes welling up. We walked into her room together. It was dark and the machines beeped steadily. She was on her back with tubes sticking out all over her mouth and arms, her ankle in a cast. I felt helpless, standing over her, suddenly aware of my own strength and stamina. The surgeon had repaired her ankle, and she was heavily sedated. I covered my mouth and reached to hold her delicate hand, her fingers limp. Mom sobbed by her bed.

It was like we had stepped into the scene of a movie and we were all bad actors. The producer had already yelled "Rolling!" and everyone was quiet, waiting for me to deliver my lines. Any minute, Willow would sit up and pull the tubes out, the cameras would back up, and the spotlights would be turned off. We'd laugh and then all go have lunch that was catered on the set.

A strong chemical smell snapped me back to reality. *I should have gone to her first.* I looked at Mom and she shook her head. It was a "I can't-believe-this-happened" shake.

There was nothing to do but wait. I told Willow to stay strong, to not give up, she was a super girl, remember? I pressed my lips together and hummed her a little song— her favorite, about playing down by the river under the sun all day. I thought she started to smile, but in reality, it was just me remembering her smile. I wanted things back to normal. I wanted us to be kids again, playing.

She was taken to explore possible damage to her internal organs. Her immune system had gone berserk.

Three hours later, the surgeon came out of the operating room with a meager smile to tell us she was in a tough spot and needed rest. She was in serious condition. They would keep close tabs on her, but that was about all they could do for now. They advised all of us to head back home and get some rest, too. It was an insane suggestion. But Mom and Dad agreed to take shifts. They were ready to step up and be by her side. I didn't want to leave her, too, but they insisted that I go and get a good night's sleep in my own bed.

"We've got Willow covered," said Dad. He stayed at the hospital, and Mom and I headed for home. Actually, she needed the rest more than I did, since morning sickness had struck her full on this week.

Dad would call us if anything changed. But the day hadn't ended for me. I expected to feel drained but somehow, I was still running on adrenaline and the natural boost from the tea.

Outside in the thick air, I gasped to find a pocket of pure oxygen. The inversion was terrible again. I could barely see in front of me as I walked to my car, the lab address searching on my GPS.

The fall of footsteps behind me wasn't alarming until they quickened when I sped up. My heart raced as I reached for my phone and tapped on the flashlight. I shone it in front of me, then turned around, shedding the bright light on someone in a hoodie. Their head was down, and they were walking fast toward me. They reached out to grab me, but I took off running, out of their grasp. Flinging my bag securely across my shoulder, I ran, swinging both arms. I glanced around and realized that I didn't know the area well and it was dark, two strikes against me. But I was fast, so I could outrun the loser behind me.

I headed toward the woods, which were hard to navigate, but I remembered Avery driving us out of the hospital and going past the woods, sneaking around out behind the back entrance. I circled that way. The footsteps faded behind me for now. I was gaining ground. I took a deep breath, focused, and picked up my pace, heading into the woods. By the sounds around me, the fall of my footsteps and the noise of cars in the area, I figured that the trees were thick but probably backed up to a neighborhood. I slowed down and clicked on the map app on my phone. I wanted to head toward the lab. My phone took a while trying to find a satellite signal, which was weak among the tall trees. The little circle kept on ticking around searching for a connection. Shit, nothing.

I stuffed it into my pocket. I was on my own, using my instincts. If this guy had anything to do with Ty, he probably wanted me to lead him to the lab, but I'd figure out a way to ditch him first. As I got deeper into the woods, my surroundings got darker, and I tripped over a rock. I got up quickly and put my hands up to protect my face to avoid branches from scraping my face and eyes. The ground was uneven; branches had fallen all over from the recent storm. I mis-stepped and grazed the top of a rock I couldn't see. Damn, this was tricky. Down I fell, getting my knees wet. A splash of dirt got in my mouth and I crunched on some grit. Springing back up, I started running again. I had no time to lose. A streetlight ahead shone through the darkness, breaking the curtain on top of me.

When I dashed that direction, the person chasing me yelled, "I'm gonna get you!" It was a female voice trying to sound different, like a man. A fast female runner. Adrenaline surged in my veins and I sped up. The voice was familiar: Oceana or Liv.

When I reached a streetlamp at the corner of the road, I saw a break in the cars driving by and dodged quickly across the street, hoping my pursuer was worn out and not able to cross as quickly. I stopped for a second and looked back. She was stuck, a flood of cars driving by.

There was no way she could cross without getting hit.

I gave her a sign, you know, something vintage along with flipping her the middle finger, then turned and kept running. After my confrontation with Liv at the lacrosse field, I guessed it was her by her skinny legs and the curve of her hips. She'd regret even thinking she could chase me down. I had to get to the lab now. Securing our trials was crazy urgent.

The cool nighttime run had energized me. I settled into a solid pace that I held as my mind drifted off to the lab and what I needed to do next. After thirty-two minutes, I arrived in the parking lot of the university. I scanned the top edge of the building and saw that cameras were everywhere, outside and inside. My eye and fingerprint scans would track the time I entered and exited. Ximena had told me she got an alert on her phone and tablet every time I entered her lab. She was logging my hours and time at the lab. Someone was always watching, and no doubt Mom was tracking me with my phone. I was alone, but technically not. I unzipped my jacket.

Before I had a chance to open the door to the lab, I heard glass drop inside. My hand froze on the door handle as I gripped it so hard my knuckles were white. It was too late for Ximena to be there; she said she'd left hours ago. I stood still and waited, then I heard some movement and glass crunching, like someone was stepping on the broken pieces. Ximena's years of hard work was at risk of being stolen, and I was not about to let any sample slip away from potentially helping Grey get better. We were too far along, and it was too valuable. I gripped my bag and felt for something, anything that could be a weapon. I found pliers and a screwdriver. I couldn't even remember why I had them, but regardless, I gripped the screwdriver in my right hand.

I opened the door as quietly as humanly possible. I sensed the perp was examining something as he was still in the room. The lab was dark, but my eyes had adjusted, and I saw dark outlines of the equipment; shadows in familiar places. I ducked down low, below the line of the tables to hide. Across the room, I saw the shadow of a person looking through a microscope, the faint light in front of them. They had a small frame and were hunched over, engrossed in what they saw.

I snuck up closer from the side and could smell a familiar scent—a soap smell that was dusty from sweat. It had to be Tyler. There was no way I'd allow him to get his hands on anything in this room. He pulled his phone out of his jacket pocket, its glow lighting up his face. It *was* Tyler. His button nose crinkled, and his long eyelashes blinked. His thick lips parted slightly as he inhaled, and a smile stretched across his face, pleased and surprised at what he saw. His fingers worked fast as he texted someone. Lifting himself off of the chair, he put his phone up to the slide and was about to take a picture.

It was then that I grabbed the chair out from under him, making him fall hard on his tailbone, his phone slamming to the floor. I reached down and picked it up, quickly slipping it into my pocket, then took the slide off the microscope, pocketing that too. Startled, he tried to get up, but he stayed sitting, before rolling over onto his knees, rubbing his ass. I turned on him quickly and held him by his shoulders.

Ty stared back at me as if he'd done nothing wrong. "Sienna! What are you doing here?" he asked, as if I hadn't been granted access.

"Me? I work here, you jackass. What are *you* doing

here?" I pinned him down on his back harder, with my knee digging into his shoulder. I waved the screwdriver over my head, as if I was ready to plunge it into his neck the second he moved. I was in a fury and knew I was capable of seriously harming this thief.

"Heh, heh, you don't have to go nuts on me. Your mentor said I could come in," he lied, his teeth clenched.

"Yeah, right. She wouldn't do that, you jerk," I said, kneeling on him harder.

"Whatever. Just get off me." He tried to get up but could barely move.

"No way. You broke in here and are stealing our research. And you sent someone to follow me, again."

"Look, I don't care what you think. It's me, Tyler. It's all fair game. Besides, you're not sending me all of your data." He smiled and winked at me, desperate to use his charm. It wasn't working. "You're one of us, and we're all sharing our intellectual property, right? Just roll with me and my plan, and it'll all work in our favor. Trust me. Look, I'll let you in on my project."

He couldn't be serious. Ty, Liv, and Kellen had their own motivations to get past me. He winced in pain from my knee then reached for my neck, but I was too fast and pulled back. Clearly, he'd had enough.

"Now get off of me!" he yelled and tried pushing me off. I was taller, but he was stronger than I thought. I brought the screwdriver to his throat, grazing his skin that was beaded with sweat. He freaked out and I shook him, trying to hold him steady; but he mustered enough strength and pushed me so hard the screwdriver fell out of my hand and into the air across the room, hitting a computer screen. As I fell back, he looked for his phone, but with nothing in sight, he started running, grabbing random stuff off of the lab counters. I hit my head hard against the floor, which stunned me momentarily. As I got up, I saw him running away from me.

"It's not too late. We need you!" he yelled, jumping out the window into the night.

Ty didn't have a clue about me. I rubbed the back of my head and looked around the lab. It was a mess, with stuff on the floor and a computer shattered. I surveyed the damage. My hand was bleeding, and I was sure I had at least a few bruises, the blood pooling under my skin. I had to find an ice pack. I searched for a fridge. Most labs had one for samples that needed to stay cool, and sure enough, I found a small ice pack in the freezer. I held it to the back of my head, where I felt a small bump forming. The cold was soothing. I rinsed my hand under the sink and dabbed the top with a tissue, where it was trickling blood.

I had no idea how long he was in there before I had found him and what he got his hands on. He worked in the dark, probably hoping the cameras wouldn't catch a clear view of his face or body and what he stole. I hoped at most he had only viewed a slide or two; I had one in my bag, which might be of use later. Still, Ximena would freak out. I limped over to the smaller fridge where we stored some of our most recent vials of our EBEX fighting meds. My hip was sore, but I let out a big sigh of relief when I saw them. From my assessment, Tyler didn't know much—maybe only some superficial info—and I'd keep it that way.

Time to get to work. I took the tray of vials out, pipetted a few drops from each and prepared them on slides. Then I looked at them under the microscope— these massive high-powered scopes were sick with their

LED lights and state of the art optics. Damn, they were awesome.

Gloves on, I took some tiny samples of EBEX infection from a locked cabinet and pipetted that onto the slide with the antibiotic. Within seconds, the medicine attacked the infection. The attack was slow at first, then the medicine was waging a full-on hyper war! But after a few minutes, it stopped as soon as it started. I repeated this same process at least five more times. All of the reactions were a little different. I'd need to tweak them based on what I saw. I boxed a few of the slides and with my back to the camera, slipped them into my bag under the table. I needed to get this to Greyson.

I texted Ximena and told her plain and simple there had been a breach in the lab. That was all. It was like three in the morning, so I'd leave it at that. I'd wait a few hours and call her with the details. I was fine, but we needed to be smart about our next steps.

I turned the lights out, and as I walked to the door, I swooped a few syringes into my bag, right off of the counter. I had almost forgotten that I still had Tyler's phone. It vibrated in my bag. I pulled it out. There was no text message. I bypassed the security code easily but could only get to a few of his settings. I disabled the tracker, which Avery had shown me how to do, then decided to hold onto it for now. I'd get rid of it later, once I had a chance to hack into it.

Once I left the lab, my exhaustion and hunger finally hit me. When I exited the building, it was still crazy foggy. I needed rescuing, like now.

Avery answered my call, sounding groggy. She agreed to secure her phone and take back streets to get to the lab. If she thought she was being followed, she would have to ditch and would let me know, somehow. I imagined myself waiting for hours, then finally running home, but I totally didn't want her being followed by drones. That wouldn't be cool. She agreed to meet me outside the lab as soon as she could.

23

Avery didn't ask any questions. That was one of the things I loved about her. She knew when to talk and when it was best to just be patient and wait me out. I wanted to tell her. I needed to tell her some, if not all, of what was happening. I was still shaken up by Tyler's intrusion, and my head was sore and my thoughts spinning.

She took twice as long as it should to get to me, and for ten minutes I thought she had to ditch me. But I knew she would be careful about her route. When she arrived, I was beyond tired, my eyes red, and my feet, hands, and head sore. My hunger had passed. When she pulled up in her little car, I noticed her shoulders tensed when she saw how I looked.

"Ah, Avery, thank you so much. I thought for a moment that you had to ditch." I slid into the passenger seat.

"Sorry, it took a while to secure my phone and figure out the back streets here."

"You weren't followed, right?" I looked behind us and then checked above us.

"I don't think so. You okay?" Avery turned to look me in the eyes and took a deep breath. Her exhalation appeared faintly in front of us, ghostly looking in the dark. Her breath smelled of mint, as if she'd taken a few minutes to brush her teeth in the wee hours of the night.

"I think so. I mean, yeah. I'm just a little on edge right now. A lot is going on."

"It's unusual you'd be at the lab this late and then call me to pick you up. Where's your car?" Avery was not being patient with me.

"It's at the hospital."

"Okay, do you want to get it now? I promise not to ask another question, but you gotta fill me in a little. You woke me up in the middle of the night and I want to help you. I'm here for you."

"You're the best, Aves. I'm sorry. It's been a crazy night and I don't know where to begin. Let's get my car later. It's better I don't have it now anyway."

"Okay. Fine. But what about your hand?"

"Avery! I need to catch my breath." I stared ahead. "Let's go to your house. I'll fill you in later, I promise. I need your help, really I do."

We drove back to her house just before dawn. While driving, I texted Grey's mom to let her know he was at Avery's house and I was taking care of him. He was safer hidden at Avery's. She texted back that she wanted to get him, but I insisted he was safer with me. I was the only one that could help him.

I'd been awake almost 24 hours. I followed Avery down to her basement. Greyson was still sleeping soundly but stirred when he heard us come in. His bedhead was crazy cute.

I hated to wake him but had no choice, really. It was crucial to move him before daylight. He'd be slow with his hurt ankle and knee and still fighting an infection. He wasn't nearly out of the woods yet.

It took us awhile to get Grey over to our greenhouse. He was weaker than I'd expected. Once he was in and settled in a hidden, safe area in a makeshift bed, I told Avery to leave, to stay safe and healthy. Neither of us could get what Grey had—I needed her. I gathered up any of our somewhat decent and viable vegetables and fruits. I took them into the house and cut them into small bite sized pieces, put them in a bag, grabbed a few slices a of bread, jam, and honey—our golden prize—and warmed up some tea.

He took small, deliberate bites, slowly chewing and swallowing. I wanted to rush him but knew better. Patience wasn't my thing, so I sat tight as I watched him eat impossibly slow. I couldn't sit still in my seat and shifted every ten seconds. Whatever he could digest and keep down would only help him in the long run, I kept telling myself, pretty much every ten seconds.

Finally, after he had eaten some food and supplements, I thought about giving him his first dose.

"Have you told my parents where I am?"

"I texted your mom to let her know you were with me and that I was going to take care of you."

"What'd she say?"

"She wanted to come and get you, but I told her you would be okay and that it was for the best. And that I'd drop you off in a couple of days. She wasn't happy, but I told her I had something special for you, to help you. I was able to convince her, and she eventually agreed."

"I'm sure she wasn't happy, but she wants what's best for me, too."

"Maybe we can set up a secure call to her after you eat."

He nodded. "That'd be perfect."

While he was eating, I couldn't stop thinking about Willow. She had to pull through, dig deep, and give it all she had. She'd struggled before and recovered, she could do it again. I took out my phone from my bag and scanned photos of her. She and I, her and Mom on the beach, her grinning. I stared at her round, pale face, her thick, auburn hair, and a strange, sinking feeling washed over me. I clicked off my photos. It was time.

I looked over Grey's leg and noticed that the spot on his lower leg was healing, but I worried about his ankle developing EBEX. A fresh open wound was a feeding ground for bacteria. I saw a small pustule near his ankle, but at least the swelling in his arm was down. He couldn't wait another minute.

I took the syringe and prepared to give Grey his first shot of our new antibiotic combination. He'd be the first. He had nothing to lose. It was me they were after and the sooner I got our treatment to Greyson, the better chance he had of surviving. I didn't care if Ty and his friends came after me. If the medicine worked, Grey would be getting better and stronger by the hour.

I got him comfortable and told him the shot would hurt like a long bee sting. He'd been stung before. It was worth a few minutes of pain compared to the pain he'd already endured. Luckily, I'd given Willow some injections in the past. Mom had shown me how to do it before she went out of town for work once.

"Just do it. Stop talking and do it already!" His voice cracked as he firmly insisted. I got that he was moody because he felt so sick. I'd felt that low before.

I raised the syringe and paused. *Please, make this work. Heal Greyson*, I prayed. The needle pierced his pale skin and he didn't even wince. It wasn't one of those fast flu shot injections either; this one was long and slow to go in. He took three deep breaths, and by the time he let it the last one out, the full amount of the antibiotic was in his body. It was done. I pressed a bandage over the site and held my hand over it for a few seconds. This had to work. Grey had to get better.

"Now we wait," I said and leaned back against the wall.

24

My body twitched, waking me from a deep, dream-filled sleep. I'd dreamed about climbing a mountain in the freezing cold. I was shivering down to my core and was thirsty. So thirsty I reached for some snow to eat, but it was so cold it stung my mouth. I held it there, but I couldn't swallow. I desperately wanted to swallow, feeling it melt down my throat. The wind whipped around me and I was alone. I couldn't remember why I was there, but I looked down and my foot slipped. I began to fall and fall, then my body jerked, and I woke up. I was now awake, scared, alone, and still thirsty.

I was back with Grey. My right side leaned against him; he was still asleep. My left side was cool. I moved to pull the blanket up and over my shoulder. Grey's face was relaxed and peaceful and I noticed the color had returned to his face. I felt a flutter in my stomach. I couldn't get ahead of myself.

The full effects would take some time, which we didn't have enough of. I took some deep breaths. I was probably getting a little too excited. I looked and thought of other positive signs—the fact that the sun had finally peeked out of the clouds after being hidden for days was good. I believed in these good signs. I believed. I closed my eyes.

In my pocket, my phone vibrated. I pulled it out, and a bunch of message notifications appeared on my lock screen. Crap. Crap. Crap. Dad then Mom, then Dad, then Mom, and Ximena, a million times. My hand and fingers shook as I unlocked my phone with my fingerprint and fumbled to tap on Dad's name to call him.

"Finally, where are you?" His voice trailed off.

"It's Willow," I said without answering his question. "She's gone. I can tell in your voice," I whispered, my throat locking up.

"We tried everything. She didn't respond to anything." He could barely speak.

"Oh, Willow." My head dropped back and a primitive cry from deep, down inside, bellowed from my throat and erupted from my mouth. A piece of me had been ripped from my core. Died, dead, withered, ripped away again over and over and over. Gone forever, my sweet sister. Gone to the heavens before I could say goodbye.

My phone fell to the floor and hit with a thud. Grey moved and opened his eyes. He saw my anguish, leaned into me, and gently hugged me. I had no words for this gift he was giving me. He felt the hurt, but not like me. His hurt was for me. Nothing like the pain I felt. Suddenly, I didn't care about anything else, or who heard me. His affection made me wail even louder.

It took a while, an hour or two, but I pulled myself together. Mom and Dad said they'd take care of details at the hospital and see me at home. I hated the idea of leaving Grey, but he needed to rest and let the medicine take over. It was still sinking in that Willow was really gone. In my heart she was here, close by, recovering at the hospital just a few miles away. Her voice clear, her breath warm and fresh on my cheek. But my mind knew differently. I knew that I'd never smell or feel her breath again. It really was crazy to think she was gone. A part of me didn't want to believe it to be true or real.

As I got up and moved my sluggish, chilled body. I felt a void and yearned for my parents. Suddenly, I craved hearing their voices and looking into their eyes. A dark moment of death had gripped me, and I felt compelled beyond my control to be with them.

I was careful leaving the greenhouse, almost sneaking out. It was very possible that drones could be hanging around outside our door. I looked up and scanned the sky with my dry, red eyes. Thankfully, it was quiet, and none were visible.

I snuck back to the house to clean up. I smelled terrible and my hair was in knots. I could hardly stand myself. Shivering, I ran a shower and thought about all the germs at the hospital, which happened to be the one place that was a breeding ground for serious harmful bacteria. My skin itched, as if it was crawling with microscopic bugs. I cranked the heat up in order to "burn" them off. Finally, after what felt like an hour but was more like fifteen minutes, I forced myself to turn the water off. I was lost in another world in my shower, the water cascading over me.

I emerged from a daze when Ty's phone rang. I knew it was his by the unfamiliar ringtone; a quirky rap-rocker song. It was laying on my bed and didn't stop ringing. Finally, I got to it and saw that it was Kellen. I had disabled the passcode, so I was able to answer.

"Hello," I said quickly, in a voice deeper than my own.
"Who is this?"
"Who's this calling?" I retorted.
"Kellen. Is this Sienna?"
"Surprised? Ty dropped it by accident. I'm sure you can figure it out," I said.

"I want to talk to you anyway. You need to cooperate," he said bluntly.

"Ya think? Hmmm, why should I? So we can let people die?" I raised my voice.

"You just don't get it, do you? We're gonna take over, whether you like it or not. It's just the way it is," Kellen said matter-of-factly, but with a softer tone than before. It sounded like he was holding back information. He was totally serious and believed the nonsense he was spouting. "I want you on board with us, Sienna. You really are amazing, and I'd like you on our side. Please consider."

"Look, this is all wrong. What our parents did to make us... I mean—it's all wrong and unethical. We can't just kill people because they're weak. It's not our place," I insisted. I hoped he had a glimmer of compassion buried in his cold body.

"You know, Ty told us at our last meeting, the one you missed, that we weren't the only generation of designer kids. Just one of many groups. There are thousands, probably hundreds of thousands and growing, who are younger than us."

My stomach felt like it dropped to my feet. My breath was shallow, so I took two deep breaths. I should've known. I had a gut feeling there were more.

"Kellen, you know this is really wrong."

"It's not up to us to decide," he squeaked out.

"I don't buy it. I don't think you really think this."

"Yeah, well, it doesn't matter what you think. This is beyond us."

"Well, I care. What, is Stevenson responsible for all of these genetically engineered projects, even the ones that go wrong? It must be her spearheading this whole thing. I mean she's freaking unbelievable," I said, shaking my head. I got up and started pacing. She'd roped my parents into having another genetically engineered child.

"It's a whole team."

"What else do you know?" I asked, suddenly not so eager to hang up.

He lowered his voice. "Not all of them are perfect. Some are messed up. Hell, our siblings could be from one of those generations. You know Ty's situation, Oceana's, and yours."

"Hmm. You think or you know for sure?" I asked, realizing Stevenson's project was much more complex and troublesome than I thought.

"Yeah. I overheard my mentor talking to your mentor, Ximena, I think. They're figuring out what to do next."

I sat silent on my end, my head and stomach flipping out. I should've known they were keeping critical information from us. Could Willow have been engineered, too? What about Maya, Ty's sister? How could he not think about her?

Kellen went on. "You know they share information about our projects all the time. All the mentors know what we're doing. They have no rules for themselves. It's the big pharma companies that have us by the balls." He said what I'd felt deep down in my gut all along.

"We're freakin' puppets." I sat down on the edge of my bed, towel still wrapped around me and my wet hair dripping onto my shoulder. *Freakin' puppets.*

"Basically, yeah," he agreed.

I chuckled at first, but it burst out to a full-blown belly laugh. I went from wailing to laughing.

"What's so funny?"

"Here we are, the smartest kids, and we didn't realize that from the beginning of this sham contest? I mean, technically, we're smarter than our natural born mentors who are what, like thirty years older than us?" I laughed again. I was not about to let these ego-driven scientists destroy anyone or anything. They had done enough damage. And my parents were along for the ride. "You must see this, too, Kellen."

"Yeah, I guess you're right about that. Us being smarter than them. Like we've said, we want to do this without our mentors. Screw them. Tyler's got a plan."

"What, to steal my stuff? Steal everyone's research? You think they haven't safeguarded and locked down all of this stuff? He's random and reckless, and he'll just fuel the fire."

"You don't know the details."

"I'll find out." I'd dig until my nails were raw. I would not lose anyone else. I paused. "The only way I'd be on board with you guys is if we take all of our discoveries and allow everyone to benefit."

Kellen was relentless. "Think about it. Would you rather have some of us get access to medications and inventions that will stop the world from deteriorating and our own human destruction, or none of us? 'Cause that will happen if you put a stop to our research and this contest explodes. Nothing will get accomplished."

"No, it won't. The designer kids can't have it all."

"Well, we're on track to have it all. You will, too. Why not, Sienna? Just think what the two of us can do. We are an amazing team. I see the real you, Sienna, and we can be unstoppable. I've always known we were special. You know we've got the resources and the intelligence to do this. You're one of our most valuable assets. It's not too late. Our success will lead to domination and all the social status anyone could imagine." Kellen believed this and wasn't backing down. "It's just a matter of time. We need you on board with us. Just think of the consequences if you don't—we have the potential to save millions of people and your family."

My family was already destroyed. We wouldn't be able to save everyone. With this foreign type of EBEX spreading quickly and out of control, something had to be done soon. Too many people would suffer and die—some had already, and I had the key to help. I just needed some more time. And now Kellen saw us as a couple. A team. But if I fell into his spell, I'd be siding with the others, too. Siding with Ty, Kellen, Liv would just get messy. Although maybe there was a way to manipulate them, forcing them to change their minds. Or maybe they were in too deep. My head was spinning, and I suddenly felt dizzy. I caught myself from falling off the side of the bed.

"We both know what's the right thing to do," I said boldly.

Kellen sighed. "It's just a matter of time. You've got to know that."

Just a matter of time. Kellen had no idea who he was dealing with.

25

I threw Ty's phone down on the bed. The gravity of Kellen's words settled in. Errors, mistakes, and wrong gene editing triggered unwanted changes. DNA manipulation didn't work perfectly all of the time. Of course, Ty was angered by what happened to Maya, and now he was planning to steal everyone's projects and take over. For all I knew, he probably knew what was coming down the pike and was a step ahead of our mentors. Maybe he had more research than I imagined, and all the designer kids were actually sending him their research. I stared at his phone. He must have some contact information in there. His phone was his lifeline.

I got dressed and took his phone down to my work room. I had set up my own mini-lab workstation in the basement, just in case Ximena wasn't cool with sharing her part of the research with me. I had already picked Tyler's tracking system apart on his phone, so he couldn't find it or me. Next was uploading any and all of his encrypted information onto my tablet so I could depict it.

I put on my microscopic glasses and started working, but my mind soon wandered to Willow. I tugged it back to the task at hand. If I stayed focused, I'd be done quickly, I kept telling myself.

Then I heard the subtle motor of the garage door, though it was muffled through the walls of the basement.

I knew the sound and my ears were sensitive. I was an engineered child, after all. I worked fast and was done and upstairs by the time Mom and Dad had unloaded the car and walked into the kitchen.

I stood still in front of them, numb. Mom's eyes were shallow and distant. Dad's body softened when he saw me and walked toward me to give me a hug. It was as if he was sad for me, too, for losing my sister, that he felt my hollowness. Mom stared out the window. Dad and I sobbed together for what seemed like an eternity. The house was still and quiet without Willow there, although we still felt her presence.

A knock on the door shook me back. Silence. Then another light tap. Mom walked like a zombie to the front door to greet friends who had brought some food. They chatted and cried. Dad went to say hello, looking worse than I'd ever seen him. Dark circles lined his eyes and his greasy hair was slicked back. He'd been to hell and back. Every movement was like slow motion.

The next hours and days were dreadful, but we all tried to celebrate Willow's short life and how she would want to be remembered: happy despite her situation and thankful for all of us.

In Willow's room, I clung to her favorite things—her stuffed puppy, her patchwork blanket, and her pillow, the most sacred of things. Her sweet smell still lingered on the soft edges. I was almost afraid if I held it too long, my smell would overcome hers and her scent would be lost forever. But I also realized, sitting at the edge of her bed, that these earthly things were just that—things. Willow was so much more than what she possessed. Despite these things, in the end, she was a kind, loving, caring, funny, soulful, opinionated, young girl. I squeezed her pillow as hard as I could and soaked up her smell for the next thirty minutes.

~~~~~~

I ignored my phone and tablet for a few days. It was terrible and impossible to think I could do this, but numbness took hold of my mind and body. Nothing else really mattered. At the same time, Ximena was frantically trying to get in touch with me. She was hardwired. She was almost robotic in her moves and in her lack of empathy. Was it so hard for her to leave me alone for two days to let me grieve! Totally impossible. She insisted that I come to the lab to discuss something.

Oh, yeah, the breach. I'd left her with that, literally threw it in her lap. Not really fair of me to do, I guess. We had a few more hours of people visiting, so I snuck out to meet her at the lab. It'd been a long few days, and I was surprised to find I looked forward to doing some work. I'd be doing something other than grieving.

~~~~~~

I accessed the lab as usual, with my eye and fingerprint. Ximena's petite body was bent over one of the large microscopes.

I startled her and she nearly fell off her chair. "Sienna! You're so quiet!"

"Sorry. Habit."

"I'm engrossed in this slide. Sienna—this is good, very good, but I hesitate to tell you much more. You said there was a breach and then you don't tell me details? I see a computer monitor is shattered. Any serious breach of security you must tell me right away," she said, burrowing her eyebrows deeper than I'd imagined possible, like one of those pug brows.

"I was able to handle it. Nothing was taken."

"And how do you know that for certain?"

"I chased the intruder away and he had nothing in his hands. Everything is locked up anyway."

"These crazy, greedy people have their ways. You should've reported this to me immediately," she said, her voice deep. "Higher ups need to know what's at risk."

"That day was unbelievable." The traumatic events buzzed through my brain. "I'm sure you heard about the shooter situation at the hospital. My sister was involved. It was tragic. Very tragic." I left out details about Grey. The less she knew about him the better.

"I heard bits and pieces. I'm sorry about your sister, truly sorry." She paused awkwardly, then stuttered and went on, "Did they catch the sniper?"

"The FBI has some leads I guess, but there's no one in custody."

"That's a real shame. They'll find him, they always do. Dr. Stevenson is calling me in for a meeting today. She wants answers. She doesn't tolerate behavior like this, and certainly someone stealing our research puts our entire project in jeopardy."

"Stevenson has her own issues," I mumbled.

"Excuse me?"

I gave Ximena my version of what had happened that night of the breach, telling her about Ty. It was Ty they should be watching closely instead of pointing fingers at anyone. Ty was the perfect diversion for me. In fact, with Grey now involved with the "trial," it was literally mine. I could tell she wasn't completely satisfied with my story.

I'd glossed over a few details, so what? I seriously believed Ty had gotten his hands on nothing of importance. I was careful to lock and encrypt my findings so no hack could access it using traditional methods. Nonetheless, Ty must be stopped. I suggested Ximena order a drone or two to follow him. Two was best. We'd see how he felt about being followed and watched.

Secretly, I knew Ty had his hands on many more projects than ours and that Ximena was keeping information from me, too. I could trust no one. I'd be lucky if Ximena and Stevenson kept me on the project a few more weeks. I rubbed my hands together, thinking of ways to download as much data as possible before going completely on my own.

Ximena frowned. She said she'd discuss the drones with Stevenson later. I asked her if she needed me to do anything right now. I had some samples I had prepared that I wanted to analyze. Ximena told me to finish up and then she wanted me out of the lab. She took off her glasses, flipped her hair, and flat-out told me that she needed some time to think and work. I felt her cold shoulder and couldn't stay in the same room with her a minute longer. I snuck some of my samples into my bag, left the lab, and logged out.

~~~~~~~~~

It was dark now and I'd taken Dad's car, which was fully powered up, unlike mine. I also figured a drone might not recognize the make and model, so I'd slip under the radar. I took the back roads home, but it didn't take long until I spotted a drone low over my back. Jerk. Ty or Liv or whoever must have locked into a special satellite and just couldn't leave me the hell alone. I gave it the finger in my rearview and made a quick U-turn, then stepped on the gas. It darted straight and sped through a yellow stoplight turning red. Ha! That'd teach Ty to lock a drone on me. I could shake 'em.

I sped over to our greenhouse to check on Grey. He had to be gaining energy and hopefully was feeling better by now. He needed his ankle and knee to heal and keep the EBEX bacteria out of those vulnerable areas. The timing was perfect to give him an injection of my new antibiotic. I imagined him peacefully sleeping for days before he was better and could be at home with his family. I parked Dad's car in the woods near the greenhouse and slipped inside.

My stomach lurched when I saw him hidden underneath a pile of blankets, his head buried in a soft pillow. "Hey, Grey."

He stirred. His face was pinkish now, his lips less chapped, and gradually getting rosy. His hair was matted down with a few stray curls coming to life. I put my hand on his arm and gently squeezed. He opened his eyes and squeaked out a sliver of a smile.

"You hungry?" I asked, maybe a bit too loudly in my excitement. He paused, as if his body was questioning if he was in fact hungry. He nodded. I patted his head and went in search of a few fruits and vegetables he might be able to tolerate. Herbs were always good to munch on and some would help settle his stomach. I collected some parsley, a baby zucchini, a couple of carrots, and a measly apple.

"Here, start with these and I'll get you some tea, berries, bread and some supplements from the house. Take small bites. Whatever you can get down will help."

He sat up as best as he could and took my offering.

"Move your leg a bit, too. You don't want to get a blood clot from sitting or lying still too long." His eyes widened, and I kneeled down to rub his calf. He leaned back and I couldn't tell if I was hurting him or it felt good.

I kept massaging as he reached for a carrot. I pulled up his pant leg to peek at his skin. His blister was looking better. The antibiotic was working! I looked up at him, hope in my eyes.

"I'm kickin' ass, right?" he asked.

"You're kicking some ass right now. Keep it up, will you?"

"I plan to, babe." He smiled deep enough that his dimple appeared. Oh, his dimple was back—truly gorgeous.

"Hey, babe, you can't call me that."

"I just did. 'Cuz you are."

"Eat! I'm going to get you stuff from the house." I got up. It was so good to have a bit of him back. After he ate and drank some more, I gave him another dose of antibiotic. He took it well; in fact, he was eager to get it since he was feeling better. He tolerated the slow injection I prepared for him. It'd be like this for five to ten days depending on how his body responded.

"Rest some more, Grey, and we can move you back home today. Also, I'm going to need you to help me soon," I hinted as I put away the syringe in my bag.

"I'm ready to get home. Help out with what?"

"I'll explain later. It's serious, so hang in there and be patient with me." I stood, my legs wobbly and tired. I wanted to tell him more, but I was suddenly exhausted.

"Look who's talking about being patient!"

"I know, I know, I'm terrible at that. I'll check on you in the morning. Early."

"Can you stay here?" His eyes told me he was lonely.

"I wish. Maybe after I do a few things. I'll try to come back and bring some more clean blankets." I hesitated, my knees weak.

"Yes, blankets are good." Grey rested his head again on

the pillow and closed his eyes. He reminded me of how it felt to be crazy sick to your stomach and finally feeling better after puking. You could then sleep for hours. I pulled the blanket up just under his neck and leaned over his ear.

"I'll be back," I whispered, and his dimple showed again.

26

I tried to sleep, but I tossed and turned instead. I got a few hours in and then, with a stiff neck, tiptoed down to my work room. I skipped the two creaky steps and caught myself from falling down the stairs. Flipping on a dim light, I pulled out the sample antibiotics in the banker's box-size fridge and prepared to make more. It was working for Grey.

Once those were prepped, I pulled out my tablet and squinted at the light, trying to re-focus. I clicked on the encrypted file I had decoded and uploaded from Ty's phone. He had layers of security and firewalls I had to work around, but with updated malware that I'd found on Dad's work computer, and the use of a proxy site Avery explained how to use, I accessed Ty's data. I rubbed my neck—my eyes were dry and tired, but my mind couldn't slow down. I sifted through his contacts, calendar, voicemail, email, websites he visited, pretty much everything on his phone. There was a lot.

I noticed that he used code names for project mentors. There were RIX, ZANA, JIPS, and POBW, all acronyms I guessed. These names and others were listed on his calendar. I looked at this week—something was on his calendar every day. Yesterday was 9 a.m., RIX @ the museum. Tomorrow night he had a dinner meeting with the EPELs @ Jayme's in Wicker Park.

I searched to find out what EPEL stood for. After a few

minutes, it popped up in one of his mail messages: Eden Project Elite Leaders. This must have been the close-knit group he formed after his announcement at the Morton's second party. I looked up Jayme's Restaurant in Wicker Park. It was a small, inconspicuous bistro and not too far from the train station. I could get over there some-time beforehand and place recording devices where they planned to meet, so I could "sit" in on their meeting. I had a few computer filter chips, so I could click into the restaurant's security system, if they had one. I'd say 98 percent of public places had security cameras to deter terrorism, fraud, and identify theft from happening. I'd watch their meeting from wherever I could that night.

I set everything aside, locked my work room door, threw on a light jacket, then took an extra blanket off our sofa and headed over to the greenhouse. The Halloways agreed he'd be better off one more day there. They had visited and saw he was improving. With my plan in place, I could rest for a few hours, right next to Grey.

~~~~~~

The sun was just about to rise when my eyes popped open. I was so used to waking early that, go figure, being exhausted didn't change my body clock. Grey was breathing deeply, almost snoring. I wondered if he even knew I had slept right next to him all night. I got up slowly, trying not to disturb him. His body was fighting inside, and every minute of rest helped. I'd give him an in-jection after he'd eaten something.

I poked around the greenhouse and found a few pieces of lame fruit: a pear and an avocado. I was ravenous and ate them as I searched for more, hoping something big and juicy was hiding in the thick, green leaves. I felt like an animal hunting just to stay alive, my mouth watering, eyes wide, stomach growling. I was embarrassed to return to Grey with anything but a plump piece of fruit.

I danced in and out of rows of seedlings, vines, and flowers, my thoughts drifting to Willow and how we'd play hide and seek in the greenhouse when we were little. It was so quiet in there, you could practically hear the flowers open up, petal by petal, so we'd have to be extra quiet to hide from one another. Then she'd bump something or one of us would sneeze or cough and we'd pretend we didn't hear one another just to keep our game going longer.

I rounded the corner and stopped when I saw a bright red flower on one of the plants. It was like it was speaking to me, as if Willow had been hiding in here all along and not really gone. I swear I saw one of its petals flop gently to the side, like it was telling me to come over and smell, touch, and look. A cool breeze whispered against my cheek.

I blinked and touched the soft petal. It was still crazy to me that my little sister was gone, really gone, like forever. Every minute of the day I ached for her and her sweet voice. I thought I heard her voice now, in the greenhouse. A moth flew in front of me and landed on my hand. It was soft and brown, so peaceful. Its wings fluttered and then went still. I took it and the flower as a sign of Willow being there with me. I sensed things would be okay, and for that moment I completely relaxed. The moth flew to my elbow and shoulder, then landed softly on my nose before flying off. I stared after it, hoping it would return.

Mom and Dad were in a funk. We would lay Willow to rest after her body was completely examined and investigators determined the actual cause of death. They needed to confirm she didn't have the EBEX virus. If she did, they needed to see who else she had come in contact with and who might be infected. The nightmare was continuing to spiral out of their control.

All of Mom and Dad's hope was now on their unborn baby, the perfect son they dreamed of, one of the modern saviors of the world. But what I definitely noticed was that they were more of a couple again. Losing Willow so suddenly and tragically drew them closer together, and Dad was back at home all the time. I liked having him around, but not just for this reason. I wondered if over time he'd bond with this baby like he had with me.

Nevertheless, they were so preoccupied that they had no clue what was going on with the Eden Project kids. These kids their friends had created to be brilliant, were in fact, so brilliant, they were outsmarting their incredibly talented and intelligent scientist-makers. I believed my parents, scientists themselves, would side with Stevenson's group, anyway. It wouldn't be the first time they'd stopped me, thinking they knew what was best. But they didn't know what was best. They never had known. I was forced to do what I had to do, regardless of what my parents thought.

~~~~~~

It was Saturday late morning, and Grey was now at home. I'd been to check in on him. He was slowly gaining strength and his blister looked as if it was healing. I gathered my bag and headed over to the train station.

It took me a thirty-minute train ride to get into the city and find Jayme's Restaurant. It was cozy, with twenty tables of four set up and a few for two by the windows. The walls were decorated with oil paintings that had an Italian flair from local artists. They were open for lunch, so I sat down at a table for four and ordered a chicken and avocado sandwich.

My stomach churned from both hunger and nerves. I acted like I was waiting for a friend, which I was, really. On my way into Chicago, I called and left Avery a message to meet me there. I had no idea if she'd show, but I pretended. I also texted Blue. I missed her and her laugh and really wanted to catch up. Ten minutes later, Avery called me back and told me she was on her way and that she'd picked up Blue. They would be there in about half an hour.

I felt a twinge of guilt being happy for a moment, excited for my own selfish reasons, but knowing they were meeting me took the edge off. I probably shouldn't have involved either of them in all of this craziness. Avery was patiently waiting for me to tell her the whole story, like a bad itch on her back that she just couldn't reach.

"Hey, girls!" I said, pleased to see them both when they arrived.

"Sienna, we are so sorry to hear about Willow," Blue said, reaching out to give me a hug. Her jean jacket buttons and full chest pressed against mine.

"Thanks." I held her as tears formed in the corners of my eyes, then stretched my arm out for Avery, and the three of us stood close together and hugged tightly. "It's unbelievable."

I shook my head, choking back a flood of more tears before we sat down. "The reality is just starting to sink in. It's tough on all of us." I took a sip of water and dug out a tissue from my bag.

They were silent for a painful minute, then Blue crossed her legs under the table and said, "I've missed you. Avery said she was there when all this happened, and she drove you to and from the hospital."

I locked eyes with Avery and could tell she hadn't given Blue all the sordid details. Avery smiled, lips together.

"Yeah, it's been literally crazy. I've been working on a science project and it's gotten kind of messy, to tell you the truth." I took a sip of water and nibbled on my nail.

"Well, I'm glad you called us to meet," said Avery. "It's probably good that you stay busy. And we're here for you."

"Yeah, me too, I'm glad you called. We've been worried about you," said Blue, looking at the menu.

"It's so cool you guys came. I need some girl time. I wish Jazz could've come, too. I've been in shock, and this project is a good distraction, but I've been a mess. We've got to eat, so order a sandwich," I said.

Avery looked up from her menu. "Jazz has gotten worse in the last couple of days."

"Oh no, really?" I asked, leaning in toward Avery.

"Yeah, she hasn't been at school. Yesterday she texted that she was going to see her doctor," said Blue.

"I hope it's not EBEX. I'll check in on her later. If either of you hear from her would you let me know?" I sat back in my chair, remembering the red spot on her neck.

It was getting late. I'd been there for almost 45 minutes and my dish had arrived, but I hadn't gotten around to placing the devices. I nibbled on my sandwich and then looked around, scouting out the restaurant.

"Are you in the city for anything special?" asked Blue, always curious.

"Yeah. I can't get into it right now, though. I'll tell you more later." Just then the waiter came over to take their order and handed me another drink.

When the waiter left, I pushed back my chair. "Hey

guys, I'm going to run to the bathroom. I've already had a few lemonades. I'll be right back." I grabbed my bag and looked around behind the bar and the computer where the waiters rang up the bills.

Behind the counter was the computer system, easily accessible but highly visible. I asked the hostess which room the EPEL meeting was in tonight, saying I'd be back to attend it later. She pointed out the small dining room and I thanked her and headed to the bathroom.

In the stall, I texted Avery that when I came out, I needed her to call the hostess over and ask her a question. Something that would keep her occupied for a few minutes. She texted back, OK.

After doing my thing and getting out the devices, I slipped them into my jacket pockets, which were large and deep. I'd picked this jacket precisely because it was oversized. I walked to the dining room and canvassed the area, sliding three tiny recording devices under the tables, unsure of how many people would be there. It was quick and easy.

When I came out, I paused near the service checkout computer and locked eyes with Avery. She waved her hand for the hostess and waiter to come over, and I ducked down behind the counter. The security system was cheap and basic, clearly the little restaurant trying to save money. I opened up the front cabinet and slipped the chip into a slot, then linked up the system to my phone. The app searched, found the restaurant's system, and synced. Now I'd be able to see the EPEL group through their camera system and I could hear them through my own planted devices. I just needed them to show up.

Avery could be a lawyer if she wanted. She was a natural debater and negotiator for as long as I'd known her. She was diplomatic, too, so whatever she was arguing about with the hostess and waiter, she'd win. She always won arguments, no matter what. Even if you thought you might have won, you hadn't.

By the time I got back to the table, they had settled everything, and Avery got her way. Something wasn't right with her order, she said. They were comping her dessert.

I sat down. I took off my jacket and patted my lips with my napkin. I was nervous enough that I'd broken a little sweat. I guess thinking about Ty meeting with his ballsy leaders in that room in a few hours had gotten me worked up. They thought they had this all figured out, but they were wrong.

"Nothing for you to worry about. You have enough on your mind," Avery said, smiling. I'd hear her story later. In fact, I wanted to hear about her clever negotiation.

We ate our lunch in the quiet room. Spending time with my two friends was rejuvenating. I knew later that night I'd be on the edge of my seat again, biting my nails.

Avery drove us both home. After dropping Blue off, she turned her car off and looked me in the eye. "What was that all about?" she asked point-blank.

"It's a long story," I said looking out the window. My hand and fingers came to my mouth. I tried to stop myself, but it was too tempting. I didn't know where to start with the story, honestly.

"You're gonna have to start telling me what's going on. You're calling on me too much to keep me in the dark. I get it the first few times, but not now. Now you're in deep, I can tell."

"Yeah you're right." I thought about my approach. She

waited patiently. "What are you doing tonight?"

"Nothing."

"Can you come over? We can watch something together, and I can explain things then." It'd be easier for her to understand the situation when she saw these jerks in action.

~~~~~~

Avery and I settled into my work room at home. She was quiet while I pulled up the monitor and got things ready. As I accessed the devices I planted, I could hear them starting to gather.

Before Avery came over, I gave Grey another injection and took a small blood sample to check his white blood count level. I'd have to get back to the lab to test it. That's if Ximena hadn't changed my security access and computer login codes. Greyson was doing much better today, even joking around, making fun of my bulky jacket and saying I looked like a vagabond. Whatever, he felt better. I was glad to see him smiling, even if it was at my expense. His parents knew they needed to protect Grey and did their best to stay under the radar as much as possible.

Avery knew little about Grey's situation. Actually, when I told her he was getting better, she gave me that look—a stare, really. Her eyes bored deep into mine, searching for answers. I could tell she sensed I had something to do with his getting better. I nodded that I did, and it was all right here in front of us, in my work room.

There were about eight people I didn't know in the meeting room at Jayme's. Four guys and four girls. I recognized them from the pool party, and of course, Oceana, Liv, Kellen, and Tyler were there, too. The others seemed familiar, but I didn't know their names. I leaned forward in my chair as they gathered, making small talk before they took their seats.

"Okay, so this is an elite group meeting we are about to witness," I told Avery quietly.

"Oh," she leaned into look closer, "so they're at the restaurant we had lunch at today, right?"

"Yep. And I know that guy," I said, pointing out Ty on the screen. "He had us followed by drones that day Grey and I were at the train station."

"Oh, and that guy and girl." Avery pointed to Kellen and Liv. "That's Kellen. And that girl, and that other guy, Ty, came out to the lacrosse game, too."

"You got it." I nodded and put my finger up to my lips. Ty was starting the meeting. Avery leaned in to listen.

He cleared his throat. "Hey, guys. Thanks for coming tonight. This is a little out of the way, but we're meeting here for good reason. I appreciate you taking some time away from your projects to get caught up on the latest with our endeavors and our dealings with Onyx." Ty sucked in a deep breath. "It's been a long time coming, but we finally have intercepted communications between Onyx and our mentors. We have evidence they've been manipulating us, tracking our moves, and accessing every step of our research, like we suspected." He paused and then was interrupted by someone speaking up from the corner.

I couldn't see who it was but could tell by her voice it was Oceana. "How do you know they aren't listening to us right now?"

Another said, "Yeah, maybe it's someone in this room who's leaking out all this insider stuff."

They grumbled and Kellen got up, leaving the room. After a few minutes, my visual was cut. He must've pulled the security camera cables. Good thing I planted the recording devices. Not visible to the naked eye. We could still hear them talk. Avery looked at me, surprised, but then smiled.

Kellen spoke next. "I've taken care of it. None of what goes on in here is traceable. Before we go further, power off your phones and tablets, if you haven't already." It was quiet, except for some clicking. You'd think they would have done this already.

Ty continued. "We've thoroughly been tracking you guys as well and we don't have a mole in the room. If you decide to become a mole, you'll be dead like that." He snapped his fingers. "So, don't get any ideas. We have our ways of knowing more about you than you probably know about yourself."

He paused to let that sink in. "Anyway, back to business. With all of your help, we also have access to all of your research as well as that of the other designer kids. That's about fifty projects. It's taken some time, but they are on a secure database." He paused again, hesitant to reveal too much information. "Very, very secure," he emphasized.

He was a shark and he wanted them all to know not to mess with him. I believed he would stoop to any level to steal and get what he wanted: pure and ultimate power.

Hmmm. I raised my eyebrows. Avery did, too. We started thinking of where this database might be. I clicked on my computer to get to Ty's phone files and flipped through them. There had to be something in there related to the database he had just mentioned. Avery knew what I was thinking. We kept listening.

A guy asked, "So what do you plan to do with all the research data? No doubt Onyx will get it too, if they don't have it already, and take it into their own labs to accelerate and take over our projects."

"Where've you been these past months, kid?" Ty asked, his tone condescending.

"Working my ass off on my project... and listening to your stupid plan," he snapped back.

"You don't have to be here, ya know," Ty said, his voice shaking in an effort to stay cool.

Kellen jumped in. "We're a step ahead of Onyx. You see, they think they have all of our research, but they have something else entirely." He stopped and after a long pause said, "They have fake data." He couldn't not tell them.

Brilliant. I should've figured they wouldn't give up precious test results and hours of priceless research that would help save the world. Of course.

"Kellen, that's enough," said Ty, pissed that he'd revealed this bit of information.

I sat back in my chair. So, all the data Onyx and the mentors thought they had was fake. They'd be working on nothing of significance while the designers took hold and claimed the real results of our hard work. Good. I nibbled on my thumbnail while I thought. The better of the two evils had the real data, and it'd be more attainable to hack into Ty's database than figure out what Onyx was doing. They were global and more complex than Ty, Kellen, and Liv.

They argued over their next moves. Some wanted to expose the mentors and Onyx for who they really were— grand manipulators who wanted to take over the world, while others wanted to see them flop on their face and come up empty-handed, wasting their time.

Ty and Kellen told each leader what they needed from them, delegating scud work, basically. Downloading more data, and to be honest, it sounded like they were trying to keep them busy and preoccupied.

"So, you've been at it with Ty, Kellen, and Liv this whole time, wanting to stop them from stealing medical advancements so they don't keep it to themselves," Avery said, nodding.

"Yep, and they want people who aren't genetically engineered to die off. Darwinism as its most basic and inhumane level." I shook my head. "I won't let it happen. Ever."

They were about to wrap up the meeting and let the servers in when Ty said, "Oh, I can't believe I forgot to mention. If anyone communicates with Sienna Yardley, let me know right away. She's bad news. She's on to us and we must keep her out of our files. Anyone talk to her recently?"

"Sienna, the one we first saw at the pool party?" a girl asked.

"Yes," said Ty.

"Didn't her sister just die? She was at the hospital where the sniper went crazy, right? And where Anish's dad bit the dust," another commented.

There was a long pause. I guessed that Kellen was waiting for Ty to answer.

Finally, Kellen, his voice shaking, said, "Yeah. Tragic." I bet he shot Ty a look. I told Avery that Kellen had called me and tried to convince me to go with their group. Begged, really. I refused.

Then Kellen said, "Ty messed up, and she was weak, anyway."

"I'll respectfully ignore that comment," snapped Ty. "We intended on gathering data from the hospital. And then Sienna and her friend, who's got killer EBEX bacteria, got in the mix. Like I said, it's a mess that is better off eliminated—more than I'd like to go into right now..." He trailed off.

There was silence, then he took a deep breath. "As we've implied, taking over Onyx Pharmaceuticals is the ultimate goal—destroy the mentors associated with it and our projects for this contest and we're in. We will lead the medical and scientific industries to save the world. I'll need to some back-up to help me and Kellen get behind the scenes at Onyx. You know, get into their labs and computer systems. Then we'll take them down. Completely down. And then start the real damage." He seemed to stop, as if he was imagining total victory—or was thinking about what he was going to say next.

Avery was on the edge of her chair and almost slipped off but quickly caught herself. We heard the waiters and waitresses enter with food and drinks. There was a lot of clanging of plates and utensils and mumbled small talk again. I turned the volume down on my device and sat back, pulling my hair back into a messy bun.

"We'll stop them. We have to. We've got to get their database and destroy it and stop them from taking over Onyx and doing whatever damage he's talking about," I told Avery, my mouth cotton dry. She didn't know it yet, but she and Grey were part of my plan. The elite group had been plotting for weeks and were ready to pounce. I rubbed my wet hands on my pants. This was all happening so fast. I'd been so focused on helping Grey and getting him healthy, that Ty and Kellen had slipped further out of my hands.

"And how do you think you're going to find their database? It's got to be hidden."

"Or in plain sight, just where we wouldn't expect it," I

said, standing up and pacing, deep in thought. My thumbs were getting raw. "This is where I need your help, Avery."

"Of course! We could use drones to follow Ty, Kellen, Liv, and these EPELs. Or install cameras in their homes and cars." Avery squinted.

"I think drones are too obvious. We could install cameras, but that'll take too much time to buy so many and secretly set them up. I have some and Dad has some old ones, but not too many."

I shrugged and then had a quick thought. It was time I checked on Dad's revolver. He kept it hidden in a crawlspace in the basement. He bought one right after their identities were stolen. I saw him put it away one day, but he didn't know I knew where he'd hidden the key to the gun box. I'd practiced on the shooting range a few times with him soon after he got it. He wanted me to know how to handle a gun, just in case. There was always a "just in case" scenario with him. My parents had completely freaked out by their identity theft. And with this whole sniper thing, the virus spreading, and Willow dead, I wouldn't be surprised if Dad had his hands tightly around that gun or bought an even bigger one.

My phone rang. It was Ximena. Not now. I needed to think. But, instead, I reflexively picked up. "Hi, Ximena," I said politely.

"Sienna, glad I caught you. I just got out of my meeting with Stevenson. She's very rattled. She's very upset that someone broke into our lab." She paused, waiting for me to answer. I said nothing.

"I can't blame her. I feel the same," Ximena added. I was silent. What did she expect me to say?

"Is there anything you want to say, Sienna? Anything to add to the story?"

"Well, no. Only that I didn't break in. You're making me out to be the bad person in this. I did what anyone would do—chased him away."

"I agree, but like I said, you failed to report all the details. We still don't know if he got any sensitive data."

"To be honest, I'm pretty certain he didn't get anything. I think I walked in soon after he got there, and I checked out the lab after I chased him off. If you care to know, I scared the hell out of him." I really thought they were wasting their time.

I'd patted Ty down when I had him pinned down and pulled out a USB drive from his pocket, slipping in an empty one. One that I was going to use to download our data. Ty was going to do my work for me. I actually owed him one. He might have hacked into the lab's computer while he was there, but he also could have done that remotely.

"Regardless, Stevenson issued a warning. If anything happens again to compromise our data, she'll suspend you from our project. Stevenson is requiring that I keep closer tabs on the lab and review cameras every day and send her assistant our login records."

I sat back in my chair. I was pissed that I was taking the heat for Ximena's lab security issues. Stevenson and the mentors seemed to have no idea that they were being targeted, with a big bullseye on their backs. A human dartboard. She didn't know how much she needed me right now. She'd be groveling later.

We hung up. Avery was typing away on her tablet, listing ideas on where the data may be, including the school, field house, lacrosse/football/soccer fields, storage units, food storage units, and drone video tapes.

"I've got a small list," Avery said, "but I think we'll

have to hack into their computer system to find out where they're sending data or else follow them. Do they have computer techies who set up their computers? I bet they have multiple computers of drives with all the data on them. If we can find out who set it up, they can lead us to the data sources. Do you think we need to physically destroy it, or can we wipe it clean remotely?"

"You're so right. Probably wipe it clean remotely. Here, let's sort through more of Ty's phone data. There's got to be something here. Do you mind starting while I check on Grey? It's been awhile."

"Of course! Hope he's doing better." She totally got me.

I gathered my things and organized my area. When I was at the door, ready to leave, Avery shouted, "Here it is! I think this is it!

27

Avery accessed Tyler's history from his phone's GPS. Once she unlocked the restrictions on his navigation settings, it traced his last fifty trips. He had taken multiple trips to the same locations. This kid was all over the place: school, library, Onyx, Northwestern University labs, U of Chicago labs, De Paul, and hospitals, too. He was at the Lake Shore hospital three times, where Willow, Anish, and Anish's dad were admitted. In the last month he'd visited every university-based science lab in the city and the top three major hospitals. Recently, just before he'd dropped his phone at my lab, he had been at Onyx every day.

"Ty gets around." Avery paused. "Ya know, the headlines say EBEX is spreading. Do you think Ty has anything to do with it? Have you thought of that?" She took a loud, deep breath in and slowly let it out.

"Now that I see his footpath here, yes, it's possible." I started pacing. "That would be a disaster. This morning's headlines state that the number of patients showing up at hospitals with symptoms of EBEX is doubling each day."

That morning I'd checked EBEX headlines on my tablet and read that the CDC was putting out bulletins to hospitals to enforce strict safety measures and recommending that patients with suspected EBEX be quarantined immediately. The influx of patients into the ER with bacterial infections had skyrocketed the last two days. People were dying every day and night. I had to get them my antibiotic. Too many people were resistant to this infection. It needed to be mass produced quickly—which meant I had to get it to the CDC. One of Dad's friends worked at the CDC and handled investigating weird diseases that came into the U.S. from other countries. I'd send it to him, if I could get his contact information.

Tyler was also on track to align with Onyx while deceiving them.

"I bet he's established a relationship with Onyx, probably Stevenson specifically, so they think he's on their side. He's sapping data from them each time he goes there, right under their noses." I raised my voice. "He's breaking into the mentors' labs at the universities and stealing their research, just like he did mine. Although I didn't let him get anything." I shifted my stance.

"He's got to have one computer or several laptops with the data on it. He wouldn't be so stupid as to keep it all in one place and on one hard drive or portable USB drive, or cloud," said Avery. I loved her. She was a techie, always up on the latest computer systems.

"You're so right! Now that I think about it, Ty's initial computer science project won him the Powell Scholar Award." I searched for the Powell Scholar Award winner projects online, then searched Tyler Brundel. A picture of him and the title of his project came up: "Securing Data in a Vulnerable Information System Environment: Breaking Down New Age File Sharing." It gave an abstract of his research paper, and sure enough, laid out a system designed to abolish all possible forms of hacking, explaining a new way for secure file sharing.

"I hate to say this, but he's brilliant," said Avery

quietly, after reading the abstract.

"He's good. Really good." I was mildly deflated, but only for a few seconds. He was intelligent, but so was I. I bit my thumbnail again. It hurt, so I stuck my hands in my pockets and resumed pacing. "Tyler and the designer kids had a network set up all over Chicago. He was sending intranet data back and forth via secure file sharing, like from one secure electronic medical record system to another. Typically, this is impossible, but Tyler found a way. We first have to get my antibiotic over to the Chicago CDC and tell them what's going on. They can mass-produce it quickly and get it to the hospitals. Then we have to stop Ty and the designers."

I needed to check on Grey and check his progress. I needed his help. I told Avery to shut and lock things down in my workroom and asked her to come to the CDC with me after checking on Grey.

I texted him: *hey need to see you can I stop over now?*

He texted back: *actually I'm on my way to you in search of a hug, food and a shot haha*

I responded: *haha I can give you all of those meet you in the GH*

Avery and I walked over to the greenhouse. Its door was slightly open. I heard a rustle, then Grey walked around the corner eating an apple, smiling, his dimple deep. He finally looked like himself.

"Oh, you found something crisp to eat!" I smiled and wrapped my arms around him, his body warm but thin.

"Yeah, I'm starving." Grey held me, and I didn't want to let go. He took another bite of his apple and chewed slowly, savoring the juices.

"Keep eating. You need to bulk up. I've got another injection here." I pulled out the syringe from my bag.

"Whatever you say. That medicine is working, so I'll take what you have." He sat down next to me and offered me his skinny arm.

I gave him his shot, we gathered up what few things he had, and Avery and I took him home. On the way, I told him what we'd discovered yesterday and that we'd need his help soon. He was ready to do whatever we needed him to do.

Once we dropped him off, I went back home and sat alone in the kitchen. It was eleven o'clock and my parents were asleep. The quiet house made me ache for Willow. I longed to look into her eyes again. Just knowing she wasn't upstairs in her bed made me feel off. The only time she wasn't in her own bed was when she was in the hospital. I always felt off then, too. But this was different. The hollowness of our house made me feel empty. My eyes welled up and tears flowed.

I put my head down in my arms and bawled, letting it all go. Nothing would be the same without Willow. She was always on my mind. Either I was worrying about her, mad at her, or I couldn't wait to see her. I couldn't just turn off my thoughts and feelings like a switch. I still thought of her all the time and there was nothing more I could do to turn back time. Nothing I could do to save her. I'd failed at that already.

I leaned back and cried harder, tears rolling down my face and my nose full. What I feared the most had happened—that Willow would slip away after fighting so hard and so long, and there would be nothing I could do. I reached for tissues and blew my nose.

My crying echoed in the kitchen, and I hoped I didn't wake Mom or Dad. I settled down a bit and waited to feel some sense that she was with me. My eyes stung. Five minutes passed. I heard nothing and felt nothing from Willow. Empty again. The trill of a bird outside seeped through a crack in the window. Then I heard the creak of the stairs and heavy footsteps. Dad was awake and stood at the kitchen door. He sighed heavily when he saw me and walked over to give me a hug. I cried so hard, and we both shook together and sniffled, blowing our noses.

"I miss her, too, honey."

"I know, Dad. This is so painful."

"It's unimaginable," he said, wrapping his arm around my shoulder. We just sat staring out the window in disbelief. He shifted in his seat before getting up and going to the fridge.

"What are you going to do now?" I asked, wondering what he was thinking.

"Right now? Get a drink of water. Honestly, my head is spinning. I know we will honor her and her life. She was a strong spirit."

"She was. But her body was so fragile. She never seemed to fully recover after each of her setbacks. Well, maybe early on. Did you hear from the doctors what actually took her life?"

"I never got a definitive answer. That's why they're doing the autopsy. They aren't one hundred percent certain. I think it could be multiple system failure. They did admit her that night for some testing. She was feeling horrible."

"I know it's uncomfortable to even think about, but I'd like to know." Sitting up, I took the glass of water that Dad handed me. "Thanks."

He sat back down next to me, shoulder to shoulder. His warm arm rubbing next to mine gave me a little bit of comfort. Silence hung in the air before a nagging thought popped into my mind. "Hey, Dad, can I ask you something kinda weird?"

"Sure, Sienna, anything."

"Was Willow a project like me? Like this new baby?"

"What makes you ask that?" he asked, taking a drink and shifting in his seat, moving slightly away from me. My arm was chilly again.

"Well, a friend brought it up, and I got to thinking she probably was. Engineered. Right? There were some projects before me, right?"

He stood up and put his water glass into the sink. "Well, let's just say I wasn't aware of it." He let out a long breath.

"So she was, then?"

"I don't want to get into this right now. We have to plan her funeral. She was my daughter, and now she's gone. That's all that really matters."

"So, you didn't know? Mom just took care of it all? Mom was in on the experimental project? I'm just thinking that if Willow was a project, then something or someone didn't do it all right, and that's a problem." My heart raced thinking of all of the possibilities and scenarios of lab mishaps.

"Don't get all excited, Sienna. Let's focus on what we can do going forward from this unfortunate situation."

"Dad, are you kidding me? I feel like she's been a discarded child." Tears welled up in my eyes again.

"Look, let's be proactive here. My buddy from college, Dan Reeves, reached out to me about Willow. He's with the CDC."

"I remember Dan! I was just going to ask you about him. I think he can help. I've discovered a breakthrough medicine that can help people with EBEX."

"That's incredible, Sienna! Let's get in touch with him. Hey, is Grey okay? Didn't you say he wasn't feeling well?"

"He was seriously sick but is doing much better thanks to this medicine. I think Dr. Reeves can help stop others from getting sick."

"I'm sending his contact info to your phone now. Let me know what he says. I can call him, too. I'd like to talk to him."

I tried to refocus on the bacterial virus. I looked at the contact Dad sent me: Dan Reeves, MD, MPH, lead investigator, CDC, Chicago. I'd call him in the morning. Getting him the antibiotic could help save lives. Thousands, if not millions of lives.

"Thanks, Dad. I'll call him in the morning. I'm super tired, gonna go to bed. You?"

I'd tell Dr. Reeves about my research, the designer kids, and warn him that he'd have to keep the vials hidden and confidential for the time-being.

"Yes, hon. We'll get through this. We have to. I love you." Dad hugged me tightly.

Before trying to get some sleep, I checked my supply of the antibiotic in my work room. It was there, locked up. I suspected Ty and Kellen would be watching my every move. I'd hide the vials and be careful that they didn't know where I was going next. I thought of Jazz since she might need some, soon. It was late but I texted her.

hey, how are you? been thinking of you

Ten minutes passed before she responded. *hey, thanks for checking in. i'm better. fever gone and slowly eating again*

oh great! so good to hear...how's your sore?

it's actually getting smaller i can't believe it

wow that's amazing so happy some sort of miracle I think

yeah a miracle ☺

well get some sleep and let's touch base tomorrow xox
sounds good – g-night!

I was astonished that she was feeling better. It was completely possible that she didn't have EBEX after all, but if that was the case, what did she have?

~~~~~~

Dr. Reeves agreed to meet me in a coffee shop a block away from his office at the CDC. I took the train into the city and two Ubers to the coffee shop. I didn't see anyone or anything following me but was still on edge.

I wore a plain baseball hat, sunglasses, and a black baggy shirt. Reeves was in khaki pants and a blue button-down shirt—he was probably early 50's, I'd guess. He walked up to the counter to order a drink then turned to look around, stroking his thick, dark beard that had streaks of gray. When we spoke briefly late last night, I told him I'd be in a subtle disguise. He looked like he was just under six feet tall. He got his drink and took a seat at my table. I was looking down at my tablet, my bag on my hip.

"Hi, doctor," I said quietly but as normally as possible.

"Hello," was all he said, stirring his drink.

"Thanks for meeting me," I said, looking around at the busy cafe. At 7:30 a.m., people were ramping up their caffeine for their morning jolt.

"Sure, it's the least I can do for your dad. I owe him one. Hey, I'm so sorry about your sister, by the way," he said, taking a sip and running a hand over his bald head.

"Thanks, it's been a nightmare," I said, swallowing hard. "Like I said, I've got something of great use to you and your organization. Well, the entire city, really."

"I hear you. Glad we had a chance to catch up. I tried to talk with Langdon, but we didn't connect. He did text me that I should hear you out. I'm interested."

I reached my hand into my bag and showed him a peek of my vials that were in a larger envelope. "Here. I'm going to give you these in greatest confidence that you'll get this to the right people, who will then duplicate them quickly as possible and distribute to those in need. Actually, anyone and everyone. You know what I mean."

My hand shook slightly when I took a sip of my coffee and then looked around. No one seemed to notice us.

"Does Langdon know everything?" he asked, uncertain I had any idea of what I was talking about.

"He knows some." Well, he would by the end of the day. "I need you to trust me, Dr. Reeves."

"And why should I?" He leaned toward me, his elbows on the table.

I figured I might as well tell him. He'd understand. "I'm genetically engineered, and I've been working on this project for months now for Onyx."

"Oh, really?" He sat back and cleared his throat, assuming I'd fed him a line of bullshit.

"You may know Dr. Stevenson?"

He nodded. "Sure. I know Stevenson very well, as a matter of fact." Reeves looked hard at my face and hands, then rubbed his beard. Suddenly I wondered if this was the wrong thing to do. Maybe Reeves was in on this so-called contest with Stevenson. Holy crap.

"How well do you know her?" I asked, clutching my bag tight.

"We went to medical school together, then into separate residency programs. Lost touch. Just saw her at a conference in town last year. Tell me about this project, will you?"

Okay, so he didn't admit to having worked with her

lately, but he could be lying. Everyone lied. I sensed an edge in his voice. The tension didn't release in my shoulders. "You know my dad well, right? You two trust each other. You go back years?"

"Oh gosh, yes, Sienna. Langdon and I knew each other in college. Took a few classes together and lived together for two years. No, actually, it was four or five." Reeves laughed. "Man, we had some good times together! He knows things about me my wife doesn't even know!"

"He mentioned you guys lived together. So, I can trust you, too?"

"Well, it's your call, but I promise I wouldn't do anything to harm Langdon's family. Ever."

I stared at him, holding my breath, wishing I could read his mind, and looked deep into his eyes, the window to his soul. I inhaled, then gave a long exhale. "Like I said last night, it's a new antibiotic that combats EBEX. My friend got sick with it and this antibiotic helped him. We think he got it from a kid on his lacrosse team who picked it up from his dad, who had traveled to and from Saudi Arabia. And who knows, maybe someone originally planted it there. It's a super freaky bacterium. Now others are getting it. We suspect someone is spreading it around. On purpose."

"Ah. I see." He rubbed his chin again.

I bit my nails anxiously before continuing. "So, here are a few vials of the drug. Test it, if you want, but don't take too long. I'm telling you, it works. As you know, EBEX is spreading like crazy. Deliver it by drones or armored trucks if you need to, I don't care, just mass produce it and get it to people." I stood up. I had to go to the bathroom, and I was nervous we'd been in the cafe too long already.

Dr. Reeves chugged the rest of his drink, looked straight ahead, and followed me to the bathroom. As we walked next to each other, I slipped the envelope with the vials into his coat pocket, then I went into the bathroom while he walked out the door.

I was back at school by lunch and found a spot at a table with Avery and Blue. I felt so out of it, since I hadn't been at school for weeks. Willow's passing and the time I had spent at the lab, kept me away. Mom and Dad had notified the school of my situation and the need for some time away. Eyes flickered on me, then off. Kids didn't know if they should look at me or not. Blue assured me they were not staring at me. She told me no one really cared where I'd been, they just felt bad that Willow was gone.

I shifted in my chair and put my head down to whisper to Avery that all had gone well with Reeves. She whispered back that she'd kept an eye on Kellen, and he was skipping classes, pacing the halls, and hiding out in the bathroom. A few friends who were in his classes reported back to her. Avery knew everyone.

After lunch we walked toward our lockers to get books for our afternoon classes. I imagined Dr. Reeves with the vials, taking them out of the envelope, slowly preparing a sample to test, and then later, he'd have a huge smile on his face, thrilled with the results. Then he'd plan. I so wished I was there with him, to see his look of amazement. To be honest, it felt incredible to share my secret.

When Avery and I walked outside to the athletic building to change for lacrosse, Tyler came out of nowhere and started following us. Yes, *the* Ty, who I thought would be off stealing data all day and night. He caught up and nudged my elbow. "Excuse me," I said between clenched teeth.

"Oh, am I in your way?" he asked with a fake, innocent smile. It made him look like a fourteen-year-old instead of a seventeen-year-old.

"Jackass." I wanted to say more but held my tongue. I knew he wanted to get me mad and make me look like the idiot.

He backed off enough, and I picked up my pace. "Look Sienna. We all know you're hot shit, but really, you have to back off. Like now, seriously."

Avey and I stopped, and I clenched my fists tightly. I wanted to punch him in the face so badly. "I'm not sure what you mean, Ty. I think *you* should back off. Seriously."

"I know you're up to something, and I'm going to find out. You can't hide from me. Don't ever think you can hide from us." He smirked.

"Oh, believe me, I can hide from you. You should know better now not to mess with me," I retorted before walking away with Avery.

Avery and I bolted into the athletic building. We stood in the entranceway catching our breath. I was mad and my heart was racing. "Let's skip practice and follow Tyler. I have a gut feeling he's up to something.

"I agree. Let's go. I'll text coach and let him know we can't make it. I'll tell her we are meeting with teachers about an exam."

I nodded. Avery and I walked to my car. I was in the driver's seat this time since we planned to watch Ty leave and follow him. I could play his game and one-up him. We headed toward his car and saw him quickly pull out. He backed up fast and almost hit the car behind him. The driver laid on her horn as Ty zoomed off. We dodged around the kids walking and driving until we were one car behind Ty. Avery opened her window and we heard a drone overhead, but it was closer to Ty's car than ours. I guessed either Stevenson or Reeves were on Ty's trail, too.

"He's heading toward Onyx, I'm sure," I said to Avery. "We need to stay back enough so he doesn't see us."

"I'll tap into the drone's camera overhead via satellite so we can watch him, in case he gets too far ahead." She clicked on her tablet and then on her wrist computer.

"Perfect, thanks." I focused on the road and Tyler ahead. "Hey, can you see if my scrubs are in the back seat? I have an idea."

Sure enough, they were there. I had taken some of Mom's medical office scrubs and liked to wear them around the house or when I worked at the lab. They were loose and comfortable, and I didn't worry about getting them dirty. After about thirty minutes, he pulled into the Onyx entrance gate and showed them his badge.

"The jerk has special access!" I exclaimed, throwing my hands up in the air. I noticed the long, high fence surrounding the building. How we were going to get in hadn't occurred to me yet. I looked up, and the drone was up and over the fence, no problem. We needed to fly, of course.

"There have to be cameras everywhere around this place. I don't know how we can get in—if that's what you even want to do?" Avery asked.

I surveyed the area. It was a fortress. "Where's the drone going? Can we see the views from the drone's camera?"

"Yeah." Avery and I looked at her watch and saw that the drone had followed Ty as far as it could. He was inside, but the drone was hovering over the building. The security guard was making a call, looking up at the drone. No doubt he was warning others about it. We saw guards moving on top of the building with guns in holsters at their sides. While we waited and watched, expecting to see the drone taken down in a single shot, I changed into the scrubs, throwing my jeans and shirt in the back of my car.

Instead of the drone being shot down, a helicopter appeared overhead and landed on top of one of the buildings, as an ambulance pulled up to the entrance security gate, barely stopping before the gate opened. The guards held their weapons and surveyed the ground. The drone was staying hidden. We couldn't see what was going on the rooftop, but when we looked at Avery's watch, we saw someone being rushed out to the helicopter on a stretcher. They were wrapped in a blanket, with a paramedic hammering on their chest.

"It's Stevenson!" I exclaimed.

28

The helicopter took off toward the hospital, and I called Dr. Reeves. After his phone rang about ten times, he finally picked up,

"Dr. Reeves, this is Sienna," I said breathlessly.

"Are you okay?"

"I just saw Dr. Stevenson being life-flighted away to the hospital from her office at Onyx. She must be very sick."

"Oh, no! Are you sure?" he asked.

"I'm sure. Do you have the antibiotic for her? I think she may need it." As I spoke, my eyes were glued to the entrance and exit of the Onyx building, waiting for Ty to leave. I wouldn't put it past him to have infected Stevenson and the whole Onyx building.

"I do. I'll call the physicians at the hospital to check in on her. This antibiotic could be lifesaving. Well done, Sienna."

"Let's hope we can get it to her in time."

"Yes, and what about her co-workers?" he asked. "They'd be susceptible to EBEX, too, if she has it."

"Yeah, I know," I told him. "We'll need you to get on mass producing it."

As I hung up, I looked at Avery and we saw Tyler cross the courtyard. He was with someone and, together, they began to jog. Then the person he was with collapsed.

"Oh man, they're going down already," I said to Avery. Ty kept on jogging. The drone was right there, swooping in. He looked up and saw the drone and gave it the finger, cursing. Avery looked at me wide-eyed, then at her tablet; she was taping the video feed from the drone.

I called Greyson. "We're sending you some insane video footage. Are you feeling good enough to go into my work room and log in to my computer?"

"Of course, anything you need." I gave him the codes to get into my house and to access my video files, so he could store it with the others.

"Stay safe," I told him, my voice jittery.

"You, too."

Avery and I waited, hiding in a thick row of bushes near the entrance gate. We decided that I'd try to get into the building while she kept an eye on the outside, letting me know what was going on. If I needed help on the inside, I'd call her.

Fifteen minutes passed before another ambulance arrived at Onyx. The gate opened, and I grabbed the door handle on the back of the ambulance to ride with it onto the campus, my face mask and gloves on. I couldn't get sick now. I'd been lucky to dodge it so far. But was it really luck?

We drove up to the front entrance of the main building. I jumped off the back, then followed the paramedics into the building when they stepped out of the truck. There were three others, wearing scrubs, masks, and gloves like me. My heart was beating fast, and I pulled my mask up to cover my nose and mouth. I probably could be seen on-camera, but since there was a medical emergency, I doubted anyone was paying close attention to the video. Thankfully, I was able to get in and past security with them.

"Hey, who are you?" one paramedic asked through his

face mask.

"I was sent over from a different squad. We were on the other side and they radioed me to come over here to help your team," I explained.

I was breathing hard, even though I was just jogging lightly inside the main lobby. I scanned the area. It was a stale environment, clean and stark white.

Someone yelled, "Over here!" and we were waved toward the outside courtyard, where there was a garden, path, and picnic tables for breaks. We approached the person Ty had been with a moment ago; the kid was lying on his back, convulsing. My jaw dropped. I recognized him from the meeting—he had been with Ty at the restaurant and must have been one of the engineer kids in his elite group. As the paramedics rushed to him, I darted into a dark conference room. I leaned on the wall and caught my breath. Now what?

I pulled out my tablet and sent Avery a message. *i'm in. now i've got to find Ty. need map of this place.* She sent me a map of all eight floors inside of the Onyx Pharmaceutical building, with good luck wishes. I took a deep breath and enlarged the map to get a sense of where I was on the first floor.

I quietly dictated into my tablet, *thx any idea where the computer servers are located?*

2nd floor outer room, she replied, sending me another map marking the spot. Not that hard to find but I was sure there were high security doors to get through. I walked down the hall looking at the map of the second floor on my tablet. A guard appeared, walking toward me.

"Hey, where are you going, miss? I need to see your security clearance." He stopped and I lifted my tablet just enough to take a quick picture of the security badge clipped to his waist.

"Hi, um, I was just told there's someone upstairs who needs medical attention. Where are the stairs?" I said to the guard.

"Ah, you got clearance?" he asked, in a deep voice.

"Oh, you mean this?" I waved my school ID badge so he couldn't make out the logo or color. I noticed the "stairway" sign and sprinted to the entrance straight ahead, running up the stairs, two steps at a time.

"Hey, wait! You can't go there!" yelled the guard.

I opened the door to the second floor. The hallway was empty.

Avery texted me: *paramedics still working on the kid. lifted fingerprints when Ty put his hand on your locker and from his phone. LMK if you need them.*

I let out a long sigh. Avery was brilliant, a step ahead. I wasn't sure how that would work. I looked at the map on my tablet and followed it as best as I could. I found the conference room with desk modules everywhere; it was like a maze. It was late in the day, but I'd have thought someone would be working into the evening. I went toward a long hallway with windows on the outer edge. It overlooked the courtyard and a small lake. The sun was setting as I saw the paramedics lift the kid onto the gurney and shuttle him off toward the ambulance. A pit in my stomach formed and I started jogging.

Straight ahead I saw a door, with a keypad next to it. There were no markings, just the pad and a badge scanner to open the door. It looked like there was an option for the machine to read the card or else physically scan it. I texted Avery: *badge scanner. i'm gonna use the picture of the security guard's badge to sign in.* I held up the picture.

Nothing. I wiped off my phone screen with my shirt and tried again. The door clicked open.

I entered the room quickly, hoping no one had followed me into the room.

My tablet vibrated. *you in?* Avery wrote.

yep.

Then she typed, *Grey confirmed he has the video safe.*

Phew, one less thing to worry about, as long as my room stayed a secret. I heard a loud thud and then another. Silence. Could the two people have collapsed? I dared not open the door just yet. I darted around the room full of computer servers until I found the main desk. Now I needed it to access the servers. I was hoping the security guard had high level access.

I wiped my forehead. I felt small and on the edge of panic from the heat from the computers. The door clicked in the distance, followed by a piercing alarm that sounded off all over the building. I covered my ear with my one hand and tried one last time to get into the computer with the badge. It searched and clicked, and I waited for exactly three minutes, then BAM, I was in! I covered both ears as the computer loaded, then took my tablet and held it near the main computer, using the USB link to sync the computers. I searched for the files I wanted to sync and disabled Ty's account and password. I instructed it not to reset it. And yes, I was very sure.

I jumped up with both ears still covered and ran to the door. The sound was excruciating. Multiple alarms were sounding. I opened the door to see two people lying face down by the doorway. One of them looked familiar. They had blisters all over their hands and faces, so it was hard to see their features. I ran back to the stairwell to head downstairs. I wanted to contact Avery but didn't have the time. She'd be waiting, I hoped, safely. In the stairwell, others were running too, and screaming.

One yelled, "FIRE! Fire in one of the labs!"

I flew out of the building from the first floor, and more ambulances were lined up as a fire truck pulled up. Water sprayed everywhere, from the courtyard out to the building. An internal sprinkler system turned on in the building. I coughed repeatedly, looking for Avery. I called out to her loudly. "Avery, where are you?"

"I'm right here," she said in a monotone voice. My arms tensed, and I turned the corner at the entrance gate. Tyler had his arm around her neck and a gun pointed at her head.

I almost lost my balance completely, then collected myself. "Ty, stay calm. No reason to hurt anyone," I said, holding out my hand like a crossing guard. I swallowed hard and looked him right in his cold, stoic eyes.

"What are you two doing here?" he asked.

"Just checking things out. We heard someone was sick," I said, clicking my tablet quietly behind my back, dialing Reeves to FaceTime. He needed to see and hear this.

"Yeah, well, I'm handling all this just fine," Ty lied.

"Really?" said Avery, "because people are going down fast, and we think you had something to do with spreading it."

Ty shoved the gun into Avery's neck. She tried to pull back, but he squeezed tighter. "Shut up! You know nothing!" He clenched his teeth.

"Ty, calm down. There's a lot going on, and hurting Avery isn't going to make anything any better." I took a small step toward him.

"Back off. I told you I was going to go forward with or

without you."

"This has gone way out of control."

"No, no, no. I've got it all under control." He smiled and backed away with Avery. She knew I had my dad's gun in my shoulder bag. We locked eyes as I reached down. A helicopter flew over us, and the moment Ty looked up, Avery jabbed her elbow into his side. Stepping hard on his foot, I pulled my gun on him. He bent over in pain and when he came up, I was pointing the gun in his face. Avery kneed him in between his legs, right in his engineered family jewels, and he dropped his gun.

"The helicopter is on its way to deliver antibiotics to the hospital. Everyone will have a chance to survive your spread of EBEX, Ty. Everyone," I said, staring him down, "whether you like it or not." I was inches from his face.

Bent over in pain, Ty couldn't speak. When he gained some composure, he said gruffly, "It's too late anyway, pretty. EBEX will be rampant in a few days, and you won't be able to keep up with it."

"Watch me." I smiled and looked at my tablet. Dr. Reeves had heard every word that came out of Ty's mouth on FaceTime.

Dr. Reeves blinked. "Sienna, hang in there. The FBI are just minutes away."

My hand shook as I kept pointing the gun at Ty. I hoped that I could hold this for a few more minutes. Avery saw me struggling and grabbed Ty's arms, holding them tightly behind his back. We were a force, the two of us.

But Ty was strong, and despite a cracked rib, he pulled and kicked Avery until she lost her balance. I cocked the gun and fired at Tyler's left leg.

29

Tyler screamed in pain and the gun fell from my hand. I had actually shot him. Honestly, I wasn't sure I could do it, but I had to stop him from hurting my best friend. Avery got up, trembling all over. My hand was shaking uncontrollably. I looked up at the helicopter getting lower, its blades spinning and engine deafening. There were four drones now in the area, fire trucks, and ambulances in and out of the entranceway. Avery waved, then yelled at one of the paramedics running by, and that's when we saw our first FBI agent. I called to one of them that we needed help.

"This kid was just shot and needs help!" The agent radioed a paramedic. Ty was lying on his back, writhing in pain. I pulled up his pant leg to look at his wound and saw his leg was red and swollen, blisters everywhere.

"Oh no! He may have EBEX!" I shouted at the agent and then looked at Avery, both of us in shock. "Be careful, and wear gloves if you touch him," I said. Ty's genetically engineered immune system wasn't undefeated.

"We are life-flighting some more victims to the hospital. We can put him on the next one about to land," she said loudly over the noise of the copter. He'd need to be quarantined.

Ty screamed to all of us, "I'm doing this all for us, Sienna! For the entire world and don't you ever forget that!"

He wasn't giving up just yet. I looked around and found my tablet a few feet away. I dialed Reeves again, but no answer.

The paramedics took Ty away, and Avery and I dropped to the ground, exhausted. I pulled my mask down for the moment as we sat there.

"Are you OK?" we asked each other at the same time.

"I'll be fine. I can't believe you shot Ty."

"Me either, but he didn't leave me any choice. He was about to hurt you. I couldn't let that happen."

"Thanks for stopping him. He was out of control. Did you disable his access to the computers?"

"I did, just in time. There were two people who collapsed right outside the door to the server room."

Thinking about their bodies gave me chills. I paused and took a deep breath. "You wouldn't believe it, but I honestly think one of them was Ximena."

"Are you sure?"

"I was running past them, but her haircut is short, she's distinctly short, and always wears high heels. And that nose of hers... I'm pretty sure," I brought my hands to my mouth to bite my nails.

"Are you kidding! Don't put your hands in your mouth!" Avery scolded.

I obviously wasn't thinking straight. "I've probably got an immune system of steel because I've been biting my nails for so long." It wasn't funny, but it was true.

We got into the car, and I drove as quickly as possible to the hospital. All along, above us, were copters loaded with medicine on their way to help people. Or it might be too late, and people were deathly sick. Either way, we were all headed to the same, dire place.

30

All chairs were taken, so people stood and leaned against the walls in the Emergency Department at the University Hospital. Physicians ran to attend to patients, people coughed, sneezed, and who knew what else came out the other end. I gagged thinking about it. The pandemic was in full force. At first, I wasn't sure where to go or what to do, so we just stood there. The sounds made my ears ring, and when I finally came to my senses, I told Avery to leave; to go home or at least far away from this place so she didn't get sick, if wasn't too late. I knew my immune system could handle this more than hers could and so I told her I'd keep in touch but asked her to check in on Jazz. She was better but maybe not completely out of the woods yet. "Hey, if you can stop at my house and get an injection for Jazz out of my mini-workstation. You know where they are? If you have trouble, call me. Take it to Jazz, just in case she's not better," I instructed.

When she left, I suddenly got the urge to throw up. I jogged over to a garbage can in the corner and hacked in there, then searched for a drink of water and a quieter place to contact Dr. Reeves.

It took a few tries, but I finally got a hold of him and told him I was at the ER. "Are you able to get in touch with someone at Onyx to mass produce the antibiotic?" I asked as I leaned against the cold wall.

"Luckily, I know some ethical people at Onyx, other

than Stevenson. It took some digging and convincing, but they pulled some strings and worked overnight. I got what we could to the major hospitals in Chicago and specifically, to some select severe cases. They're still producing. Now it's just a matter of time. We'll have wait to see how it works." He was willing to wait and be patient, unlike me. I wanted everyone better, now.

"What can I do?"

"Sienna, you've done quite enough. Beyond anyone's expectations, in fact. Get some rest and be with your family. We can take it from here."

"I don't know if I can stop, ya know? How's Dr. Stevenson?"

"Well, she's had the medication for a few hours and is hanging on. I think she was blindsided and had no idea what was going on."

"I don't think so. She was the leader. Is she at this hospital? The U?" I asked. I wasn't completely convinced that Stevenson had no idea about Tyler and all of his backhandedness.

"Yes, she is. But be careful, Sienna. I advise you to get far away from there. I have to go." Someone in the background urgently called for Reeves.

"I'll be in touch. Thanks, doc." After I hung up, I looked for a computer station to find Stevenson's room number. I approached a young nurse working on one.

"Um, I need to find my mom. I'm not feeling good, and I can't remember what room she's in. Can you help me?" I asked, holding my stomach, which still hurt."

"I can't give that you that information." She looked up at me and then put her hand out to hold my arm. "You okay?"

"No. Not really. I really want to see my mom. Dr. Stevenson? She arrived here about an hour ago, I think. I'm really worried."

"Oh, what harm can be done? Let me see." She tapped on the computer screen and a bunch of Stevensons popped up in the computer. "Date of birth?"

I had no idea. I scanned the screen over the nurse's shoulder and saw her address. On her way out of the lab once, Ximena said was on her way to meet Stevenson at her house in Lake Forest. Her birthday was listed next to her address, so I blurted it out. "There she is," I sighed.

The nurse tapped a few more times and located her chart and her room number. "She's in 306."

"Thanks so much. You're a lifesaver. Thank you!" I limped at first, but when I was out of her sight, walked fast to the elevator, holding my stomach.

I stood, head throbbing and throat dry outside of Room 306. I leaned against the wall, my legs weak, and closed my eyes. I never would have thought it would all come down to this. Ugh. My tablet vibrated in my bag, two, then three times. I didn't want to check it. Everything ached. I just wanted to rest. After two more vibrations, my shoulders tightened, and I reached in my bag. It was Greyson.

I read his text: *i've got it all on video. safe, where are you?*

Ha! I almost laughed out loud, but I was too tired. He's asking me if *I* was okay. He was asking *me*. I sank deeper into the wall, but it didn't give. I tilted my head back and tried to gain some energy. *awesome thx...I'm hanging on will call you soon can't wait to c u!*

Ah, the thought of hugging Greyson warmed me up and gave me a shot of energy. I could do this. I pushed on Stevenson's door before a nurse was about to walk up. Once I was in the room, I stopped. She appeared to be sleeping, tubes in her arms and an oxygen mask on her face. Probably not a good time to talk to her. I pulled a mask from the box of them on the wall and approached her bed slowly. At this point I couldn't be too cautious, even though I'd already been exposed.

Just then, a nurse came in. "Everything okay here?"

Stevenson moaned and moved her head to the side.

"Yeah. I just wanted to visit my mom," I lied. The nurse nodded, handed me a face mask and gloves before she left. I put them on before entering her room.

I touched Stevenson's arm and she opened her eyes. She squinted, trying to recognize me.

"It's Sienna. I think you're going to be okay, Dr. S." I gently pulled her mask off so she could talk.

"Ugh, what happened?" she moaned.

"You're in the hospital with a drug resistant EBEX, and you're being treated."

Her eyes opened wider. "How can this be?" She tried to sit up but was unable to move.

"Tyler and some of the other genetically engineered kids spread this around Onyx, trying to take over your company and spread it so millions of people die. He's responsible," I blurted out.

She frowned, confused, but then I could tell by her pause and a tiny nod that it did make sense to her. She would figure out all of the details, eventually.

"Is he being stopped?" She breathed heavily.

"I stopped him, and he will be punished. He wanted all of our discoveries to be kept to himself and the privileged."

"It can't. He can't do this. But wait, there's more..."

"He can't and he won't. My antibiotic is helping you and others." I paused and reached for her hand but stopped myself, sitting on the edge of my seat. "More, what do you mean?"

She sat up and stared at the wall across from her. "Everything was planned to the last detail. I don't know how Tyler even got into Onyx, let alone caused this chaos." Her voice tightened and raised when she said "chaos."

She turned her head. I waited to see what, if anything, she'd do next. She was out of it. Heavily medicated, not sure what she was saying. A long silence blanketed the room.

"You were the one creating chaos," I said in a low, calm voice. "You. You've destroyed lives and doomed families. You played with fire. You can't change what happened in Eden. You can't. And now you continue to give false hope to kids like me and my parents. False hope and security. You can't change the past by creating and controlling the future."

She stared at me, speechless, as I got up and pushed open the door. I ripped off my mask and gloves and threw them in a biohazard bin across the hall.

Greyson stood next to me. It was like I was dreaming when I saw him waiting outside the door in the hallway. He was smiling and back to his old self, so content, as if this had all been a bad dream. I flung my arms around his neck. We stood for what seemed like forever in the hall hugging. I melted. My knees buckled and my body shook.

"It's so good to see you," I said.

"You, too. You're going to save all of those sick people, everyone." He ran his fingers through my hair. "You saved me."

I wiped my eyes. We were not done yet. I straightened up and backed away, but not far. I reached in my bag and got out a tissue to wipe by teary eyes. "You have the video. Well done. Let's upload this. The news outlets will get this for breaking news and people will see it right away. We can post it everywhere on the Internet." I was breathless and my words tumbled out quickly.

"I can do this with one click." His eyes drilled into mine with anticipation.

"Let me see." We sat down in the hallway outside of Room 306 as Greyson clicked away. My jaw dropped as I reviewed the footage of Tyler, Kellen, and even Liv's well-planned out steps, with not an ounce of regret.

When it was finished, I nodded, and Grey knew what to do. In just a few minutes, Tyler and Kellen were exposed. The video of him at Onyx, holding a gun to a young woman was posted for all to see. People would be wondering why so many were in danger of dying and would now know Tyler spread the EBEX. The CDC would warn people to stay at home until the epidemic could be controlled and announce that it was being treated by a new antibiotic that was effective to this resistant disease. The antibiotic was available to all who needed it. Absolutely no one would be excluded.

"There's one thing that you need to know. This may not all be over. Do you have any idea if the FBI or police stopped Kellen and Liv?" Grey asked me as we rode down in the elevator.

"Haven't seen them since I left school when Avery and I followed Ty to Onyx. I'm guessing they were either at Onyx already working on their plan of infecting everyone there, or they found out about Ty at Onyx and are on the run."

"I thought maybe they were at Onyx in that mess and the FBI got both of them, but I've been scouring the news and haven't heard. I have no idea about Liv. They're just saying that Ty's accomplice was being hunted down and was still on the loose. I was hoping it was old news and that they had captured him."

"Yeah, the FBI finally got to Onyx, but it was total chaos there. Kellen and Liv are smart, and I'd think he'd have a backup plan. They tried to stay a step ahead of everyone else this entire time." The thought of Kellen and Liv out there made my stomach sink. Even if it was just Oceana and the other kids in their group, they could all be on the run with damaging information. While they were out on their own, they could be hiding and securing all the information they had gathered. It was as if we were back at square one.

When the elevators opened, Mom and Dad were there. I collapsed in their arms, the weight of the past weeks hanging on us as we gripped each other tightly. I closed my eyes and saw the four of us back in the greenhouse. An emptiness opened into my soul. I hummed to Willow's soothing voice as all of us worked together among the plants in the warm, humid, clean air.

31

The man who sat across from me had a day-old beard and thick, black, bushy eyebrows. He seemed familiar as he reached down into his bag. I didn't know what he pulled out but realized that I'd seen him in another train station somewhere. The stale, dirty smell of the train wafted in the air as the car rattled and squeaked on the tracks as Mom, Dad, the Halloways, Grey, and I headed to the FBI headquarters in Chicago. The man's hand emerged from his bag, his knuckles hairy and old-looking. It hit me; he was the same man I had bumped into at the train station when I saved Greyson.

Grey's leg firmly pressed against mine. I pushed his harder to get him to look at me, and I shifted my gaze to the man across from me. The man was focusing on his book now, some sort of journal, so Grey couldn't get a good look at his face. The man's eyebrows covered his eyes as he looked down. I looked away, hoping he wouldn't recognize me, just in case he hadn't followed us. I hoped this was a random chance meeting, but the sick feeling in my stomach told me otherwise. I scratched my leg near Grey's and played with my ponytail. Avery looked down at her phone.

"Hey, is Jazz ok?" I asked.

Avery looked up. "She started to feel bad again so yeah, I gave her an injection just in case."

"Oh, good that was smart. Glad she's ok, I was worried.

Um, anything new about, well, you know?" His name was on the tip of my tongue, but I held back.

Avery squinted hard at her screen. Her lips moved as she read. "Um, it says he's been cited, but they can't verify for sure that it's him. He's got to be disguised and out of the country by now. Canada or Mexico, is my guess."

"Agree. The FBI can't seriously think they can find him now. It's been like, more than forty-eight hours," said Grey as he wrapped his hand around mine. His warmth filled me with a comfort I'd never felt before.

Grey's hand squeezed, telling me, *it'll be okay, even if they don't find him, we're in this together.* I sighed deeply and my shoulders dropped, but when I crossed my legs, I caught the man staring at us. He didn't appear to recognize us and quickly looked back down at his journal. He shifted, but I wasn't convinced he didn't recognize us. I could tell that he was the kind of guy who had a good poker face.

"Not unless they're sick or hurt too, ya know," I added.

"For sure, a possibility," Grey agreed.

The announcer said Argyle was the next stop, and we all looked up at the train route colorfully outlined across from us over the man's head.

"Hey, show me your big, beautiful eyes," Grey said as he lifted up his phone to take a selfie of us. When the train slowed down, the man stood up to get off. The train jerked and he reached for the railing, and when the doors slid open, he stepped off the train. Grey nodded. He recognized him, too.

"What do you think?" I asked.

"I think he followed us," he said firmly, without doubt.

"Yeah, you're right, this time. Too much of a chance that he'd get on the same train, same time, and sit across from us. Too much in the news about us." I squeezed his hand tighter. It was over, but at the same time, we'd stepped into new, unchartered waters for both of us. We were in a different set of circumstances now.

"I got a picture of him when he looked down at his book, or whatever he had in his hand. Our selfie, ya know? I like you, but I don't need a picture of us riding on the train." His dimple was deep again when he smiled. Grey looked at the photo and nodded, before handing me his phone to look. I enlarged the photo and noticed a small inscription at the bottom of the book. I enlarged it again to see it better.

What I saw sent my stomach into a knot. In tiny, block print it read, "L. Yardley." My throat locked up, and I looked over to Dad, who was oblivious to this man. Two more stops and we'd be off. We nodded at each other, silent. That guy was creepy. Either it was a coincidence that he had a book with an inscription with the same first initial and last name, or it was an indication that his name was similar.

I could only imagine what this man might have been scheming since we last saw him at the hospital, and what would happen now that Kellen and Liv and possibly others were on the run, loose with the data, unless Ty, selfish Ty, had somehow secretly kept the files hidden only for himself to ultimately gain access. I wouldn't put it past him to change locations of the data, passwords, and firewalls, to postpone any hackers, even Kellen and Liv, from getting into his sensitive files.

Our stop arrived and all of us got off the train and stepped onto the platform to grab an Uber to the FBI center.

"I'm so proud of you all," said Mom, looking a little

pale from morning sickness.

"Couldn't agree more," said Dad as we walked toward the ominous FBI building.

"I still can't believe all that's happened and how you linked Tyler to this crime. Just unbelievable that anyone would engineer people and then try to destroy others, like Greyson," said Mr. Halloway. Mom and Dad looked everywhere else other than at Mr. and Mrs. Halloway.

"You saved him, you know, and we'll never forget that. Ever. You've always been so special and now this! How can we ever repay you and thank you enough!" A tear formed in the corner of Mrs. Halloway's eyes.

"He's a special guy and has always been an amazing friend to me, Mrs. Halloway. Wouldn't have it any other way," I said as she gave me a hug.

Grey, Avery, and I had corroborated our stories. We'd tell them the facts—but leave out my hidden lab at home. There was no reason for them to raid that and disrupt all the work I had done already. Only Grey and Avery knew about it anyway, and they swore they thought it was just a closet in my house. It was, partially.

Anyway, I was ready to get this over with. We all were.

Just inside the entrance, we were screened by security. They already had Dad's gun and kept it as evidence. None of us would dare bring in even a pen.

We shifted through the process and told our stories. After several hours and countless cups of coffee, we had told them everything we knew about the Elite group that Tyler and Kellen had pulled together and what we knew of their carefully orchestrated plan. We even handed over the video and audio tape of their secret meetings and Ty's phone. We had downloaded everything we could. We told them everything we knew about the Mortons, Onyx, Dr. S, and the mentors, too. I was thoroughly exhausted.

After we were cleared to leave, we took the train back to the suburbs. Avery, Grey, and I decided to hang out for a while at Avery's house. We sat around a table on her back porch. The warm sun blanketed our bodies as if it was recharging us and filling us with spaciousness. We took off our socks and shoes to free our stifled feet, and Avery served us glasses of cold water. My mouth was dry from being so nervous and talking for hours with FBI agents. We sat in silence for five minutes before Grey spoke. "You two were amazing!"

"You were, too! We couldn't have taken Tyler down without you," I said, and Avery nodded.

"Seriously, Grey, we're so happy you are better and could help. We needed you," I said.

"What do you think Kellen, Liv, and the other elites are up to now?" Grey asked. He didn't know everything about their hidden agenda.

"Well, I think they have all of the research data and are on the run, figuring out their next move," I said.

Avery added, "I bet they'll lay low until the spread of EBEX is controlled and we all finish school. Then they'll pop up somewhere with some crazy idea of getting rid of the weaker class again with all of the data they've collected. My brain is in overdrive, obviously!"

"You're probably right, Avery. We can't rest completely. Any ideas of how we can get on their trail?"

"Maybe there's a way I can connect with Liv and you with Kellen," said Avery. "Surely, he's ditched his phone. Maybe copied his data and got a new one. Who knows."

"Yeah, maybe. Kellen was trying to talk me into siding with him."

"Maybe with some of Ty's location info we downloaded from his phone, we can track him down. He may revisit some places. You may need to flirt with him, so he gives up info," said Avery.

"Hey, wait a minute! I'm not good with that!" Grey said, raising his voice.

I laughed. "I can be a good actress, Grey!"

32

Later that night, I crawled into bed, my head throbbing from the long day and the flood of caffeine. My heart was still racing, but my eyes were heavy. By telling our story, a heavy weight had been lifted from my shoulders. All would be calm for now. I felt this in my bones, while another stirring in my body was brewing. I picked up my phone to check one last time for messages before texting Grey and Avery goodnight and turning off my light to try to get some sort of restful sleep. One message had been sent almost an hour ago. It was from Kellen. I opened and read it.

So, things didn't turn out as I had planned. I hoped you'd see through the fog, Sienna, and join us, join me in becoming something much bigger than this virus, than this unattainable goal of saving everyone you are so drawn to. It's not too late, though. I feel a tug between us and a little light guiding us toward a path together. A path to a brighter future and one where we can make a major difference. We can find the other engineered kids and discover something so unimaginable right now. It's out there. I feel it. Just take that step toward me and a new beginning. We have the power for change right in our hands.

I dropped my phone onto my bed and resisted responding with the pure tightness I felt in my chest and discomfort in my gut. My brain said to slow down and think about how to respond. I took a deep breath in, then out. He hadn't given up and was on a war path. As his written words sunk in, I found I had no words for him. He was a new force that had risen from this destruction, and I'd have to contend with that.

On the other hand, Kellen had opened the door for me to find him. I rested my head on my pillow and closed my eyes, trying to clear my head of jumbled thoughts. Where was he? What was his next move? What did he know about the other engineered kids? How would I stop him from doing more damage? My phone rang. It was Grey, Face Timing me.

"Hey, you okay?"

"I'm not sure, to be honest with you." I rolled over to my side while lying in bed, my hair falling over my shoulders. "Kellen texted me. Can you believe it?"

"Oh, wow. That's crazy. What did he want?

"He is still trying to convince me to join him and Liv. He's not giving up but pushing forward on finding more engineered kids."

"Well, doesn't surprise me really. After all that's happened. What are you going to do?"

"I'm going to think about it, but my gut is to go along with him to find him, figure out his plan, and find a way to stop him. You know, play him."

"Could be dangerous, so be careful. Let's talk about it tomorrow. Right now, forget about him. I miss you. I was dreaming that you were next to me, then I woke up and had to see you." Grey combed his fingers through his hair.

"You're right. Thanks for Face Timing! I wish I was with you, though."

"Me, too. So now what?"

"One day at a time," I said, reminding myself.

"Hey, I hate to say this, even mention it, but I noticed a

little spot on my elbow as I was changing my clothes earlier. Do you ya think it's back?" He had a concerned look on his face, and my stomach sank.

"Seriously?" I sat up in bed.

"Yep. It's small, but thought I'd mention. Probably nothing."

"We can only hope. But we can't be too careful. Can you show me?" I sat up fully on my bed and crossed my legs, wide awake.

"Sure." He moved the camera on his phone to show me his elbow.

"That spot is red, brownish and flat. It can't be that you're getting this again. The antibiotic should cover you."

"You mean this is something else?" he asked, confused.

"Either that or else the antibiotic isn't completely effective and the EBEX is back in your system. But that doesn't make sense. Do you have a fever?"

"I don't think so."

"Ok, good. Come over. I need to give you another dose. I can't not be with you tonight. But we need to be careful." I truly didn't think I could fall asleep without him, especially knowing what I did.

"Really? You think your parents will let me?"

"Just come..."

Grey jumped out of bed and our connection was lost. Fifteen minutes later, he was at my front door, wrapped in a warm jacket and in his pajama pants, wearing his slippers.

"So glad you didn't change." I smiled and wrapped my arms around his neck, rubbing my nose into his clean, fresh smell. He was not hot with a fever, thank goodness. My nose tickled from his short neck hairs. I closed my eyes and held on. I didn't want to let him go, not ever.

He took off his jacket, and we walked together over to the couch. "Let me see your elbow," I asked as he pulled back the sleeve of his top. "Hmm, that's not great. I can't believe this." I sat staring at it, thinking, maybe this is what Stevenson meant when she said there was more.

"Whatever are you thinking, Sienna, it doesn't seem good." Grey twisted his elbow so he could see it.

"Yea, I'm thinking that this is something else completely."

"You're kidding, right?" Grey let his sleeve drop down his arm and sank back into the couch.

"Look, I'll give you this antibiotic, and we'll see how it looks tomorrow. We'll take it day by day. You can fight this." I stared into his eyes and ran my fingers through his hair, which was finally back to his usual smooth, clean-smelling curls.

We were silent for a while until I finally got the courage up to say, "I can't believe I shot a gun."

He looked directly at me and said, "You were brave. You had to. He left you no choice."

"I know, but I still did it. Something I never imagined I could do. What would Willow think of me?"

"Hmmm. It all happened so fast."

"Too fast."

"Willow would be proud of your courage, I think."

I was silent and nodded. He was probably right. If I didn't shoot, Ty would've killed Avery, and I couldn't let that happen, not to my best girlfriend.

"She'd want us to go after Kellen, Liv, and everyone else, I know that."

"Yeah, you're right, again, dammit," he said, then gave me a quick kiss on my cheek.

"We're going to fight this—whatever you have, if it's EBEX or something else, we'll go after it, and we'll go after Kellen and Liv. Anyone or anything that's sabotaging our existence."

Grey and I cuddled on the couch, his sickened elbow away from me. Once he drifted off to sleep, I grabbed my phone, set the alarm to wake him and send him home before the hour was over. Dreading the moment he'd have to leave.

I opened up my email. I pulled up Stevenson's contact info and typed her a note: *Hey, Dr. Stevenson, I don't know if you're even able to read this, but I think eventually you'll be feeling better. When I saw you in the hospital, what did you mean by, "Wait, there's more?" I need to know as soon as you get this. Thanks, Sienna.*

I hit send and sat next to Greyson, watching his chest rise and fall with his breath. *As long as he's still breathing,* I said to myself. I can do this.

END OF BOOK ONE

Made in United States
Orlando, FL
20 November 2021

10578745R00153